PRAISE FOR ABBY COLLETTE'S
ICE CREAM PARLOR MYSTERIES

"Fun! Fresh! Fabulous! Abby Collette has crafted a delicious addition to the cozy mystery world with her superbly written *A Deadly Inside Scoop*. Delightful characters and a puzzler of a plot kept me turning pages until the very end. I can't wait for my next visit to the Crewse Creamery for another decadent taste."
—*New York Times* bestselling author Jenn McKinlay

"A deliciously satisfying new cozy mystery series. It's got humor, a quirky cast of characters and ice cream. What more could you want?"
—V. M. Burns, Agatha Award–nominated author of the Mystery Bookshop Mystery Series

"With an endearing cast of characters ranging from [Bronwyn's] close-knit, multigenerational family to her feisty best friends, this intricate mystery plays out with plenty of suspects, tons of motives and an ending I didn't see coming."
—*New York Times* bestselling author Bailey Cates

"With a host of quirky friends and family members, Abby Collette's new series is a welcome addition to the cozy mystery scene, and life at Crewse Creamery promises plenty of delectable adventures to come. Only one warning: *A Deadly Inside Scoop* causes a deep yearning for scoops of homemade ice cream, no matter the weather."
—Juliet Blackwell, *New York Times* bestselling author of the Haunted Home Renovation series and the Witchcraft Mystery series

"What do you get when you put together a tight-knit, slightly quirky family, a delectable collection of ice cream flavors and an original mystery? A tasty start to a new cozy series. *A Deadly Inside Scoop* is a cleverly crafted mystery with a relatable main character in Bronwyn Crewse."   —*New York Times* bestselling author Sofie Kelly

SOUL
OF A
KILLER

Abby Collette

BERKLEY PRIME CRIME
New York

BERKLEY PRIME CRIME
Published by Berkley
An imprint of Penguin Random House LLC
penguinrandomhouse.com

Copyright © 2022 by Shondra C. Longino
Excerpt from *A Deadly Inside Scoop* by
Abby Collette copyright © 2020 by Shondra C. Longino

BERKLEY and the BERKLEY & B colophon are registered trademarks and
BERKLEY PRIME CRIME is a trademark of Penguin Random House LLC.

ISBN: 9780593336205

First Edition: October 2022

Printed in the United States of America
1 3 5 7 9 10 8 6 4 2

Book design by George Towne

To old friends and good food.

SOUL
OF A
KILLER

Chapter One

"I HATE LIVING in the future."

That was Mama Zola's response every time my twin brother, Koby, mentioned to her she needed a cell phone.

"I like the past better. Simpler times," she said. "Just give me a rotary phone, a typewriter and a transistor radio and I'm good."

And that was the line she gave when he told her that a cell phone wasn't a thing of the future, people had been using them for more than twenty years.

But that was Zola Jackson. She wasn't much for change.

We were at Mama Zola's church, Everlasting Missionary Baptist Church on the outskirts of Timber Lake in the unincorporated limits of Porter. We were dropping her off, and Koby wanted to be sure she could reach us if she needed to.

I was with her on the cell phone, though. I rarely kept mine on, the bookstore and my house had landlines and I was always one place or the other. Plus, I didn't have many people to talk to.

Mama Zola was so excited about the day. It hadn't been long since she'd moved to our lakeside town. She'd come to help me and Koby at our café and bookstore, Books & Biscuits. This was a new church home for Mama Zola. She hadn't wasted any time joining the month after she settled in her new place, a few blocks from our store. Koby wanted to make sure she was okay since he would no longer be in the City to keep an eye on her.

Koby and I had driven her and Pete Howers to the church so they could get set up for the Annual Founder's Day Potluck. A red brick church with a white wooden steeple, it was one story and had had two additions added over the years, one on each side of the atrium, the original building where the chapel was located. The additions were long and L-shaped with lots of closed doors. We'd come in through the chapel.

Today would be Mama Zola's first time participating and she was trying to show out. She'd been up cooking since three a.m. And if she didn't turn us loose soon, we were going to be late opening our place of business. It was already a quarter to nine.

Everyone in Timber Lake who'd been to Books & Biscuits knew she was a great cook. An awesome cook. She was the one we gave credit to for our soul rolls. They were bringing in people in droves. Juicy greens or hoppin' johns inside a flaky, crunchy egg roll wrapper. And then Koby had even come up with dessert ones—sweet potatoes and apple crumble.

I sure was looking forward to anything Mama Zola was going to serve today for the church event. Koby and I had planned on coming back around lunchtime to eat. But now she was nervous just the same. And excited. And driving us crazy.

"I hope I cooked enough." She surveyed the spread of

food. Worry etched across her face. "I bet a lot of people will come."

We were in the church's kitchen. A spacious area off the back of the main church in one of the additions. Right behind the baptismal area. Cabinets and counters flanked newer-looking appliances, and the walls were painted a cheery, but faint yellow. We helped Mama Zola unload her foil-topped dishes onto the large aluminum countertop island.

It seemed we were the first ones there and probably the ones with the most food. Most potluck attendees, at least in my experience, only brought one covered dish. She probably had about twenty.

"I think you'll be fine," Koby said.

"I don't know. I ordered four bags of peaches for my cobblers, and they only sent three." She turned and looked at me. "And you ate two of those, Keaton."

"I only ate two *peaches*." I held up fingers that could have denoted the number or a peace sign. Both gestures I hoped would help my cause. "Not two bags." A sheepish look on my face, I hung my head. I had eaten them. Couldn't deny that. And I knew I was going to hear about it from her. She did not hold her tongue at all. But they were ripe and oh so sweet and juicy.

"I didn't say you ate two bags. But those two made a difference."

"Sorry," I said. Again. But she had moved on.

"Are you sure you got all the pans out of the car?" She looked toward the door as if she could see it from there.

Pete, her designated assistant for the day, although his usual job was in the bookstore with me, had gotten a serving cart from inside the church with the help of Rocko.

Rocko Jackson (no relation to Mama Zola) looked more like a bouncer at a corner bar than the church's designated security and parking lot attendant. Muscles popping out everywhere, buzz cut and dressed all in black—T-shirt, pants and combat boots. He sat in a wooden booth, glass windows on all four sides, centered in the middle of the parking lot. Country gospel on his radio and a plastic container filled with umbrellas. It didn't take much convincing for him to let us in the building early, once we pried him off his cell phone and with Mama Zola's promise of an extra heaping serving of her peach cobbler.

"Yes, we got everything out of the car," my brother answered.

"What about the sweet tea from Biscuits?"

"Our soon-to-be-famous sweet tea?" Koby asked. It was intended to be our signature bestseller when we opened, it and Koby's buttery, flaky golden-brown biscuits, but it had been surpassed by Mama Zola's soul rolls.

"Did you spill anything?" She started lifting the foil covering over the aluminum containers. The smell of the food came wafting out, making my stomach grumble.

"Nothing spilled, Mama Zola," Koby said. "We were careful."

He knew how to handle her. She'd been one of his many foster parents.

We were separated when we were two. I was adopted into a great family, who gave me a loving home and an awesome childhood. Koby wasn't adopted. He spent his formative years in group homes and other people's houses and lives. That was until he got to Mama Zola's. She'd been his real first mom.

Starting when he was thirteen, Koby had put on a sleuthing hat and somehow, over the course of a few years and out of the seven point six million people in Washington State, found me.

But, even with Kobe's skills, our birth mother's present location was unknown, but, now together, we were working on that. Hopefully, though, we'd find our biological mother. I know Koby wanted that more than anything.

In fact, I had written to the King County Adoptions Department of Family Court Services to get any identifying information on her we were allowed by law to have. Morie Hill. That was her name. We'd gotten the correspondence from the county around the time when Koby's foster brother, Reef, had been killed. Inside, we'd found out a couple of things that may help on our search for her—like a last known address, where she went to high school and that she had attended a community college. And hits on our genealogy account with other people with matching DNA were also helpful. Meanwhile, the two of us together had started a family business, Books & Biscuits, a soul food restaurant and bookstore, and we were trying to make up for all the lost time from being separated for all those years.

"Oh." Mama Zola placed a hand on her cheek. "I hope I didn't leave anything at the restaurant . . ." Her eyes wandered back toward the door.

"You didn't leave anything," Koby assured her.

"I think you took all the food we had," I said, teasing.

I ran the books side of Books & Biscuits, so I didn't know about what went on over on the Biscuits side. My brother was the cook and manager of our café. I knew better than to try to give my input into anything on that side. I took my cooking skills after my mother—well, my adoptive mother, Imogene Rutledge—who, I had discovered since eating my brother's and Mama Zola's cooking, could win a place on the Food Network's *Worst Cooks in America*.

"I didn't take everything," Mama Zola said, using a napkin to wipe the sweat from her forehead. She turned her mouth down into a frown. "Just the things I made for the potluck."

"Nope, she didn't," Pete said. "She left a box of salt."

We laughed, even harder than we should have. Probably because Pete wasn't one to make jokes.

"It's not funny." Mama Zola didn't laugh, and she raised a finger and opened her mouth, ready to tell us why, but we were saved from her wrath by Reverend Calvin Lee. Her entire demeanor changed when she saw him.

He was standing in the hallway talking to a tall woman. Holding hands, they smiled at each other before he left her to come into the kitchen.

As they parted ways, I glanced down at their shoes. She had on the highest heels I'd ever seen, and the pair she wore were an emerald green, matching her green-striped dress. *Nice shoes,* I thought. I'd never seen any that color. I smiled. Certainly wouldn't be something I'd be seen wearing out, but for some reason I found myself admiring them.

The pastor almost outdid her in the shoe department. His were pretty. (Can you say that about a man's shoes?) They were polished and gleaming. They looked as if they had a spit shine put on them and then they'd been shellacked. They were brown with a gold buckle at the instep that glistened. I wondered if I could see my reflection in them.

He was dressed in a tan suit, lavender shirt and a purple-and-tan tie, and he seemed to have a habit of stroking his neatly trimmed beard.

I'd only seen him once before, when I went with Mama Zola the first time she visited the church. She insisted on introducing me to him. Who knew why? At first, I thought she was trying to be a matchmaker, even though he was quite a lot older than me. But then I found out he was married, and I realized that perhaps she was worried about my soul.

"Morning, Pastor," Mama Zola said, a big grin appearing on her face.

"Morning, family." He nodded his greeting. "Sister Jackson." He gave her a smile just as wide as hers. "I knew you must be here. I smelled your good cooking as soon as I walked through the door." He shook his head. "Made my mouth water."

"Aw. Thank you, Pastor. I'm just happy to be able to participate."

"And we're glad you became part of our church membership—"

He was interrupted by a loud and boisterous man. He was tall, slender and had excellent posture. Looking at him made me throw back my shoulders and stand up straighter.

He strode through the kitchen entryway like he owned the place. Dress to a T, too, he rivaled the pastor's look, kicking it up a notch with French cuffs, diamond-looking studded cuff links and pointed toe, black leather saddle shoes. A gold bracelet on his wrist had a single, small charm hanging from it.

In my opinion, his attire looked more expensive than the pastor's. More like Wall Street or the boardroom. He was what my father used to call "snazzy."

"Calvin," the newcomer said with a voice just as smooth as his dark skin, "why are you milling around with the help?" He came over and put a hand on the pastor's shoulder. "We need to get you into your office."

"Austin. I saw you pull up. Thought I'd make it to the office before you made it inside." A big grin came across the pastor's face. "But the aroma coming from Sister Jackson's food stopped me in my tracks." He licked his lips. "Had to take a detour."

"You knew that brute you've got guarding the parking lot was going to give me trouble. But he didn't know that I am not one to mess with before I've had my morning coffee."

I saw his eyes scan the countertops in the room and I followed suit, not quite sure what we were looking for.

The pastor let out a hearty laugh. "He helps me keep devils like you out."

They both laughed. The Austin guy's laugh didn't seem as genuine to me, or like he was even paying much attention to the conversation. Although, I couldn't be sure. I was finding more every day how much my twin and I were alike. We were growing closer. I enjoyed so much being around him.

But there were things, naturally, that one was better at than the other. For instance, my brother, Koby, was better at assessing people than I was. I mostly noticed people's clothing. He noticed their actions. After our involvement in and subsequent solving of Reef's murder, I had decided to try to be more like my brother.

"Pete Howers." Austin must have just taken in the other people in the room. "Who let you indoors? Aren't you used to camping out under the trees? Or in doorways?"

The pastor frowned. "Austin. We don't do that here. Pete is welcome and he knows it."

"He's with me," Mama Zola said and stepped in front of Pete. Our employee didn't usually have much to say. It seemed that Mama Zola thought she needed to speak up for him. "And *who* are you? You're looking out of place yourself." She looked Austin up and down.

"I've got oxtails!" We were interrupted again. This time by another potluck cook. Thank the Lord. Mama Zola had no problem speaking her mind, and I was thinking that might not be a good thing in a church or in front of her new pastor.

"Oh, I love your oxtails," Mama Zola said. A true compliment coming from her. She smacked her lips. His eyes twinkled.

Oxtail Guy had a deep voice and a jovial face. And like I always did, I noticed what he was wearing—a red apron, made like the black one that Koby wore at work, with BILLY RAY emblazoned across the front. A white button-down shirt underneath and black pants. A pair of Crocs on his feet.

"Brother Patton," the pastor said, that wide grin returning to his face. "You got cornbread to go with that?"

"I sure do. I got hot water cornbread," he said, rocking his head from side to side in rhythm with his words. "Came in to see if I could find the cart to bring everything in. I got banana pudding and string beans in my SUV."

"Ray," Austin said, calling the man who just came in by what, according to his apron, was his middle name. "Looks like you've been eating all of your cooking." He pointed to Ray's large, round belly.

"You just can't stop, can you?" Mama Zola said. She looked up at Austin, who must have been at least a foot taller than she was. "Somebody needs to cut you down to size?" She cocked her head as if she might be the one to do it.

"Ignore him," Ray said. "He just likes to hear himself talk. And he probably just needs a few more shots of caffeine." Done with Austin and his insults, Ray pointed to the cart that we'd used to bring the food in from Koby's car. "Can I borrow that?"

"Sure," Mama Zola said. "Pete, give him the cart."

"We're going to go," Koby said. "Everything good with you?" he asked Mama Zola.

"Yep. We're good." She pried her eyes off of Austin, who she'd been trying to bore a hole in with her laser stare. "We're going to get our stuff squared away and then help set up the hall. If . . ." She looked to the pastor. "We're still needed."

"Of course. Of course." Pastor Lee came over and put his hand on Mama Zola's shoulder. "We appreciate you. God bless you. Do whatever you need to do." He threw a glance over toward Austin. "C'mon. Let's go to my office and chat."

"If you need us, Mama Zola," Koby said as Austin and Pastor Lee were leaving, "Call down to the store."

"On what?" she asked. "Only phone around here is the

one in the pastor's office and I'm not using that one. If I had to go anywhere around that Austin guy, I might just wring his neck."

Ray laughed. "Oh, I like this one," he said. "Feisty."

"Beg your pardon?" Mama Zola turned her attention to him.

Ray threw up both his hands. "Didn't mean anything bad. And if you need to use a phone, you can use mine." He reached down in his pocket and pulled out his flip phone.

Koby looked at me, leaning in as he lowered his voice. "Being around these two"—he waggled a finger between Mama Zola and Ray—"you would think using a smartphone involved rocket science."

Chapter Two

"MAMA ZOLA CALLED." Koby had come and stood in the archway between the two stores to speak to me.

"Oh," I said and smiled. I looked up from my calendar. I was trying to schedule some book events for the store, sending out email invites to authors and keeping my fingers crossed they'd respond back. "She found a phone."

"Seems so."

"Are they ready to go?" I glanced up at the clock. It was only one. The event was supposed to go until three thirty and we had planned on going back around two. We'd take a long lunch. Grab a plate, eat, help Mama Zola pack up and then bring her and Pete back to the shop.

"No," Koby said and walked over to me. He leaned in over the counter, lowering his voice. "She said she thinks she's getting ready to be arrested for murder."

"What!" I screeched. Pretty loudly, I found out by the startled look on my clients' faces. "Who in the world could she have killed? She's in church, for God's sake."

Before I had met back up with my twin brother, I had

led a pretty calm, quiet existence. But not anymore. There was always something. And this was the worst kind of something. Still, I wouldn't trade us finding each other for, as the current murder suspect often says, "all the tea in China."

Koby shrugged. Nonchalantly. Standing up straight, he didn't seem as upset as the level I was presently ramping up to. "I'm letting Georgie close up the kitchen." His voice was still low. "You riding with me?"

"Of course I'm riding with you!" My words again at that same high pitch.

How could I not go? But I needed to calm down. No need to get worked up. Not yet. And no need of freaking my customers out. I wanted them to finish their browsing. It would be nice if they bought something before I pushed them out the door.

I looked around the Books side of our business. There were two people browsing and I'd just rung one customer up, but something had caught her eye as she headed for the door, and she was now perusing again. I needed to get them out of the store without causing them to become disgruntled.

"Give me minute," I said, trying to use a calmer voice. I nodded toward the two customers in the back of the store. "I don't want to rush them out."

Usually, I would have had Pete there to hold down the fort while I left. But he was with Mama Zola.

"Pete's involved, too." Koby nodded as he spoke, like he'd read my mind. We seemed able to do that sometimes. Know just what the other was thinking. Even verbalize the other's thoughts or say the same thing at the same time. Twin telepathy? Whatever it was, it was uncanny. It was a real thing between us even with our twenty-year separation.

But then I thought about what he was saying meant . . .

"They murdered someone together?" My voice up an octave. My face all scrunched up.

Oh, my goodness. What in the world could have happened at a church's potluck dinner?

"Shh!" Koby shot a glance back toward the browsing customers. They were looking at us, both with worried looks on their faces. "You'll have them running out the door, no books in hand and never returning."

I smiled at my customers. I hoped they couldn't tell how fake that smile was.

"How do you want me to react when you tell me that two of our three employees are mixed up in something like—" I turned my head to see what the two in the back were doing and then, turning back to face Koby, I leaned closer over the counter and mouthed, "Murder."

"Think how I feel." His eyebrows doing an upward arch. "I thought I was moving to small, idyllic Timber Lake. Life at a slower pace. Safer. More like suburbia." He leaned in and lowered his voice, mimicking what I'd done. "No murders." He cocked his head to the side, a smirk rising up on his face. "You sure had me fooled."

"Yeah. I should have known. This place is textbook cozy mystery setting," I muttered.

"Cozy mystery?" Koby asked.

"Yeah. You know. Like Cabot Cove. Although there probably isn't anyone left there."

"Where?" He shook his head in confusion. "What are you talking about?"

"*Murder, She Wrote* books." I pointed to the mystery section of my bookstore. "I probably have half of the fifty-some books in stock. "Some are back in the storeroom." I hiked a thumb in that direction.

"I didn't know there were books," Koby said.

"Lots of books," I said. "Now written by Terrie Moran. Tales of the amateur sleuth, Jessica Fletcher, who had to start traveling around to solve murders because there probably wasn't anyone left in Cabot Cove."

Koby chuckled.

"I'm sure," I continued, "over the course of all the books"—I nodded my head at Koby, acknowledging his familiarity with the series—"and with the TV shows and movies, that small coastal town probably heralded more dead bodies than wherever the real-life murder capital of the world is." I shook my head.

"You're being dramatic."

I probably looked like a bobblehead. I was nodding up and down at a fast clip. "No. I'm serious." My face likely showed just that sentiment. "This is just how it started in Cabot Cove."

"Which now is becoming Timber Lake?"

"Oh my gosh. I hope not," I said and threw up a hand. "Let's just hope Mama Zola is exaggerating."

That was when we heard the sirens soar past us and all my hopes just evaporated into thin air.

Koby and I looked at each other.

"I'll go get the car," he said.

"I'll get these people out of here."

ALL KINDS OF thoughts raced through my head on the fifteen-minute drive over to the church. I couldn't have imagined who Mama Zola could have been accused of killing.

At least it wasn't Pete. He had a shaky start with me and a shady past. And I didn't know how far in his past the shady part went back. Right now, I wasn't even sure where he lived, although I had an idea.

When we got back to the church, it looked like what Channel 8 News called an "active crime scene." And it reminded me of the last time I'd been at one—when my brother had to rescue me from the clutches of Reef's murderer. It made the skin on my arms crawl.

There was yellow tape, with police cruisers, news trucks, Timber Lake Power trucks and a scattering of bystanders milling around. And there were lots of police officers. More than I thought we had in Timber Lake.

The first person I saw that I recognized was Pastor Lee. He was talking to one of the many officers and a guy in a yellow construction hat. I was relieved he wasn't the victim. I couldn't imagine what would happen to Mama Zola's "everlasting soul"—her words, not mine—if she'd killed a preacher.

Koby spotted Mama Zola. "There she is," he said, tapping my arm to get my attention. He pointed. "C'mon. Let's see what's going on."

Standing with her were Pete and Avery Moran, aka Capt'n Hook. Wasn't sure why he was there and how he'd known what was happening.

Thankfully, there were no handcuffs attached to Mama Zola.

Maybe it wasn't as bad as I thought.

"Koby!" Mama Zola called out to him. She saw us before we'd even made it over.

"What is going on?" Koby asked once we got to them.

"One of the church members died," Capt'n Hook said. "I think it's got Zola upset. He had a bowl of her peach cobbler in his hand when he expired."

Expired.

That didn't sound like *murder.* But Avery Moran had a way of putting things to make them go over easier. He was an ex–police captain for the Seattle PD and another new fixture in Timber Lake. He'd bought the marina in town, where Koby docked his houseboat just after we'd opened shop.

He'd gotten the nickname Capt'n Hook from the kids Koby had hung around when he was younger. Foster kids that Detective Moran had said he wasn't going to let get "lost out" and become part of the juvenile system. He meant "get into trouble out in the streets" just because they didn't have a real home. They were his Lost Boys and he was their Capt'n Hook and Koby had taken right to him. I, being the avid reader that I was, and fan of J. M. Barrie's work, *Peter Pan, or The Boy Who Would Not Grow Up*, knew that those boys and that pirate did not have a good relationship. Koby liked to ignore that fact.

"I don't even know how he'd gotten into it." Mama Zola drew in a breath. "I didn't even remember him coming up to get any from us."

"I don't remember seeing him either," Pete said, chiming his agreement.

"Mama Zola's peach cobbler killed someone?" I asked. I thought about the two peaches I'd eaten. "What did she do to it?"

"I'm standing right here," she said. "And I didn't do anything to it. Nothing different."

"Maybe he just had a heart attack," I said, wanting to dismiss it as being anything else. I'd had enough of murder. Especially if Mama Zola was involved. We'd just dealt with one. Reef Jeffries, Koby's foster brother, had been killed on the light-rail. And somehow, I'd been the one to figure out whodunit right when the murderer was ready to strike again. That was scary. Didn't want to do it again.

Koby shook his head. "Not with all the police here." He glanced around the parking lot and I let my eyes follow his. "Something is up."

"James Austin is dead, that's what's up," Mama Zola said.

"Austin James," Pete said, correcting her.

She waved a dismissive hand. "Whatever his name is. He's dead."

"The snarky guy from this morning?" I asked, remembering how she hadn't been too keen on him.

"Yep." Pete nodded his head. "The one she said she was going to 'cut down to size' and 'wring his neck.'"

"I didn't say *I* was going to cut him down to size," Mama Zola said, this time correcting Pete. "I said *someone* needed to do it."

"Same difference," Pete said. "And you did say you were going to wring his neck."

"Yeah, yeah." She rubbed a hand over her forehead. "I did say that." She turned to look at Koby. "That's how I know they're going to arrest me. There was a room full of witnesses to my words."

"We aren't snitches," Pete said.

"It seemed to me," Koby said, "he was good at rubbing people the wrong way. I wouldn't be surprised if someone did kill him."

"Or maybe he had a heart attack." I tried to get my suggestion in again, this time with a little more emphasis.

"They are not going to arrest her," Moran said. "You don't have to worry about that."

"Good," I said and gave a nod. "And no one said there was any foul play either, right?" I wanted reassurance about Timber Lake not being the new Cabot Cove.

"Nope," Moran said. "No one has said that. But they really aren't saying anything."

"See," I said, a confident smile on my face, wanting to calm Mama Zola's fears. "Things are going to be fine."

"Where's the body?" Koby asked.

"Over there." Mama Zola jerked a finger over her shoulder, keeping her eyes from looking in that direction.

"Outside?" I asked. I didn't see anything in the direction she pointed. Not an ambulance, medic or even a sheet-covered gurney.

"No." Capt'n Hook pointed to the church. "He's still inside. I think they'll still processing everything."

"I don't understand then what all the commotion is about," I said. "He wasn't poisoned. A lot of people ate the peach cobbler, right?" My head was nodding as my eyes looked to Mama Zola and Pete.

"Are you still thinking that I put something into the peach cobbler?" Mama cocked her head to the side as she spoke to me. "Koby has already cleared me. He said that that guy had rubbed lots of people the wrong way and you said that others ate my peach cobbler and no one else died."

"Right," Pete said, before I could respond. Mama Zola kept her lips tight.

"No," I said leaning toward her. "I'm not. I'm just wondering what all the hoopla is about." I gestured out to all the commotion going on in the parking lot.

"You're right," Koby said. "It wasn't poison. I think he was electrocuted."

Chapter Three

MY BROTHER HAD an eye for details. He was, in my opinion, a lightweight Sherlock Holmes. Noticing people's actions, things they said and getting clues, he could make assessments about what they had done and what they were up to. Me? Not so much. I noticed what people were wearing. My superpower—a clothing guru. It, of course, hadn't helped me solve anything yet.

Sure, I saw the Timber Lake Power truck when we pulled up, but I did not once associate it with anything that was happening. Not sure why my brother had.

"I knew I didn't kill him," Mama Zola muttered.

She wasn't going to let me live down my comment, but she'd been the one calling to say she was being arrested for murder.

I shook Mama Zola out of my head and turned to my brother. "The power truck tells you that, how?" I asked, my eyebrow raised a few ticks.

"The power truck doesn't tell me anything, the guy

from the truck does." Koby gestured in that direction. "He's talking to law enforcement and to Pastor Lee."

And so he was.

I noticed that he had on gray chino pants, matching shirt with their blue lightning bolt emblem badge sewn across the top. Older guy, the gray in his hair showing on the sides of his yellow hardhat.

"That's Ross Franklin, interim Timber Lake chief and, today, acting detective," Avery Moran said.

"Figures," I said. "Timber Lake is such a small place, I'm sure we wouldn't have a homicide detective." The last homicide we'd been involved in had happened in Seattle, so the police here initially had no jurisdiction. But when the murderer was found in Timber Lake, I'm sure they'd been in the ranks during the arrest. I was too out of it to notice. I glanced over at Mama Zola, who was still giving me the stink eye. "Not that we'd need one."

"I heard about him. He's just standing in until the town could vote in the permanent chief," Koby said.

"Yeah, and I heard that Chow is running for the job," Avery said, sharing more news.

"Daniel Chow?" My eyes got big. "The homicide detective from Seattle?"

"One and the same," Avery said.

"When is the election?" Mama Zola asked.

I wondered if she was even registered to vote in Timber Lake.

"Two weeks from Tuesday," Avery said. "And I do believe Chow is the only one in the running."

"So he's gonna get the job," Koby said.

"Oh geesh!" I said, nearly shrieking out the words. "Is everyone involved in Reef's murder moving here?" I glanced around our group. "No offense meant."

"I wasn't involved in Reef's murder," Mama Zola said. She put her hands on her hips.

I took a step behind Koby.

"I just meant I don't want to go through this all over again. Murder. With the same cast of main characters. In the same place."

"How would you like your murder served?" Mama Zola cocked her head and stared at me.

I'd like it better somewhere else, I wanted to say. But murder anywhere wasn't a good thing. I was having visions of Jessica Fletcher sitting at her typewriter, big glasses on, eighties hair piled high, writing about us.

Although, when I found out about a death in a church, another book came to mind. Kathryn Dionne's cozy *Murder at the Holiday Bazaar*.

In it, the pastor was murdered, keeled over with a chicken leg in hand sold at the bazaar, and found by his secretary. This one wasn't the church's clergy who had died, but someone who seemed to me, to be his right-hand man. It wasn't chicken, but Mama Zola's sweet peaches concoction that had been found with the victim. And, in Dionne's book, the cook was the prime suspect, which is just like what Mama Zola had surmised about herself. But that was not who had done the deed.

Life imitating fiction. I shook my head. This was just too much murder to happen in our neck of the woods.

Okay, yes. I knew that all of those stories were just that—stories. But at the rate we were going, if this was another murder in our quaint little town and we somehow were being drawn into it, our real lives were all set to intersect with Dionne's fiction.

Timber Lake was not a place where crime ran rampant even with two murders (was this truly our second murder?) under our belt. And it seemed to me that a Seattle homicide detective coming to work in our fair town would just seal the deal. I had voted in every election since I'd been a resident of Timber Lake, even special elections like this one. I guessed I'd been busy with the shop, because I hadn't heard about this one. But I was wondering what to do. Did I want my vote to usher in a man like Daniel Chow? He had listened to Koby in the end, which helped to save my life, but initially, he'd made me and Koby his prime suspects.

"Look," Pete said. "That Acting Chief Ross Franklin and the Timber Lake Power guy are going inside."

My eyes followed them as they walked to the door. Then I glanced back at Pastor Lee, wondering how he was feeling. Austin, it seemed, had been his friend. And now he'd died in his church.

And maybe Austin had been more? It seemed that Pastor Lee and Austin James had some business to discuss. At least from the conversation they had had while in the kitchen that morning.

Wait! Was I starting to think like my brother?

That made me smile.

But then when I looked at Pastor Lee, his eyes were staring right back at me. And I couldn't figure out what that meant or why he was looking my way with narrowed eyes.

Or maybe . . . I turned and looked behind me. *Maybe he was looking at Pete.*

Maybe my skills needed more honing.

Undeterred, I stared right back at the pastor and squinted. Yep. One of us had caught his attention. And he didn't seem too pleased with the one or both of us.

"I wonder what's going on," Avery said, diverting my attention away from Pastor Calvin Lee. "What are they trying to figure out?" He shook his head. "They haven't even brought out the body yet."

"Let's go talk to the pastor and find out," Koby said. "We won't learn anything just standing around gawking."

"No," I said, reaching out to put my arm on my brother's. "Why would you want to do that?"

"I agree," Mama Zola said. "Don't go stirring up that pot." She shook her head. "You're always too curious. Always have been. They've got plenty of people over there taking care of things."

"I just want to know where Austin is."

"You mean where his body is," Pete said.

"Right," Koby said, tapping his foot and patting his leg with an open hand, his interest on level ten. "Why, he's still in there and what they are thinking as the cause of death."

"I thought you said electrocution?" Hadn't we already settled on the method of death? I guess it just went to show how much confidence I had in my brother's observation skills.

"I did," Koby said. "And I am ninety-nine point nine nine nine percent sure it was electrocution, but it would be nice if it was confirmed. So"—he cocked his head to the side and nodded—"we should go and talk to the pastor."

"I wonder how he was electrocuted," Mama Zola said, seemingly not disagreeing with Koby interrogating her pastor. "I mean, wouldn't it have to be some live wires or lightning or something? And there wasn't anything like that *inside* the building."

"Yeah," Avery Moran said, "the voltage inside a building isn't usually enough to kill a person."

"He had a pacemaker," Pete said. "A little jolt, even from a hundred-and-twenty-volt line could cause the electrical signal to falter."

We all turned and looked at Pete.

"How do you know he had a pacemaker?" I asked.

"I worked with the man. We were colleagues. I remember when he got sick."

"Wait!" Mama Zola said. "There he comes now."

By "he," she meant Austin James. At least what remained of him.

I turned to the sound of squeaky wheels stumbling over the gravel asphalt of the church's parking lot to find two EMTs rolling out the gurney with what had to be

Austin James' body on it, covered with a white sheet. A quiet fell over the scene as they folded the legs and lifted him onto the back of their truck.

"C'mon," Koby said. "It's probably now or never. No need for him to hang around much longer now." But before Koby could get over to the pastor, a uniformed police officer came our way. He took it as an opportunity to find out more. "What's going on?" Koby stepped up to meet the cop.

"I really can't say too much," he said, stepping past Koby. "You'll have to wait until the morning newspaper comes out. That's about the most anyone'll get out of this until it's solved."

"Solved?" Avery said. "As in murder?"

"Tomorrow's newspaper will cost you a dollar," the officer said. "That's about all the info I can give you right now."

"Someone's dead," Koby said. "That's pretty obvious. You can't tell us how?"

"Nope. You can check the mor—"

"Morning's paper," Mama Zola finished his sentence. "Yes. We got it."

"Good." He gave a cordial pseudo-smile. "Pete Howers," he said, alerting us to his present business. We all turned, once again, to look at Pete. "Can you come with me, please. Acting Chief Franklin wants to have a talk with you." He put a hand on his gun like he thought he might need to draw it. "Down at the station."

"Why?" Mama Zola went and stood in front of Pete. "He's not going anywhere. You've got no reason to talk to him. I made the peach cobbler."

Oh my. Were we back to that?

Pete's expression or demeanor didn't change once he found out the police's presence (and evidently the pastor's earlier gaze) were for him.

In fact, nothing about Pete had changed. Not since the

first day I met him when he wandered into our bookstore. A lopsided haircut. Ruddy complexion. His clothes were a lot fresher and neater now, though. I suspected that had something to do with Mama Zola. She was always taking in strays.

I had been leery about hiring him and was ready to send him away when he showed up. But not my brother. He hired him. On the spot. Without any references. And without giving a second thought to his misbuttoned shirt, worn Hello Kitty book bag (which was strapped to his back even now) and him being unwilling to tell me his last name.

I didn't want to think it now, but maybe we should have looked more into him. Checked out his past. Found out exactly who he was.

"He can come willingly," the police officer said. "Or in handcuffs."

Koby stepped in that time because Mama Zola had puffed up her chest, standing akimbo. It looked like she was ready to explode all over that police officer.

"He'll go willingly," Koby said. "Right, Pete?"

Pete, his eyes not showing one spec of emotion, nodded, it seemed involuntarily.

"I'll follow along, too," Avery Moran said, evidently donning his Capt'n Hook persona—looking out for Lost Boys. He patted Pete on the back. "I'm with you, buddy."

"Unless you're his lawyer, you might *not* want to tag along." The police put a hand on Pete's shoulder, grabbing it with a tug. "Don't know that he'll be able to talk to anyone or be leaving the station anytime soon."

Chapter Four

"WE NEED TO find out what's going on," Koby said. This time I agreed with him and nodded my head to show it. "That's the only way we'll be of any help to Pete." His last words, I could tell, were directed to me. But I was already on board. Even with second thoughts and all about who he was, I still wanted to help Pete out.

But that meant on board to try and find out what was going on with *Pete*. And Pete only. As to solving a possible murder? Uh-uh. Don't think so. We'd already done this before. Had Koby forgotten what happened last time we went around investigating a death?

And God forbid this one was murder.

The officer had opened the police cruiser's back door, tucked in Pete's head with his hand so Pete wouldn't hit it as he was put into the car. The people who had been milling around the parking lot watched in awe the taking out of the body and the "arresting" (not sure that was what was happening) of Pete like it was a tennis match. I didn't know where they'd come from—if they lived closed by and heard the ruckus or if they had been there for the potluck, but their interest sure was captivated.

I watched as the car carrying Pete drove away and Moran followed in his car, before I turned to answer Koby. "Yes. We need to see why they are interested in Pete. I agree. But"—I shook my head—"no, we do not need to like *investigate* anything." Verbalizing my thoughts, I pointed to the fading-from-view police cruiser. "We need to let the police handle that."

Just then Ross Franklin walked out. Interim chief. New to me, but however capable he was, was good enough. He was accompanied by the guy from the power company. They seemed to be wrapping things up. Good. I'd had enough entanglement with snooping around looking into dead people and suspicious causes of death.

Chief Franklin walked back out of the church doors, parted ways with the guy from Timber Lake Power and started conversing with one of his officers.

I sized up Mr. Interim Chief. He looked official and capable enough. I saw no need of butting in.

"That's exactly who we need to talk to," Koby said. He had followed my gaze.

"Who?" I asked although I already knew the answer.

"Ross Franklin."

Geesh. Now it wasn't just the pastor Koby wanted to talk to, he wanted to question the police chief, too.

"Won't help." The man who cooked oxtails for the potluck sauntered up. Billy Ray, according to his apron, but I remembered the dead guy had cut that name short to just *Ray*. "He's not giving up any information," he said. "I tried." He pointed his thumb over his shoulder. "When they came through. I was packing my stuff up in the kitchen and I tried to pry some information from them. Wasn't happening. The only thing they wanted to know was who made the peach cobbler."

"It wasn't my peach cobbler that killed him, Ray," Mama Zola said. "Koby said he was electrocuted."

Seemed Mama Zola called him "Ray," too.

"Electrocuted?" Ray's hazel eyes lit up. "I knew coffee was going to get him in the end."

"What does that mean?" I asked, my face turned up in a frown. I didn't know the victim or this man. I'd seen them only for the first time this morning, but I remembered that they seemed to know each other. And it seemed their relationship was fractured.

"That old coffeemaker that he was using in the kitchen?" Ray said. "It was on its last legs."

"How do you know it was the coffee machine?" I said and looked at Koby at the same time. Had my brother noticed the coffeemaker when we were in the kitchen? I hadn't. Although it wasn't unusual for me to miss things. But I knew an old coffeemaker, and nothing more, couldn't kill on its own.

Unless it was the coffee inside?

Koby, wrong? The man's death wasn't why the power company was there? Nah. I shook my head. I'd learned to trust my brother's intuition.

So he had another reason to say something about the coffeemaker.

I looked at Ray. That he had information about the electrocution did make him interesting. At least to me. I looked at him sideways.

Could he have something to do with Austin James' death?

"C'mon, Mama Zola," I said. I took her by the arm, pulling her away from Ray. "We should go. Too much commotion going on here." I didn't want her getting friendly with a possible killer. Not jumping to conclusions, but who knew what involvement Ray had in what was going on.

"Let's talk to the pastor before he leaves," Koby said.

He seemed to be getting antsy. He'd said that same thing a few times and we had yet to make it over to him. "We can catch the two of them." He started to walk off. "We can talk to Ross Franklin at the same time."

He had said that before, too.

Okay," I said. "But we need to remember that that Austin guy was Pastor Lee's friend. We should tread lightly and with some sympathy. Even a little empathy."

"We will. And him being the dead guy's friend makes him exactly the right person and this the right time to talk to him. He might have the most information. Especially since he'd been the person the police were talking with."

"And remember, we're not talking to him in an attempt to solve the murder." I swallowed hard. "I don't want to solve any murders." I followed reluctantly behind him.

"I know you don't," Koby said. "But if we're to help Pete, we have going to have to"—he grabbed my hand and looked into my face—"find out what happened and possible reasons why."

"I want to help Pete, too," Mama Zola said. She'd caught up with us and glanced toward her new pastor. "I just hope he doesn't think my peach cobbler had anything to do with it."

I blew out a breath.

Koby was partially out of luck. By the time we walked across the small parking lot, Interim Chief Ross Franklin was getting into his car. Pastor Lee had just started to head into the building when we got to him. He didn't seem happy to see the four of us, but he did force a smile. And I didn't like that Ray had tagged along behind us.

"Pastor Lee," Mama Zola said as soon as we were in earshot of him. "Seemed like my peach cobbler wasn't the hit I'd hoped it be."

I couldn't believe she was talking about cobbler. I shook my head and crossed to stand in front of her.

"We're sorry about the loss of your friend," I said.

"Death comes to all of us," Pastor Lee said.

"Not by electrocution," Koby said,

A look of surprise came across the pastor's face. Then he looked across the parking lot like he was looking for the person who had told Koby.

"How do you know how he died?"

"My brother is good at observation," I said. "We were just wondering what happened."

"The building looks up to code—"

"It is," the pastor said. "We take care of everything around here."

"And the two additions to the atrium are new."

"It was an accident. Plain and simple. It had nothing to do with our building."

"Or my cobbler," Mama Zola said.

Pastor Lee squinted his eyes and a look of confusion set across his face. "It was a tragedy. But if you'll excuse me."

"What happened, exactly?" Koby asked, following in step with the exiting pastor.

"You seem to have a lot of information. You tell me."

"I mean," Koby said, "usually a one-ten- or one-twenty-volt line inside a building isn't enough to kill a person."

"You wouldn't think," the pastor said, his voice trailing off. "But it's what happened. Along with a frayed extension cord." He looked at Koby. "Just a combination of things all at once."

The good reverend looked sad.

"Why would they pick up Pete?" Koby asked. "He had no control over a combination of things." He repeated the words.

"Unless that combination was set up to happen. There were only a couple of people who knew Austin had heart trouble and knew how to rig an electric trap."

"And, what? Are you saying Pete was one of them?"

"I don't like hurling accusations around," the pastor said as he reached for the door handle. "I'll leave the investigating to the police." He stepped inside. "And so should you."

"Pete's a good guy," Koby said, stepping in behind him.

I followed, but before going inside, I turned back to Mama Zola and Ray. "You two stay here," I said, lowering my voice. "No need of Pastor Lee's church members getting on his bad side."

"Because Koby isn't going to let up," Mama Zola said.

I had to trot catch up to Pastor Lee and Koby after I'd left Mama Zola and Ray at the door. They'd walked down the long hallway of the addition with its shiny linoleum floors. I didn't know what Koby had said in the interim, but by the time I got to them, the good reverend's words had gotten testy.

"Look, I don't believe that any of my church members had anything to do with this. And like I said, I am going to leave this to the police. But I am the shepherd of this flock and I have to make sure they are okay."

"Are you saying that Pete makes them unsafe?"

"The Good Word says to help others because you might be entertaining angels unaware. But my advice to you, young man, is that you should think twice before you open your doors to a vagabond."

With that, Pastor Calvin Lee opened the door marked RESTROOM and, before shutting it behind him, he added, "And I don't think it would be a good idea for Zola Jackson to continue her membership here. Not if her association with Pete Howers continues. He is no longer welcome in my church."

Chapter Five

WELL, THAT WAS *a smack in the face,* I thought as Koby and I stood facing the door that had just been shut in front of us.

"Wow," Koby said, staring at the door until it completely shut and then turning his gaze on me. "He sure did do a one-eighty. Chastising Austin earlier for saying mean things and now calling Pete a vagabond."

"Yeah. He did." I shook my head. "And that's gonna hurt when we tell Mama Zola that," I said, turning to look at my brother. Still standing outside of the restroom, I lowered my voice. It seemed only appropriate. "Because there is no way she's not going to associate with Pete. They work together."

"I know. And she really liked it here." As usual, he spoke in his normal voice. It wasn't often that he felt the need to hide or be discreet.

"So now what?"

"We wait," Koby said.

"Wait on what? To tell Mama Zola she can't come back to church?"

"No. On Pastor Lee to come out of the restroom. We need to talk to him again."

"We can't wait here." My eyes big, I wasn't so sure why my brother was being so determined. Although I had learned, even after only the short time we'd been together, that determination was built into his DNA. "This does not feel—appropriate."

"Yeah. You're right. Let's go to his office," Koby said. "It's probably where he'll head after he's finished in there anyway."

"Okay," I said, following behind him down the hallway. "But what else do we need to find out from him?"

"Whatever he's willing to tell us. And"—he looked back at me—"we need to convince him not to kick Mama Zola out of the church."

"And what are we supposed to do with the information?"

"Use it to help Pete."

Of course, that answer made no sense to me. The last thing I'd heard Pastor Lee say about Pete seemed more like an indictment than an exoneration. Putting Mama Zola out of the church if she continued to associate with Pete.

I followed my brother, as I found myself doing lately, down the hallway until we heard a noise coming from the only door that wasn't completely closed.

A woman in the pastor's office, according to the sign on the door, was crying. Softly. In short bursts of sniffles. It was easy to hear her outside in the hallway.

We'd found Pastor Lee's office on the other side of the atrium in the other addition. I was worried about just marching in, having a seat and waiting for the pastor to return, but I knew that wouldn't stop my twin brother.

And neither did the crying.

I knew it was a woman from a peek through the slightly ajar door. It revealed her sitting behind a desk, her head down and her hands covering her face. It looked as if she wanted to be alone.

We'd gone there to wait on the pastor, hoping he'd return so we could finish questioning him about Pete, his friend Austin James and now Mama Zola. A fact-gathering mission that hadn't gone so well so far, but this presented a whole other dynamic to what we set out to do. A crying woman couldn't be good.

"Hi," Koby said, pushing the door open wider and walking inside the small space.

So much for her being alone.

"Hello yourself," the voice came from behind the door.

Oh, she's not alone . . .

"Didn't you see the door was closed?" the woman behind the door asked.

I stood still in the doorway. Not stepping over the threshold. Koby, on the other hand, was practically so far inside that he could touch the crying woman.

"I just came in to see if she was okay." He pointed to the woman at the desk.

"Does she sound okay to you?"

I wanted so bad to peek around the door and see who was talking.

The voice was gruff. Snide. And not so Christian-like. I wanted a face to match. And I wondered, what was she wearing . . .

"I think you should leave," the Voice said to Koby.

I tried to make myself tiny. I didn't want her to see me. We'd already seemed to make one church member unhappy.

"Is there anything I can do?" Koby asked and pulled a tissue from the box sitting atop the desk, handing it to her.

She looked up. First at Koby. Then at me. And without

saying anything, she looked at the Voice Behind the Door, her eyes pleading.

"You'd better go," the Voice said.

That's when I saw her.

Short. Squat. Round. Elderly.

She stood up, coming from behind the door, she started toward Koby. She wore a short brown wig and a small purple hat, which didn't match anything else she had on, on top of that. She had on a navy dress that looked shiny from too many times under an iron. And she clutched her purse handles as if it were a weapon. I squinted my eyes, anticipating that my brother was going to be her target.

It was all I could do not to yell "Duck!" to Koby.

"Young man. It's time for you to leave." The woman had cleared her throat, making sure she made her words clear to Koby. "My daughter doesn't want to talk to you." Her purse started a slight swing, I guessed to build up momentum. "Now I'm not going to tell you again to leave."

He turned to the Mother of the Crier (she was no longer just a voice behind the door) and spoke to her as if she had invited him in for a slice of sweet potato pie.

"I was just wondering what is going on around here. Is she crying because of what happened to Austin James?"

I couldn't take any more. Koby was making us enemies, not finding facts. First the pastor and now this little old lady. I wanted to pull him away, but I didn't know whether that would work. But I figured if I left, he'd leave to follow me. A death, possibly a murder, had taken place in these hallowed halls and he wouldn't leave me to wander them alone for long. So I stepped, gingerly, back into the middle of the hallway and headed back toward the restroom because I knew that was the way back out to where we'd left Mama Zola and where Koby's car was parked. Once there, maybe I could persuade my brother to leave.

As I walked down the hallway, I kept an eye over my

shoulder. I anticipated it wouldn't be long before Koby would notice I'd left and start out behind me.

I must've gone the wrong way, though, because I ended up at the atrium, the middle of the church, an area I hadn't remembered passing after we'd left the pastor in the restroom.

I took the hallway that led to the kitchen in back. Seeing that I was so close, I wanted to have another look for that coffeemaker that Ray had alluded to earlier. I hadn't seen it that morning, and if Austin James actually was victim to it, the police had probably already removed it. Still, I was curious.

Curious . . .

That was what motivated my brother to snoop and here I was complaining about him doing it and then doing the same thing. Geesh!

Still, as I walked, I put together my excuse for roaming about. I'd been there before, this morning. I could say we thought we'd left something there.

But I never had to explain myself because as I rounded the corner, I was stopped dead in my tracks. I heard voices. Angry voices. Speaking in a strained whisper.

They didn't want anyone to hear what they were saying, so I turned an ear.

"He was a menace and he got what he deserved."

I peeked around the corner to see who was talking. Two men. One I recognized. Rocko Jackson, the security guard. The other I didn't know, but his outfit was a dead giveaway. Yellow hard hat in his hand. Short-sleeved shirt. Lightning bolt.

That one worked for the power company. He was a different guy than the one I'd seen outside earlier talking to the pastor and the police chief. This one was younger, with a mess of curly brown hair and round, wire-rimmed glasses.

"Ugh." Power Company Guy closed his eyes and

rubbed the area at the bridge of his nose. "That was just over the top." His voice was so strained it almost squeaked. "He may have been a menace, but c'mon."

"It's done now. Can't go back."

"Keaton!"

Koby almost gave me a heart attack. I jerked back around the corner, my leg giving way from him scaring me and the odd angle I'd been in snooping. I nearly fell to the floor.

"Koby!" I whispered. "Be quiet!" I flapped an arm at him.

"What?" he asked. His voice normal. "Why? And why did you run off? You can't go walking around here by yourself."

"Shhh!"

I grabbed his arm and pulled him down the hallway, in the opposite direction of the two conspirators, breaking into almost a trot when we passed the pastor's office.

At least we were going in the right direction. I didn't even take a look at what was going on in there.

"What are you doing?" Koby said.

"Keeping us from being the next ones who get electrocuted."

Chapter Six

BEFORE WE COULD get out of the building or even close to the door, Koby stopped, stood still and became immovable. I couldn't get him to budge. I dropped my grip on him and stood in front of him, looking him in the face.

"Can we go now?" I asked.

"Go?" He frowned at me. "Don't you need to tell me what was going on in there? The reason we had to leave in such a hurry?"

So I told him what happened. The two guys. The conversation they'd had. My assumptions.

"You think they killed the guy from this morning?"

I nodded vigorously, confirming he'd understood me correctly. "So can we go now?"

Of course, the answer to that was no.

"No," Koby said. "We need to talk to them. See what the heck they were talking about."

"Really?" I said and put a hand on my hip. "Do you think they'll just tell you?"

"No." He frowned. Again. "I don't think that, but we need to hear what they have to say."

"So you can figure out what they really mean?"

"Something like that."

I know Koby's time in foster care and in groups made him more streetwise than I could ever hope to be, but in my estimation, it was nearly impossible to "read" two guys you'd never met. I just wanted to get him away from the church. I still hadn't figured out what he'd said to upset the pastor. I didn't know that I wanted to hear what it was. And we still had to explain to Mama Zola her current excommunication from Everlasting Missionary Baptist Church.

"We can't do that," I said.

"Why?"

"Because I was eavesdropping." I bucked my eyes at him. "They won't be forthcoming at all if we question what I heard."

"Or if they were the killers."

"Exactly," I said.

"Okay. Okay," he said. "But we still need to go back and see if we can find the pastor. We definitely need to finish talking to him. Otherwise"—he glanced down the hallway toward the door that led outside—"I won't ever be able to live through what Mama Zola will have in store for me."

"I don't think he wants to talk to us anymore. And"— I shook my head—"we may have already done irreparable damage." I took off walking toward what, this time, I was sure was the way out.

"Oh." Koby pulled on my arm to stop me. "Is that the power guy you saw Rocko talking to?"

"Where?"

"There." Koby pointed down the hallway behind me. "The one that's now talking to the good reverend Calvin Lee."

"What!"

And sure enough, the same guy who had just talked to Parking Lot Attendant Rocko Jackson was standing in the hallway talking to Pastor Lee.

"We can't hear anything," I said, getting nervous about them seeing us. I turned my back to them, ready to run out of the door. "Maybe we should go."

"We don't *need* to hear anything," Koby said. "Look at what they're doing." He turned my head to them. "Look at them."

So, I did. I watched as they talked. Nothing too serious, it seemed, and then they shook hands, Power Guy gave Pastor Lee something—a business card, folded piece of paper, I wasn't sure—and then they parted ways.

Power Company Guy was coming straight toward us.

We turned and, breaking almost into a trot, certainly a brisk walk, went in the other direction.

But we hadn't gotten more than twenty feet when we nearly ran into the older woman who had been in the room with the crying woman. She was coming out of the restroom. Drying her hands on a paper towel, she had a bead of sweat over her upper lip.

That restroom was giving us grief today.

"Are you two still lurking around in the hallways?"

"No," I said, which really didn't sound like the truth, seeing that we stood there in the hallway. But we were trying to leave.

"Then it's time for you to leave," she said, hissing out her words. "This isn't a time for games. We just lost a church member, and the police wouldn't want you here messing things up."

I wanted to say that the police had already left and that we weren't messing anything up. We'd only been walking (lurking in her estimation) and nothing more. But I was already a little afraid of her. I hadn't asked Koby what she'd done to get him to leave the pastor's office. Then I remembered that swinging purse.

"We're going," Koby said. "Hope your daughter feels better."

"*Hmpf*" was all we got in response.

Finally, Koby was agreeing to leave.

"I'm so glad we're out of that place. It was like a fun-house, something around every corner," I said after the door shut behind us. "And we gained nothing for it."

"Yes, we did." A look of confusion on my brother's face. "We did learn something."

"When?" I mimicked his confused look. "What?"

"From the conversations. The one you overheard, and the one we just witnessed."

"What did they mean?" I asked. "Okay. So the one with Rocko and Power Guy seemed ominous enough. But we didn't learn anything from when Power Guy talked to the pastor. We don't even know what they were saying."

"What we just watched. You know, the shaking of the hands. The passing of the business card. The nice pleasant smiles. The small talk." He nodded like he'd just explained it all to me. "It means something."

"What?" I asked again.

"Okay. So right now, I have no idea," Koby said. "But maybe it might mean something later on."

I chuckled. How was I ever going to imitate him if he didn't even know what the things meant that he did notice?

When we came back outside, the sky had turned gray and smell of the coming rain was in the air. Mama Zola and Ray were still standing in almost the same spot where we'd left them.

"Glad to see you guys made it back," Ray said. "I didn't want to leave this little lady out here all by herself."

That made me feel bad. I just realized I'd left Mama

Zola with a guy that was on my suspect list. I knew that she was capable—probably more than capable—of defending herself, but it probably hadn't been a good idea.

"Are you okay, Mama Zola?" I asked.

"Of course I'm okay. Why wouldn't I be okay?"

"No reason," Koby said and gave me the eye. "We just stayed a little longer than we thought we would."

"Yes, you did," Ray said, agreeing.

"Yes. You. Did." Mama Zola noisily blew air through her nostrils. "Now"—she raised an eyebrow—"are we going to see about Pete, or what?" she asked. She'd started tapping her foot. "While you two are running around an empty church, they could be strapping him up to the electric chair."

"Mama Zola, there are no electric chairs in the state of Washington," Koby said.

"There isn't even capital punishment," I said. "They abolished it years ago."

"So that makes it okay to leave him there?"

"No, of course it's not okay," Koby said, "and we're not leaving him there."

"Seems like they have their man," Ray said, swiping his hands together like he'd just been served a delicious meal. "All the excitement has died down."

"They don't have the right man," Koby said.

Ray had moved on. He looked at Mama Zola. "I've already got my stuff packed up, you got your leftovers?"

"Didn't have any," Mama Zola said. "Pastor Lee and the dead guy got my last. And"—she clucked her tongue—"Koby's right. They don't have their guy. Pete didn't no more kill that guy than you did."

Ray gave what I thought was a sinister smirk and let out a chuckle that was even more ominous. As if he'd been the one who'd done Austin James in. But I seemed to be the only one who noticed.

I had my suspicions. Ray knew about the coffeepot. Billy Ray was certainly on my list.

"Well, look at you. Everyone must have loved your food," Ray said to Mama Zola, which made her eyes sparkle. Yep, she definitely didn't believe Ray had anything to do with that grisly death. "I'ma have to get a private tasting of your cooking, so I can have you all to myself." He smacked his lips.

"Her cooking, you mean," Koby said. "Not her." He didn't seem to like Ray's flirting with his foster mom.

Ray grinned. "Well. I gotta go," he said. "I hear those oxtails and that cornbread calling my name." He licked his lips. "Thank goodness I didn't run out of them because that's gonna be my dinner tonight."

"Mmm, yes," Mama Zola said. "That sounds good,"

"You're welcome to join me," Ray said, smiling at Mama Zola.

"She's good," Koby said. "We're leaving, too."

"Okay," Ray said, tipping an imaginary hat. "But in case you change your mind, I'ma leave the door open." He winked at Mama Zola before he ambled back over to his car and tucked his large frame inside.

"I don't need you to speak for me, you know," Mama Zola said, referring to Koby sending Ray on his way.

"Okay," Koby said and nothing more. He knew there was no way to win an argument with her. He had told me a couple of times, when it comes to her fussing at you, just say "okay." She can't argue back if you're agreeing with her.

"I thought we were leaving," Mama Zola said after we hadn't budged from the spot we were in.

"I was thinking we should wait for the people inside the church to come out," Koby said. "I wanna see if any of them have more information than what we were able to get."

"Who?" Mama Zola asked.

"And then do what?" I asked.

"Do what with who?" Mama Zola asked.

"Rocko, the pastor," Koby said to Mama Zola, and blew out a breath. Then he turned to me. "I don't know what we should do." Koby shrugged. "Follow them?"

"Which one?" I asked. "There were five people we ran into in that building." I shook my head. "We can't follow all of them."

"Yeah, that's true," Koby said.

"Is that what the two of you were doing in there all that time?" Mama Zola asked.

This was the most disjointed conversation. And it seemed like Mama Zola wasn't getting any of the answers to the questions she posed.

"And I don't even know what you said to that crying woman and her mother," I said.

"She was the pastor's secretary," Koby said. "I did find that out."

"Who?" Mama Zola and I said it in unison.

"The crying woman," Koby said. "The other woman was her mother."

"Yeah, I got that the older woman was the mother."

"Are you two talking about Mother Tyson and Lacey Bell?"

We both looked at Mama Zola. Her words finally got our attention.

"Yes. We said her mother," I said.

"No. I mean Lydia Tyson is a *mother* of the church."

"Oh," I said, understanding. "Mother" was a term of respect and honor given to older women of the church. Younger women in the church would go to them for advice.

"But is she Lacey's actual mother, too?" Koby asked.

"I think so," Mama Zola said. "She calls her Ma."

"I don't know," I said. "Good question." I looked at my brother. "Did you get their names, Koby?"

"I guess we got them now." He glanced over at Mama Zola.

"Don't look now," Mama Zola said, "but someone is coming out of the building."

Power Company Guy had left the building and was headed to his truck, one of the few cars left in the parking lot.

"So what are we going to do?" I asked. "Are we going to follow him?" I clarified. "Power Guy." Although Ray had turned the corner, I wouldn't have been against following him. That might have been a missed opportunity.

"I think we should watch and see what Rocko does." It was Mama Zola. Hadn't she just been complaining that we needed to leave to go and see about Pete? Koby and I turned again to look at her. "Makes sense," she said. "Either he had a hand in killing that James Austin—"

"Austin James," we corrected in unison.

"Or," she continued, not giving a second thought to what we were saying, "he let the person in who did."

"So we sit tight for a minute," Koby said, evidently agreeing with Mama Zola.

"Don't we look conspicuous?" I asked. "Standing in the middle of the parking lot?"

"Let's go sit in the car," Mama Zola said.

"We're like only one of a few cars left in the parking lot," I said, noting how it had emptied out. "We'd still look suspicious."

"People park here all the time," Mama Zola said, waving a dismissive hand. She started walking toward the car. "I've come to Bible study here a time or two and there were cars who belonged to people not in the church."

"Then," I said, following her, "it looks like Rocko isn't doing his job."

"And maybe that's why that James guy got killed," Koby said.

We climbed into the car, and I realized Mama Zola

had made a good point. Two good points actually. Either he was involved directly or indirectly due to his negligence. And even though sitting in a parking lot waiting for him to emerge from a building was a long shot on finding out his involvement, we did need to start somewhere.

Although, I thought as I started coughing, remembering all the smoke I'd inhaled from our last whodunit escapades, *I wasn't all for us getting involved in another murder.*

I twiddled my thumbs and stared out of the window.

"Wondering what he's doing in there?" I muttered more to myself than anyone. *Is he getting rid of evidence? Covering up his involvement?*

It was making me a little nervous. Sitting there. Waiting on a man who might be a killer. All three of us doing nothing in a parked car in an empty lot. Car not running. The windows down. And no apparent reason for not leaving like everyone else had after all the commotion had died down.

"He has no idea what we're doing," Koby said and looked at me. I'm sure he could sense my nervousness. "It won't be long. He'll be out in a minute. Nothing inside for him to do."

That wasn't what I'd been thinking.

But Koby was right about one thing—we didn't have wait long for the parking attendant to come out.

Rocko emerged from the doors of the church like he was on a mission. Phone up to his ear. Talking low into the phone that was glued to his ear. He was taking long strides and not giving one thought to his surroundings or us hanging out in the parking lot. He rubbed his hand over his buzz cut a time or two and tugged on his ear. He seemed agitated.

"I wonder who's got his goat," Mama Zola said.

"Seems like someone does," Koby said.

Rocko headed straight for the security guard booth and, once inside, he did a few turns, looking all around on the floor like he was looking for something, then he sat down on the stool.

"What in the world is he doing?" I asked.

"Sometimes when you're upset, you can't think straight," Mama Zola said.

"Wait. What is that?"

Rocko had popped back up and this time looked under the built-in desk-like counter. It seemed he had found what he was looking for. Phone still to his ear, he cradled it on his shoulder and pulled a cord out like it was a snake.

"Is that an extension cord?" I asked.

He stuffed it into a book bag and sat back on the stool.

"Did you see that?" Mama Zola's voice was on Volume 10.

"Shhh!" my twin and I said in unison.

"We saw it, Mama Zola." Even Koby had lowered his voice.

"Don't shush me." She sucked her tongue. "And now what is he doing?"

We turned to look back at Rocko.

"Writing something down," I said, in almost a whisper.

He tore the paper out from the notebook he'd written in, folded it neatly and put it in his book bag, too. Getting off the phone, he stood up and surveyed the parking lot, which made us all duck down. By the time we'd felt safe taking another peek, he was driving off in his raggedy silver Toyota Corolla.

Chapter Seven

"SO ARE WE going to follow him?" I asked.

"Or are we finally going to check on Pete?" Mama Zola asked.

We were still sitting in the parking lot of the church. We watched as the tail end of Rocko's rusty, noisy Toyota Corolla bumped across the apron of the parking lot and turned onto the street.

"I think we should go and look around the booth," Koby said.

"We can't get in there," I said.

"He didn't lock it."

"How do you know?" My voice went up an octave. "We all got out of sight as soon as he was about to exit."

"I peeked."

He would.

I glanced toward the building. "There are still people in there," I said. "They could come out. They'd see us."

"And Pete is still at the police station," Mama Zola said.

"I'll only be a minute," Koby said, already opening the car door.

"I'm coming, too," I said. I knew my brother. He would need some coaxing to make it snappy and get out of there and he'd need someone close by to keep a lookout. The church was a public building open to everyone (but Pete?) but it was still private property. I didn't want one of the owners of Books & Biscuits to end up the same place one of its employees had.

"Mama Zola, you stay here." Koby glanced at her before he closed the car door.

"You don't have to worry about me," she said to Koby. "I am not snooping around my church. Just don't seem right."

We got out of the car and Koby, with resolve, walked to the security guard booth. I sulked behind, constantly looking over my shoulder to see if anyone was exiting the church building.

That would be all we needed, for the pastor to see us. His stipulation about Mama Zola not coming back if she was still hanging around with Pete would probably be amended to banning all of us from coming back. Forever.

"So what are you looking for exactly?" I asked. I stood at the door. Koby had stepped up into the booth and was doing what we'd seen Rocko do earlier. Spin in circles.

"I can't know *exactly* what I'm looking for," he said. "You didn't think I could *know*, did you?" He gave me a smirk. "That's not how snooping works."

"Just hurry and find something. Or nothing. So we can go."

"Don't be so nervous. If we get caught, we can just say we lost something and we wanted to see if it was here. I'm sure there's a lost and found box somewhere."

It was funny how alike our minds worked. "Because people are always losing things in the parking lot?" I hoped he caught the sarcasm in my voice. "Do you see a box? I don't see a box." I blew out a breath. "The box is probably inside the church."

"Where we should have stayed and talked to Rocko and not come and look around in a four-by-four-foot booth."

"Too late now," I said. "Do you see anything?"

"The notebook he wrote something down in," he said and held it up.

I looked at the notebook and saw the indentation from where he'd written. "Let me see that," I said and Koby passed it over. "Do you see a pencil in there?"

Koby looked over the desk and found a stub of one. "Will this work?"

I held out my hand. "Yep."

I took the side of the pencil and scratched the graphite across the page.

My brother beamed at me. "Smart."

I smiled back. "Okay. So it's a phone number," I said and showed it to him.

"Whoever he was on the phone with gave him a phone number," Koby said. He rubbed his chin, then he pulled out his phone. "We should call it."

"No we shouldn't." I shook my head. "How random." I held the notebook to my chest so he couldn't see the number.

"Already have it memorized."

"What about if it's a phone number for a girl he wants to date?"

"Then we'll warn her he's a possible murderer." He started punching the numbers in.

"Not funny," I said.

Koby put the phone on speaker and held it up to face me.

"Good afternoon." Someone had picked up the phone. "Grace Spirit Revival."

"Another church," Koby mouthed the words.

"Maybe he's looking for another job," I mouthed back.

"Hello?" said the voice on the other end of the line.

"Oh sorry," Koby said. He looked at me. It seemed he wanted me to help him think of something to say. I had no idea. I didn't even do prank calls when I was a kid. I held up a hand and shrugged.

"Uhm," he started, "I was just wondering where you are located? My sister and I"—I shook my head, indicating I did not want to be in on whatever story he was getting ready to come up with—"are thinking about visiting your, uhm, church?"

He said it like he was unsure that was what it was and then hunched his shoulders at me.

I rolled my eyes. That was why he shouldn't have called somewhere he had no idea about.

"We welcome all visitors," the voice said, her tone chipper. If the voice only knew what deception was going on at our end of the phone.

"I'll give you our address, if you need it."

"No, we have it," Koby said. "Thank you."

"Have a blessed day."

"You're going to hell, you know," I said after he hung up.

"For what?"

"Lying?"

"When did I lie?" He pried the notebook out of my hands and tore off the page that had revealed Grace Spirit Revival's number.

"When you said we were coming to visit. When you said we have the address." I could go on, the list of his fabrications was long. But I figured I'd stick to only the untruths he'd told in the last five minutes.

He typed something into his phone, then held it up for me to see. He had Googled Grace Spirit Revival and was showing me what he'd found. "See. We have the address, and you'll be the only one not telling the truth if you don't go with me over there."

"You're going over there?"

"I wouldn't want to lie and go to hell," he said with the same sarcasm I had used on him earlier. "But it seems you don't have a problem with that."

"I'm not the one who said it," I said, but then actually wondered if it wasn't the same thing. "Oh my gosh!"

He balled up the paper and stuffed it in his pocket. "C'mon," he said, an evil little smile on his face. "Let's go before lightning strikes us for all of our lying and we end up like Austin James."

I didn't know why I ever aspired to be like my brother. He was so mischievous. He had me following people around. Snooping. And standing right in the line of fire. Figuratively, right now, but I was beginning to think it might not be too long before maybe it would be literally, too.

"I didn't tell a lie."

He chuckled. For some reason he found that funny.

"What did you find?" Mama Zola asked when we got back in the car.

"A phone number," I said.

"Nothing," Koby said.

I turned and looked at him, then up to the graying sky. "Looks like there may be lightning."

A big grin broke out on his face. "*Nothing* of any importance, Mama Zola," he said, turning his falsehood into what was probably the truth. "At least not yet."

That meant, I assumed, he'd have plenty of questions for the people over at Grace even though I knew how innocuous that phone number was probably going to turn out to be.

Chapter Eight

FINALLY.

Koby started the car and I let out a sigh of relief. We were leaving.

I was happy to get away from this wretched place. No offense meant to all the members of Everlasting Missionary Baptist Church. But it couldn't be a good sign when a murder happens inside a place of worship.

Or when the pastor accuses and condemns a person before he even had an opportunity to prove himself without blame. That person being Pete. We were also finally going to get him.

"Look," Koby said and pointed. "The pastor is coming out of the church." He looked over at me. "Maybe we should follow him."

So, okay, maybe we weren't on our way to get Pete.

"I vote no," I said.

"So do I," Mama Zola said. "That man is a saint. He doesn't have anything to do with what happened today. And he certainly hasn't done anything wrong."

I watched as the good reverend the left the church. He had his secretary, if I recalled correctly, Lacey Bell, and her mother with him. It seemed Pastor Lee was giving them a lift.

I hoped they'd be safe riding with him.

"He seems to think that Pete may have had something to do with Austin James' death," I said, maybe a thought I shouldn't have voiced out loud.

"No, he doesn't," Mama Zola said and waved a dismissive hand.

"And he said that you couldn't come back to church if you are going to hang out with Pete."

"Hang out with Pete? I don't hang out with people. I'm too old for that."

"I think he meant 'associate with him.'"

"What are you talking about?" She seemed to be trying to process what Koby was saying, but it was, it seemed, hard to believe what he was saying about her pastor. "He wouldn't have said that." She looked out the window at the pastor as he held the door open for Mother Tyson.

"He did say that," I said. My word didn't carry as much clout as Koby's, I'm sure. But I knew that she knew, after spending some time with me and lots of time with my brother, who was more apt to tell the truth.

"I'm sure if he did say it, he didn't mean it like you think."

"He said, 'Tell her, don't come back.'"

"I have to associate with Pete," she said. "We work together." She shook her head. She looked puzzled. "He's my friend."

"If that's true," Koby said, "we'll have to find you a new church home."

"The nerve." Mama Zola snorted out the words. "Hmpf!" She buckled her seat belt. "What are you waiting on?" She turned to Koby. "He's getting away. Follow him!"

I chuckled to myself. It wasn't funny. I knew she liked

that church, but it didn't take much for her to turn against her beloved pastor.

"Where do you think he's going?" Mama Zola asked. "Drive faster." She patted Koby on his arm. "You think we'll catch him doing something?"

"Probably not with other people in the car," I said.

"Unless he plans on killing them, too," she said.

That time I chuckled out loud.

"Murder isn't funny," she said.

"I know. I'm sorry." I hung my head, more in mock remorse and to hide the humor that I feared was still showing on my face.

"You're going to lose them, Koby."

"No I'm not, Mama Zola." He turned to her momentarily and shook his head. "We can't get too close. They'll see us. Mother Tyson already doesn't like me."

"Oh my," Mama Zola said. "She's sweet as pie. What did you do to her?" Her face looked confused. "You done caused so much trouble for me here today. First my pastor, then the mother of the church."

"What?" Now Koby chuckled, too. "I didn't do anything."

"I think I'm going to cry."

That concerned me. I didn't think anything could bother Mama Zola.

"Don't start crying now, Mama Zola," Koby said. "He's letting the girls out of the car."

"They're not girls," she said and frowned. "Mother Tyson is old enough to be your grandmother."

"However old they are, we're going to need your eyes dry so you can help me keep up with that pastor of yours after he drops them off."

"I wasn't really going to cry," she muttered. "I've got perfect vision. And," she sniffed, "he isn't *my* pastor anymore." She turned and looked out of the window. "What a pretty house."

And it was. I didn't know if they lived together. Mother Tyson was old like Mama Zola said, but she seemed quite capable. But either way, the house was big enough for ten family members. It was painted white, with powder blue shutters and a big wraparound porch. Why they needed such a big porch in a place that got more clouds than sun was a mystery to me. But even that didn't change my mind on what a grand house it was.

We weren't far from the church. We'd gone around a few corners and up one hill and down the next. The driveway where Pastor Lee pulled into belonged to a house that was on a hill higher than any one I'd thought we had in Timber Lake. The houses on the street were so far apart that we could see into the backyard and the water beyond.

"That's a really nice view," I said, looking out the window. "I'd spend all my time back there if I lived here." I turned back to look at the house. "Right on the water."

"It is a nice life," Koby said. "Waking up to look out onto the lake."

"Don't rub it in," I said.

Koby had inherited a houseboat and had moved from his Seattle apartment to a lakefront sailing vessel right down the street from me. Only there was no view from my front porch. I was pretty sure his boat probably couldn't navigate even out of the dock where it was moored, but it still gave a million-dollar view. It was nice, but nothing fancy, and perfect for him.

And me. Now I had my brother living close to me. After being separated for just about two decades, even though I hadn't known, every second near him was priceless.

Pastor Lee got out and went around the car. He opened the door first for Mother Tyson, who was sitting in the front passenger seat, and then for her daughter, Lacey.

"What a gentleman," Mama Zola said. "Are you sure he said—"

"I'm sure," Koby said, anticipating what she was going to say. "But I'm going to fix it for you."

"I don't know if you can fix this."

Pastor Lee walked the ladies to their front door and gave each one of them a hug. Then he waited for them to get inside and close the door behind them before he went back and got into his car.

"When is he supposed to do something that will let us know he's the murderer?" Mama Zola asked.

"He may not be the murderer," I said. "So he may not do anything suspicious."

"Then why are we following him?" Mama Zola asked. Seemed she was wavering once again in her belief about her now ex-pastor's goodness.

"Because he might," Koby said and took off behind him. "He's on the move again. Let's see where we go this time."

"To his house." Mama Zola sounded disappointed. "This is his house."

We'd only gone a few blocks from where we'd dropped off Mother Tyson and her daughter, Lacey. Back in the direction closer to the church. We landed in front of a small bungalow, similar to mine but with a stained-glass window and painted two shades of gray with white trim.

"How do you know this is his house?" Koby asked.

"Because I've been here before," Mama Zola said. "Mother Tyson usually has a tea for new members, but something was going on at her house so he hosted here."

"I don't remember that," Koby said.

"Why would you remember that?"

"Because I would have taken you there."

"I am quite capable of getting around on my own," Mama Zola said. "But it was after church and one of the members drove me."

"Oh," Koby said.

I smiled. He was so protective of her. Sometimes I

wondered why he cared about finding our biological mother. I was quite happy with the one who had picked me instead of giving birth to me. And it seemed he had found a pretty cool one, too, although I knew he hadn't been with her long. Still she'd made a lasting impression on him for sure. It was where he'd gotten his awesome cooking skills.

"So are we going to go and ask him if he killed Austin James?"

Koby and I looked at each other. It was the first time she'd gotten his name right.

But then I had to speak up before Koby, because following the man into his own house to interrogate him was right up my brother's alley.

"No. We are not. We can sit and watch to see if he does anything we can report to the police."

"How boring," Mama Zola said and yawned. Loudly.

Koby thought that was funny.

"We know where he lives in case we have to do any further investigations," Koby said. "I think we're good to go."

"Thank the Lord," Mama Zola said.

"We can go and see about Pete," Koby said.

"That was the smartest thing you suggested to do all day." Mama Zola shook her head. "I changed my mind about you figuring out what happened. I think maybe you should just stick to cooking."

Chapter Nine

WE FINALLY MADE it to the police station and to Pete, although they didn't allow us to see him when we got there. And that didn't sit too well with Mama Zola.

"What do you mean we can't see him?" She put her hand on the counter, stood on her tippy-toes and leaned in. "We're here to take him home."

The police station was a two-story red brick building close to downtown Timber Lake, which made it close. The person behind the desk didn't seem intimidated at all by Mama Zola. "You can wait over there." They pointed to a waiting area, where we found Avery Moran.

Avery was quite still, unperturbed, especially for being there as long as he had. I hoped he could share some of his calmness with Mama Zola.

"What do they think they're doing?" Mama Zola said, pacing the floor. "How much information do they think they can get from him?" She threw up her hands and threw a look at the officer behind the desk. "He doesn't know anything. He was with me the entire time."

"Maybe you shouldn't say that out loud, Mama Zola," Koby said. "You don't want them dragging you back there."

"I'd like to see them try."

"Did you find out anything, Avery?" I asked.

"Not much." He glanced over at the officer behind the desk. "But they are thinking that it was definitely murder."

"Murder." Mama Zola frowned up and groaned. "What a terrible word."

"I agree," I said, although she had been the first to say it when she called, causing us to close up shop early.

"By electrocution?" Mama Zola seemed to want to confirm.

"You know, they're going to do an autopsy," Moran said. "But looks that way."

"Now that we know he had a pacemaker—" Koby started, but I finished.

"It could have been some kind of cardiovascular event." I glanced over at the desk clerk. "The pacemaker's signal got interrupted by the electrical shock."

"Yep." Koby nodded. "His heart couldn't work properly."

"And Pete"—Avery Moran lowered his voice—"knew about that pacemaker."

We all looked at one another. That wasn't a good thing.

"And," Moran added, "there seems as if there was a video."

"Of Pete killing Austin James?" I asked.

"Of course not," Mama Zola said and gave me the same look she'd given the desk officer.

"No. Not necessarily," Avery said.

"But seemingly evidence, *clear* evidence, as the acting chief put it, that Pete may have been involved with *it*."

What "it" was exactly, I wasn't sure. Certainly not the murder. And what the good chief had termed "clear," Koby and Mama Zola called "hogwash."

"Hogwash," they both said in unison.

"The chief—"

"Acting chief," Mama Zola said.

Avery Moran smiled. "The acting chief said that the church had a security tape that they were able to watch."

"Of what happened?" I said, my face scrunched up, my voice a little shaky. "How disturbing."

"Did you see it?" Koby asked.

"No," Avery said. "But not of the death. It was people going in and out of the church."

"What exactly happened to that Austin guy?" Koby asked. "Were you able to find that out? I got that it had something to do with a coffeemaker and his pacemaker."

"Yeah," Avery said. "Seems like he had a thing for coffee. Drank it not just in the morning but all day."

"I didn't notice a coffeemaker in the kitchen this morning," Koby said.

I knew if one had been there, my twin would have noticed.

"Yeah, that was the thing," Avery said. "It was always in the kitchen. Except for today."

"Where was it today?" Mama Zola asked.

"In the office that Austin used."

"Used for what?" Koby asked. "Was he like the assistant pastor or something?"

"More like the devil himself," Mama Zola said. "Didn't seem to have a kind word for anyone he ran into."

"I don't know the answer to that. Thinking he's not the devil, though"—Avery glanced over at Mama Zola—"but unsure what his role was."

"So what about this surveillance camera?" Koby asked. "How did that indicate Pete was involved and warranted him coming down here?"

"The tape, or video, I guess it's called these days," Avery said, showing his age, "showed three people going into the church before anyone else this morning."

"This morning?" Mama Zola said. "Nope." She shook

her head. "I'm his alibi. Pete was with me all morning. I could tell them that." She looked to the desk clerk. "All they have to do is ask me."

"The three people," Avery said, picking up where he'd left off before Mama Zola's unsolicited speech exonerating Pete, "were Pete, one of the deacons of the church and a woman in a hat."

"Who was that?" I asked. I was always interested in what people were wearing. "The woman in the hat? I don't remember seeing a woman wearing a hat."

"Deacon who?" Mama Zola asked.

"Don't know the answer to any one of those questions," Avery said. "Only found out what I did because of police courtesy and I'm here with Pete. No info on anyone else."

"So any of the other two could have done something to James Austin," Mama Zola said.

"Austin James," I said. She just couldn't get that man's name in the right order.

"That's right," Avery said. "Early entry gave all three of them the opportunity and the means to create the situation that killed Austin James."

"The situation?" I asked.

"The situation or, should I say, the murder weapon," Avery said. "A coffeepot connected to a frayed extension cord that was laying in a pool of spilt coffee."

"And a victim whose heart already had some electrical problems," Koby said.

Avery looked at Koby, then hung his head. "Seems like everyone didn't know that. Only certain people."

"And Pete was one of those people?" Koby asked.

"Seems that way."

"How did he know?" Koby asked.

"That I don't know." Avery looked toward a shut door that I assumed led to the back offices where they were holding on to Pete. "You'd have to ask him."

"So now what about the other people in the surveillance video?" Mama Zola asked. "Is anyone talking to them?"

"As I said," Avery said, "I don't know."

"It doesn't seem to me that anyone cares," Mama Zola said. "Because everyone we saw investigating this morning is in the back, badgering Pete." She looked at Koby. "You're going to have to figure this out."

I slapped a hand across my forehead. My brother did not need any encouragement. He was already on it, didn't she know?

"Who moved the coffeemaker?" Mama Zola said. "That could have been done at any time. Not just this morning"— she turned to the desk clerk and raised her voice—"when Pete was with me."

"It's possible since Koby doesn't remember seeing the coffeepot in the kitchen this morning, then anyone in the church, anytime before the potluck, could have moved it."

"That James man could have moved it himself."

"He didn't come in until after we got there," Koby said, reminding Mama Zola about when we'd first seen the dead guy.

"He could have done it yesterday."

"He would have been on the video," Avery said. "He wasn't."

"Where was Rocko?" Mama Zola asked. "How were all those people getting into the church?"

"Good question," I said. "The answer I think we might have already discovered when we were back at the church." I tilted my head and raised an eyebrow. "Rocko Jackson is not good at his job."

"And maybe looking for another job," Koby said.

"Sooo," Koby continued. I could see the wheels turning in his brain. "Someone came in. Moved the coffeemaker ahead of time, then set up a murdering machine by hooking it up with a faulty cord and dousing it with coffee."

"That's the story I got," Avery said.

"What kind of shoes did the guy have on?" Koby asked.

That would be a question for me.

I remembered Ray had on Crocs. Probably not real ones. They were pretty expensive. Still, they were plastic and probably a good insulator against an electrical current. Wasn't quite sure whose shoes Koby was talking about. But it mattered for victim and killer. And Austin? He'd been dressed like John Gotti.

"Black leather saddle shoes," I said, realizing shoes like that may have had a leather sole. "And like Ray's shoes, they wouldn't have been a good conductor."

"Ray?" Mama Zola said. "How'd *he* get into this conversation?"

"We have a lot to figure out," Koby said.

"Austin didn't have on any shoes," the person behind the desk finally contributed to the conversation after Mama Zola had pitched so much talk their way. "He was barefoot when they found him. And my suggestion to you amateur sleuth wannabes is for you to butt out of police business. We know what we're doing."

"Evidently you don't," Mama Zola said. "Because you're holding the wrong guy back there. We know he hasn't done anything wrong."

"We don't have to have it completely right," the desk clerk said. "We just have to have enough evidence to show he could have done it. Enough to get an indictment."

"And you don't have enough information to get a story on page six of the evening newspaper," Mama Zola said, triumph in her voice.

"If we didn't," the desk clerk said, looking back at the computer. "We wouldn't have brought him in."

Chapter Ten

THERE'D BEEN A mix of fury and glee and a whole bunch of chaos when the last vestiges of the homeless encampment had been removed at the City's Mini Park. In Seattle, nearly one and a half percent of the population were living on the streets and in shelters. But people wanted them out.

Out to go where, I didn't know. They were already out on the streets. But I hadn't ever thought Timber Lake had that same sort of problem.

But it did. And Pete Howers, our second employee in the door, was one of those people.

"Looks like he put down your bookstore and restaurant as a home address," the police officer who'd walked out with Pete informed us. "We need to know that that's where we'd be able to find him."

I looked at Koby, but he didn't hesitate.

"Yep," he said. "That's where he'll be. Where he lives." He walked over and stood beside him. "Can we take him home now?"

"You can." The police officer stepped aside. "But he's not to leave town."

"Where's he gonna go?" Koby said.

The future wasn't looking bright for Pete Howers, but as I thought about him, I wasn't how sure how much light there had been in his life, at least of late.

The police officer shrugged. "I just know that the chief is looking to arrest someone soon." He nodded in confirmation.

"But not Pete," I said, surprised that I cared so much. But really, who wants to see someone they know, someone they work with, be guilty of murder? "He's not looking to arrest Pete."

"Like I said," the officer said and looked at Pete then back at me. "He's free to go. For now."

His words, "for now," sent a shiver up my spine. I just couldn't picture Pete doing such a thing, although I didn't know him well, which might be something I now wanted to work on. But I knew, at least I hoped I hadn't assessed him wrong, that underneath that kind of weird, quirky exterior of Pete's, there was a guy with a really good heart. Not one that could commit murder.

I'd watched him work in the bookstore over the past few months.

But I hadn't checked in on his housing situation.

And now I felt really bad about that.

I didn't want his new address, even though until tonight he probably hadn't had a current one, to be Washington State Penitentiary.

And then the officer looked over at Mama Zola, his head cocked to the side as if in recognition. "Are you Zola Jackson?"

"I am," she said, puffing up her chest. "And I'm here to tell you that Pete didn't do anything."

"You can vouch for him?" the officer asked.

"I can. And I do."

"And who can vouch for you?" the officer asked.

"I don't need anyone," Mama Zola said. "You people are barking up the wrong tree." With that, she marched to the door.

We walked out to the parking lot, everyone quiet, and if like me, lost in thought about what that police officer who'd brought Pete out had said. He even seemed to want to question Mama Zola. They were grasping at straws, but we knew that could be a bad thing.

Avery said his good-byes and both Koby and Mama Zola thanked him more than a couple of times for staying with Pete.

Pete did something I'd never seen him do before. He gave Avery a hug.

He wasn't big on touching. Or talking. And I hadn't seen him be grateful. Not for the job we gave him or for the kindness we'd shown him. He took everything in stride. But not today.

We got into the car and out of the parking lot right behind Avery Moran's car. We were both heading to the same place.

Timber Lake was small and quaint. Sparsely populated compared to the nearby big city, Seattle, there were about three thousand folks that called it home. Lazy Sundays. Lakefront living. We lived in the picturesque Pacific Northwest. Situated on a spit of land nestled between Bishop Creek and the ravine our town was named for, our little town had green spaces galore—sweeping meadows, native grass. Protected and meticulously maintained grounds. Trails wound into the woods that were filled with cottonwood trees and weeping willows. And at almost every turn, the view had the calm, blue lake waters that butted up to our shoreline boundary. Looking upward on a clear day, I saw the mountains that lined Timber Lake's skyline shrouded in a thin layer of white mist.

And until a few months ago, it had been practically crime free.

"What kind of information do they have on you, Pete?" Mama Zola said, her voice low. Concerned. She turned around in her seat as she spoke to face him. "That clueless desk clerk said if they hadn't had anything on you, they wouldn't have brought you in."

"I didn't kill the guy." Pete sat in the back seat with me. Hands folded in his lap. Shoulders back. He was much calmer than I would have been.

"We know that," she said.

"So they couldn't have anything on me."

Sound logic, I thought. Didn't think that would work in front of a jury, though.

"Capt'n Hook said they had you on camera going into the church early," Koby said.

"Going into a church doesn't mean you killed someone." Pete's face showed no concern.

Getting answers from Pete Howers was going to be like pulling teeth.

"Well, Pete wasn't the only one there early," I said, coming to his rescue, seeing he didn't seem to have to the need to do it. "Rocko, the pastor."

"Ray," Koby said, taking on adding to my list.

I nodded, agreeing with him. "We don't know exactly when Ray got to the church, just when he came looking for a cart."

"Right," Koby said.

"I don't think it was Ray," Mama Zola said.

"The woman in the hat," I said, not wanting to upset Mama Zola by admitting Ray had been on my list almost from the word "murder." "And the woman in the emerald green shoes."

"Who was that?" Mama Zola said.

"She was the woman who was talking to Pastor Lee right before he came into the kitchen," I said.

"They had some kind of business arrangement," Koby said. "I remember her."

"How do you know what was between them?" I asked my brother. Although I knew the answer.

"He had a different smile than when he talked to his parishioners," Koby said. "And he shook her hand. He was more familiar than that with everyone else."

"I thought Avery said that only three people were seen on the video," Mama Zola said. "How come everyone isn't on there?"

"So, I'm guessing," I said, "that we need to figure out how early was early enough."

"To do what?" Mama Zola said.

"To move the coffeepot and hook it up to faulty wiring in the office that Austin James had been using without being seen," Pete said.

"I was going to say 'early enough to be on the video that it concerned the police,' but wow, Pete. What you said." We knew Pete hadn't gotten there any earlier—he'd been with Mama Zola all morning—and that was the only time the police questioned.

"Right." Koby looked at me, then Pete, in his mirror. "Pete, man, how do you know all of that?" Koby asked. He raised his eyebrows, blinking his eyes. "The police told you that?"

"They tried to get me to confess to doing that."

Koby gave a nod. "Okay. But you didn't confess, right?" Koby asked.

"No," Pete said. "I had nothing to confess to."

"Because you didn't do anything," Mama Zola said.

"Right," Pete said.

"Seems like they are concentrating on the people on the video," Koby said. "I wonder how we could see it."

"My lawyer could get you a copy," Pete said.

"You've got a lawyer?" basically all three of us said, in different ways but all at the same time.

"Where'd you get a lawyer from?" I asked.

"I told them I wouldn't answer any questions without a lawyer. So they got me one."

"Then you answered their questions?" Mama Zola asked.

"No," Pete said. "My lawyer told me not to."

Everyone but Pete laughed at that.

"So where was this lawyer?" Koby asked.

"I didn't see anyone else there while we were there," I said.

"He'd left already."

"Who was he?" Koby asked. "A public defender?"

"Yep," Pete said. "But you know him."

"Who knows him?" I asked.

"All of you, he was Reef's lawyer."

Koby's dead—murdered—foster brother, Mama Zola's foster son, Reef Jeffries, brought as much surprise to Koby and Mama Zola as Pete was bringing today by having a lawyer.

"Brian Jenkins?" Koby asked, guessing.

Pete nodded.

Brian Jenkins had been the one that Reef had gone to, to handle his end-of-life bequeaths, an act that bewildered everyone that knew him well. He was young and healthy and had no reason to think he wouldn't live long. But it did turn out in the end, Reef needed legal counsel.

And while he hadn't done anything to help us solve Reef's murder, some of the information he had had been useful. It had helped us to learn not only about the life Reef had been living, but who could have killed him.

And now Jenkins was involved in another murder that my twin and I were also involved in. Not in the same capacity, but it might make it easier for Koby to get the information I knew he wanted.

"How did you find him?" Koby asked.

"Not in the yellow pages," Mama Zola muttered. "I found out they don't have that anymore."

"I know," Koby said and reached over and patted her leg. "It's hard living in the future."

"They had a list," Pete said. "I told them I knew there was one and I didn't want them picking one for me."

"How did you know they had a list?" Mama Zola asked.

"Because I saw it the last time I was arrested."

Chapter Eleven

"YOU SEE WHY we should do background checks on potential employees?" I asked Koby.

It was Friday morning. I was sitting next to my brother on the light-rail when we should have been in Timber Lake opening up our shop. I checked my watch. We probably wouldn't get back until nearly noon. We wouldn't lose business. We'd left our little enterprise in quite capable hands even if one of those people was a person of interest in a murder investigation.

We were on our way into Seattle to see that person's— Pete Howers'—lawyer, Brian Jenkins.

"How many times are you going to say that?" Koby asked. Not even turning to look at me. "It's like the tenth time you've said it since yesterday when we found out he'd been arrested before."

"That was all he would tell us," I said, flapping my hands on my beige-colored trouser-clad thighs. "We still don't know why he'd been arrested before, if he was convicted or what."

"We're not hiring anyone else now, so it doesn't matter," Koby said. "With Pete, Mama Zola and Georgie and the two of us, we've got things at the shop covered."

"Still no excuse not to find out about our employees."

This time he turned to me to speak. "Pete has been a great employee. We couldn't have asked for a better one."

"I know," I said, "But—"

"But nothing. What he has done in the past shouldn't determine his future." Koby shook his head. "It was easy to see the first day he walked into our store the man was down on his luck. Didn't have money or a place to live and he was looking for employment, not a handout. Or a stickup."

"I agree, but—"

"You'd rather we hadn't hired him?"

"I'm not saying that," I said. "I'm saying that now we are taking off time from the store to take care of him and we might could have avoided this situation."

"Are you saying we should act like Mama Zola's pastor? Determine him guilty because he's poor?"

"No." I blew out a breath. There was no winning an argument with Koby about things like this—helping those less fortunate. I understood why, it was because at one time, he was one of those people. He'd lived his whole life so far among those kinds of people. He called lots of them—kids then but adults now—family.

"I'm just saying," I said, my words mumbled, my body becoming slumped.

"I hear you," Koby said. "But I think we're doing the right thing."

I didn't say it out loud, but I thought we were doing the right thing, too. He had to know that. And it wasn't that I grew up stuck up or isolated or anything. I just spent my childhood as a loner. With my nose in books, hanging out with my dad at the library where he worked and being overanalyzed by my mother, Imogene, a clinical psych-

ologist. I didn't have many friends and I didn't give a second thought about dipping my nose into other people's
business. And whatever it was that I chose to give my attention to, I had always looked at things more from a
brain-focused viewpoint than my brother, who was logical but was led in most decisions by his heart.

The lawyer's office was in the University District, near
the University of Washington. I had spent a lot of time in
that area of Seattle. It was where my father worked as an
academic librarian.

The mostly brick buildings on University Way, where
his office was located, were all stuck together. There were
awnings, glass fronts and vibrant colors that set apart the
different businesses.

The lawyer's office was not quaint or posh. We walked
in the door to a big reception area with royal blue velvet-
like love seats and lime green plush chairs. With coffee
and end tables filled with magazines. We were greeted by
a woman behind a high desk and told Mr. Jenkins would
be with us shortly.

"Shortly" came in less than five minutes. I had only
gotten through half of the article I'd found on adoption
lawyers in Seattle.

"Well, who knew I'd see you again so soon," Brian
Jenkins said. He stood up as we walked into his office.
One just off the reception area. "Sorry, it's on such bad
terms."

"Me too," Koby said. "You remember my sister, Keaton."

"Of course." Brian stuck out his hand for me to shake
it, then pointed at a chair in front of his desk.

"Hi," I said and sat at the seat he offered. Koby sat
down next to me.

"So what can I do for the two of you?"

"We want to help Pete all we can." Koby looked at me
as he spoke, dipping his head at the end, signaling that we
were in agreement on that.

I nodded.

"And we were wondering, too, if we could take a look at the video the police got from the church."

"I have a copy of it." He pulled a blue folder from a stack that sat in a corner of his desk. Clipped to it was a white DVD envelope. "I can play it," he said, pulling the disc out of the sleeve and inserting it into his desktop. "But it really doesn't show much."

"We heard that it shows Pete going in early along with another man and a woman."

"Right." Attorney Jenkins nodded. He used his mouse to click on the app's icon and started the media player. He turned the monitor around so we could see it. "The man"—he pointed to the screen—"is a deacon at the church," the lawyer said, then he swallowed and shook his head. "But they don't go in at the same time, as you can see, the times are staggered."

"And the woman," I said. I pointed to the screen at a woman in a hat, one hand holding on to the brim of it so it wouldn't come off. She kept her head down and carried a rectangular strapless purse pushed under her arm as she entered into view.

The early female intruder was slender. All her hair was under that hat, so I didn't know if it was cropped short or she had tucked it under. She had on flats, capri pants and a blouse with large pockets on the front that caught the wind as she walked.

"No one seems to know who she is," the attorney said. "Her face was obscured, as you saw on the video, by that hat."

"What time were they going in?" Koby asked. "How close to each other?"

"Relative to the time we showed up." I added. "And everyone else who came early." I couldn't imagine Pete getting over to the church and back to leave with us. It's a ten-minute drive.

"There's no time stamp on it."

"Then how do they know it was early?" Koby said. He blew out a breath. "That makes no sense."

"I agree. But you know." I tilted my head thinking. "When I worked in the library, the tape would only last forty-eight hours and then be reused. So the physical tape is limited."

"What if a crime happened a week ago? Was that evidence just lost?"

"No." I shook my head. "It went to the Cloud, or stored on a server, not sure. But I'd be willing to bet that's how the police know the time."

"A backup." He nodded. "Okay. Makes sense."

"Another question is: How long did Pete stay inside?" I asked.

"It doesn't show him coming back out."

"What?" Koby moved up to the end of his chair. "He did come back out, though."

"I'm sure he did, but not out of that door."

"There's only one camera?"

"Seems that way, so no one else was captured on the surveillance footage."

"What do you mean? No one else? Like me, Mama Zola? Keaton?"

"Right," he said.

"Not the pastor?" I asked.

"No."

"What about Rocko?" I asked. "Does anybody know what time he got there? Wasn't he the one who had to let everyone in?"

"Maybe the deacon had a key," Koby said, glancing over at me. I could see his mind getting in gear. "And maybe he left the door unlocked."

"But how did Pete get there?" I asked. "Early, I mean."

"From what I understand, Pete wasn't there early. The

first time he came to the church is when you guys dropped him off."

"You understand that?" Koby asked.

"Well, I learned it from Pete. It's what he told me."

"Did he say when he went in that door?" Koby asked.

"Why he went in that door?" I asked.

"He said he must have gotten turned around."

I squinted my eyes, trying to picture that. I mean, I had gotten turned around in that building, too, although one would think from the way it's made that it would be easy to navigate.

"But it didn't show him coming out of it?" I said, remembering that I had realized before I got to the door that I had gone the wrong way.

"No. Just going in."

"Back to the deacon. Do you know his name?"

Mr. Jenkins looked through the paperwork in his folder. "Doesn't seem like it's listed here, but I couldn't say that they haven't looked into him."

"The only person they took into custody was Pete," Koby said. "As far as we know."

"It seems that Mr. Howers knew the decedent," Attorney Jenkins said. "Knew him well."

"How?" I asked.

"It seems they worked together before."

"Where?"

"Not sure. But it was what the chief—"

"Interim chief," Koby said, interjecting.

"Right." Attorney Jenkins nodded. "Acting chief said so when he was questioning Mr. Howers."

"He—Pete—knew that Austin James had a pacemaker," I said to Koby. "Remember?"

"I remember," Koby said. "What's the reason that he thinks that Pete would kill that guy?" Koby moving on from my question.

"They don't have a reason. It's all circumstantial."

"Circumstantial?" I said. I'd heard that before. Other than using context clues, I had an idea of what it meant but no concrete definition.

"If you go to bed and the ground is clear," Koby said, "and you wake up and the ground is covered with snow, it is more than likely that it snowed overnight."

Attorney Jenkins smiled. "Textbook definition."

"So." I wanted to translate that explanation to our situation. "Because Pete was at the church, per the video, had the time to rig the coffeemaker, knew the decedent"—I pointed at the lawyer as that had been his word—"and knew he had a heart problem that required a pacemaker, he is more than likely the killer."

The lawyer touched his nose, charades style. "You got it."

"So you have to prove he didn't do it?" I asked.

"Actually," Attorney Jenkins said, "according to the law, the prosecution has to prove that he *did* do it. We don't have to prove anything."

"But you will, right?" I said. I could feel my nerve endings getting all tangled up. Pete was going to need all the help he could get.

"You do what you have to according to the law, and we appreciate your help." Koby stood up ready to go, so I followed suit. "But my sister and I will do what we have to do."

"And what's that?" Attorney Jenkins asked.

"Find out who really did it, since the police don't seem too interested in doing that." Koby turned and walked toward the door.

He'd said all he wanted to say, I assumed. But certainly, he didn't think he was speaking for me? When I asked the lawyer if he was going to do all he could because I wanted Pete to have the help he needed. I didn't mean me finding the killer to replace the interim chief's misplaced accusations.

I watched my brother leave and then turned to the lawyer and raised my hands, indicating I had no idea what my brother meant.

Oh, but I did.

"I wouldn't do anything rash," Attorney Jenkins said. "Or impulsive. You can get in trouble getting involved in police investigations."

"You are preaching to the choir," I said, cringing at my use of a church-related saying. "You don't have to tell me."

Chapter Twelve

BOOKS & BISCUITS, established 2021, was on the first floor of the corner building that straddled the intersection of Park and Second Streets, in downtown Timber Lake.

Two half-moon steps were outside our front door. Above the shop were apartments with, so far, tenants that were pretty quiet. We hadn't heard a peep from them. We didn't own the building, but Koby had often remarked since we opened that if we did, he'd keep every one of the tenants—they all seemed like good people.

The front door of our business opened to the bookstore. We had tall shelves along the wall, short ones in the middle and three chandeliers in the ceiling. Carpeted floors in the author area where I'd already hosted two author events and had another one coming up Tuesday evening. They were local authors and all those books had found a place on the shelves of my bookstore. It would probably be a long time before I could fly an author in.

Nicole D. Miller. Not a local author, she hailed from Cleveland, Ohio, but was visiting Seattle (not on my expense) and coming in for a reading and talk. Koby was going to make canapés and other finger foods and serve some of our sweet tea. Author of *Stories for the (Urban) Soul*, a collection of short stories and novellas, Miller had been thrilled when we talked over Zoom and I walked her through the bookstore.

There were reading nooks and an archway, surrounded by books, that led to the Biscuits side. My twin brother's domain. I was so excited to have her.

I'd gotten Maya, a girl I'd met after Reef died, to help me publicize the event. She was the closest thing I had to a girlfriend and she was always ready to help me and Koby. I still had a ton of stuff to do to get ready for the event. I was glad to get back to the shop.

As we walked through the door, returning from our trek to Seattle and our maiden voyage of things criminal, I took in the smells and sounds of our small business. Although the book and cooking areas were attached, I could still distinguish the smell of the books—the physical kind—and the aroma of the covers from those of the food that was being prepared and served just on the other side of the wall.

I have had many who argued the point that books do indeed have attributes that arouse all five of our senses, not to mention the sparks they ignite in our neurons. But I say that they do. The touch and feel of the outside and the pages inside. Settings and descriptions give pleasures to sight and sound even if only seen and heard through our imagination, and the words explode with tastes and pleasures.

That was what I had wanted to bring to my bookstore.

It hadn't been my idea. I had been a librarian. I had gotten the job on my dad's recommendation to the head librarian here. I had moved to Timber Lake shortly after my father died. And then my brother had found me and with him came all kinds of ideas and adventures (and ventures) for the two of us to do together.

And it had been his idea to hire Pete.

My eyes scanned the store, and as usual, Pete had everything in its place and looking good. The displays were centered just so to catch the eye of all who took a gander inside or around. Chairs were pulled out from the small table in the children's section with books scattered about, making it look inviting and as if children has just vacated the area and it was ready to house more.

Customers were browsing and a few looked at me and smiled before casting their eyes back at the bookshelves.

They seemed happy. Unfettered. Probably unaware of what circumstances were swirling around our sterling employee. The only one who'd been there with them that morning. And the only one I'd come to trust on my side of the business.

Originally, I had hired Georgie Tsai to work with me. Nearly her entire body was an exercise in creative writing. I thought she'd be the perfect fit. Pale skin and black hair, and her entire left arm and right lower leg were covered in colorful tattoos. Green. Red. Blue. Aphorisms and one-word exclamations. Some in English. Some not.

But even before we opened up the shop, and she'd worked for us for only a few weeks, I got the feeling she wasn't going to work out. I had even voiced the same to my brother. I was ready to let her go. Her nose constantly stuck in the books we'd ordered when she should have been placing them on the bookshelves. I anticipated the headache she was going to be after we officially opened, and I figured I'd fix the problem before it got in the way of us running a successful business.

Okay. To be honest and clear, neither my brother nor I had ever run a business before so we weren't quite—if at all—sure of all ways to turn one into a success. But it appeared to my common sense that employees who didn't do their job was one way a business would probably fail.

My softhearted brother took her hand, literally, led her to the kitchen and put her to work in his domain. "We've already hired her," he said to me later. "She's counting on us, just like we're counting on her. How about if we give her another chance?"

I really didn't have a say in it, just like I hadn't when we hired Pete.

Come to think of it, it was Georgie who had let Pete in, in the first place . . .

But it had all worked out. Georgie on the Biscuits side with Koby and Mama Zola, and Pete with me.

Business was good and it had to do with our team. Our whole team.

I scanned the store and there was Pete, in the back of the store, duster in hand, box at his feet. I was sure that box had been part of the shipment of new books we'd gotten yesterday—in the short time we were open.

He hadn't wasted any time getting them out and up, even in the midst of seeing to our customers.

And only then, after I had visually checked all was well with the Books side, did I smell the buttery biscuits wafting in from the other side. I turned and looked at my brother. "Seems like all is going well here."

"Why wouldn't it be?" he said and shook his head. "You are such a worrywart."

"And while I'm being one," I said, "don't forget you're going to talk to Pete about that previous arrest of his."

"How can I forget when you won't let me?" he said before he took off for the other side. "I have to see what's going on in the kitchen." He looked over his shoulder. "If that's okay with you."

We'd found out in the lawyer's office that Pete had been arrested for embezzlement, tampering with evidence and obstruction of justice. A white-collar crime and other stuff prosecutors "throw at the wall to see what sticks," according to Attorney Brian Jenkins. He'd been indicted, but the charges had all been dropped. Attorney Jenkins had no idea what the charges stemmed from.

"I just got on the case yesterday," he said and held up his hands. "I'll have to look into it. Talk to Mr. Howers about it. But this murder thing is much more important."

Murder thing . . .

Was murder just a thing? Like being fond of going to the gym to work out? Or baking cupcakes in your spare time?

Geesh.

I went behind the counter and pulled out my handwritten inventory list. I had a habit of jotting things down and then entering them into the computer. Koby thought I should carry my tablet around with me and enter it all there. "One step and you're done."

I let him do things his way.

Too bad my brother didn't do me the same way.

I hadn't been at it long when Pete came over.

"What did my lawyer say?"

I looked up, ready to shush him, warning him not to talk like that around customers, but there weren't any in the store. I should have known better than Pete blabbing his business around in front of people.

"He just said he was going to work on getting you off."

"He won't have to work too hard," Pete said.

"I know." I smiled. "Because you didn't do anything."

He nodded.

"And because you have Koby." Koby was determined to make this be over in Pete's favor. "Attorney Jenkins is all set to find the real culprit."

I thought I saw a faint smile appear on his lips.

"I used to be an accountant," Pete said.

"You did?" I said and looked down at the inventory sheets in my hand. I wondered why I hadn't let Pete take care of this stuff.

"At a big trading firm downtown."

"In Seattle?"

"Yep. Hatton & Lyndale."

"Oh wow," I said. I was impressed. Even me with no money to invest knew of that name.

"Yeah." He rocked his head back and forth. "So. A customer lost a lot of money. I got blamed for it."

I had to stop and think for a minute. Process what he was talking about. Then I got it.

Embezzlement. Tampering with evidence.

"Is that why you have an arrest record?"

"I didn't do anything then. Just like I didn't do anything now."

He said it so matter-of-factly. As if it were just that simple. He proclaimed his innocence, and it was set in stone. Affirmed. Undisputed. I think that theory would be hard to get past all of those inmates inside prison cells who make the same declarations.

Well, now I knew. No need for Koby to question Pete. He'd spilled the beans himself.

Maybe Koby was right. Pete was going to need more help proving his innocence than Pete was willing to provide.

Chapter Thirteen

"WHO WAS AUSTIN James?"

I felt like I was doing a true crime podcast.

Koby and I were sitting at one of the tables on the Biscuits side having lunch. Pete had made it back from his break—sitting out back with Koby's rescue yellow Labrador retriever, Remy, eating a sandwich made on white bread and drinking pop out of a can. Lunch for employees was free, but he always brought his own. He never seemed interested in taking a handout. But before he had left, he told Koby the same story he'd told me. Not adding one more bit of information.

Koby was having crispy-on-the-outside, flaky-on-the-inside salmon croquets smothered in peas swimming in a light brown roux and a side of sticky rice. He had no problem shoveling it in his mouth. He was on his second raspberry and lemon sweet tea. I couldn't get a sip of water to go down my throat as I picked at my curried chicken salad overstuffed inside a buttermilk-and-chive biscuit with let-

tuce sticking out on all sides and a slice of a red, ripe to-
mato wedged in between.

"I think that's the first thing we need to find out."

"I agree," he said.

"I mean, why would someone want to kill him?"

"We covered that already," Koby said, stuffing sticky
rice into his mouth. "He didn't seem like a likable guy."

Just then my phone pinged. A text message.

"It's from Maya," I said. I held up my phone so he
could see the images she'd sent over. "She's doing some
social media posts."

"I like it," Koby said. "You'll get a lot of coverage like
that."

"I hope so."

He tilted his head. I could see an idea brewing. It made
me nervous. There was no telling what thoughts popped
up in my brother's head.

"You know that letter we got from Kings County?"

I nodded. "The identifying information for our biological mother."

"Right. What if . . ."

I gave him a moment to speak, but he didn't say anything. "What?"

"I was thinking, what if we posted on her high school's
page and her community college's page that we're looking
for her? Maybe someone will know her. Know where
she is."

I blew out a breath. "What if she sees it?" I could feel
butterflies in my stomach.

"That would be okay," he said, nodding.

"I hadn't thought of doing that," I said. "Makes me
anxious, but I think it's a good idea." I scrunched up my
nose. "You gonna do it?"

"Yeah. I'll let you know if I hear anything."

"Okay."

"Okay," he answered back. "Now. Back to Austin James."

I dismissed my lingering thoughts on finding our mother and got back to the task at hand. "How are we going to find out about him?"

"Google," Koby said, after gulping down the last of his second glass of sweet tea. Georgie popped up with a pitcher and refilled it almost at the same time it landed back on the table. "Thanks." He smiled at Georgie and looked back at me. "Have you tried Googling him yet?"

I pulled out my phone and held it up. "I will now."

But that proved futile. There were a million Austin Jameses and not one picture under images that matched the man I'd seen the day before.

"We're going to have to find another way to do that."

"Oh. Speaking of 'other ways'"—he swiped the last of his croquet through the gravy—"we're going to go to that church tonight."

"What church?" I asked. "Mama Zola's?"

"No. We'll save that one for Sunday." He pushed back from the table, probably from his stomach expanding from his large lunch. "Grace Spirit Revival."

"The one with the phone number we got from the security booth."

"Yep. Remember, I said we would be stopping. Don't want to make us out to be liars." He chuckled.

"You." I pointed a finger. "Make *you* out to be a liar. I never consented to anything."

"Guilty by association." He nodded, assuring me I was part of it whether I thought I should be or not.

I smiled. Maybe it was a good thing I hadn't grown up side by side with my brother. No telling how much trouble I would have gotten into.

"So another field trip, huh?"

"Yep. One of many, I'm sure." He pointed at my food. "So you better eat up. You'll need all your energy. Plus, we don't waste food around here. There are starving children in Africa."

I shook my head. I'd heard that a hundred times growing up. Like it was possible to ship all the food left on little kids' plates off to another continent and alleviate any hunger crises. Maybe our childhoods had been similar in some ways after all.

"I won't need energy to do it," I said. "I'll need courage."

"Courage to do what?" I turned at the words to see my mother standing behind me.

"Hey, Mom," I said and stood up to greet her.

"Hi, sweetie." She hugged me and kissed me on the cheek, then went over and planted one on Koby's. "What is it you need courage about?"

My mother the psychologist, always with the questions.

"Courage to eat all the food on my plate," I said and pointed to it.

She stared at it for a moment, then at me, then came back around the table. "I know that isn't true. You should just say you'd rather not discuss it right now."

It was true, though. I didn't have an appetite. No motivation to eat. So not an untruth, just a small omission, of which I felt bad.

"Koby and I are going to go over to a church."

"The one where that man was killed?"

"No. One we got the number for from the security guard that worked for the church where the guy got killed."

"And what do you plan on doing there?" she asked.

"Ask questions."

"That's always a good thing," she said. "That's the only way to get answers." She swiped a hand under the skirt to her navy two-piece suit and sat in the seat I'd just vacated. "Happy that you reconciled the fact that lies

won't help any situation, whatever it may be, I will finish
off your lunch. We can't go wasting food . . ."

She didn't finish her sentence. The food had distracted
her. But Koby gave me a look that said everyone seemed
concerned about uneaten food but me. I was concerned
about keeping things from my mother.

She put a forkful in her mouth and closed her eyes.
"Mmmm. This is so yummy. Is there more in the kitchen?"

GRACE SPIRIT REVIVAL was a storefront establishment
with purple curtains adorning the glass front. A cheery
welcome mat was outside the recessed doorway. As we
peeked through the glass, we didn't see anyone inside.
When we went to open the door, we found it unlocked.
And once inside, we saw about forty or fifty folding chairs
lined up facing a wooden podium. A stack of prayer rugs
and shoes lined up neatly by the door.

I patted Koby on the arm and pointed. "Do you think
we should take off our shoes?"

He looked down at the floor. "Maybe we should just
stand here. Wait until someone comes out."

Koby and I had driven over to the church, leaving after
closing up the shop for the day. We'd missed the rush-hour
traffic that we would have encountered if we'd made the
trip earlier in the day.

The ride, like this room, had been calming.

In the small, square room that appeared to serve as the
chapel, there were serene scenes painted on the walls.
Soft lights coupled with the sun streaming through the
light-filtering sheer purple drapes. Pamphlets, hymnals
and extra Bibles stacked on two tables pushed against a
side wall. And at the one end, there was a coffeepot. It
was full, but looked stale. No rich color. No steam. Sugar

packets, creamer tubs, and stirrers were scattered in front of Styrofoam cups.

"I wonder what kind of church this is," I said. "What denomination."

"I want to know why Rocko was talking to the people here." He looked around. "And if it had anything to do with Austin James' death."

"This is so farfetched," I said and sighed. "A long shot. We won't find anything out chasing after a phone number."

"You never know," Koby said.

"I know one thing." I did my own observation of the room. "I don't think they'd need a parking lot attendant here," I said. I turned from the waist and looked back through the door we'd just entered. "I don't even remember seeing a parking lot within a block of this place."

"I noticed that," he said. "Maybe he just wanted to change church memberships?"

"Do we know if he *is* a member of Everlasting?"

"So far, I'd have to say we don't know much." He looked at me. "About anything."

"Maybe we can help enlighten you," came a voice from the back. A man had emerged from beyond the drapes that matched the ones up to the windows. "Hi, I'm Brother Ron. Nice to meet you."

He was bald and bearded and barefoot. His voice soft, his smile pleasant.

"Welcome," he said and stepped all the way into the room. "How can I help you?"

Koby looked at me. It looked as if he didn't know what to say. He should have known better than to ask me. I didn't like to be untruthful even it was in the pursuit of justice.

Koby shrugged and seemed to just go for it. "Do you know Rocko Jackson?"

I saw Brother Ron's smile waver for a moment. But then it came right back. "I don't know him, but I did speak to him yesterday."

"May we ask why?" Koby asked.

"He delivered some rather disturbing news."

"That Austin James was dead?"

Brother Ron lowered his head and took in a breath—it seemed, to settle himself. He looked back at us, his smile returning but not as sincere.

"Yes. From what I understand, murdered."

"My condolences if he was a friend of yours."

"More like family. Spiritual family." Brother Ron tilted his head. "May I ask why you are inquiring?"

"The police are looking at one of our employees as a person of interest and he's had enough things going on without worrying about that."

"Ah." Brother Ron nodded. "Pete." He quickly corrected. "Pete Howers. I heard."

But it was too late. Koby had caught what he'd done. Heck, so had I.

"How do you know Pete?" I asked. I was ready to jump into the conversation.

"I don't know him personally." Brother Ron hesitated. It seemed he wanted to say more but didn't.

"But?" I asked. "You recognized his name right off."

"Pastor James and Pete used to work at the same trading firm."

"Hatton & Lyndale?" I asked.

"Yes. Pastor James, Pete *and* Pastor Lee."

"Wait," I said. I had completely taken over the questioning, but Koby didn't seem to mind. And this information was almost making my head spin. I hadn't thought we'd find anything interesting by coming here. "All three of them worked at the same place?"

He nodded. "And there was some incident where they all lost their jobs."

I looked at Koby. I was almost sure that we knew just what that "incident" had been. I was sure he knew just what I was thinking.

"Why do you call Austin James 'pastor'?" Koby jumped in. "He had a church?"

"He did. I'm sure you may have heard of it."

"Why do you think we heard of it?" Koby asked.

"We just met him for the first time yesterday," I said.

"He was the pastor of Abundant Faith Tabernacle."

"The megachurch?" I asked.

He nodded. "Yes."

"I heard they folded because . . ." I didn't finish that thought. Not out loud. But it had been because of money problems. I changed gears. "What was any of their association here?" I asked. "To this church?"

"Members of Abundant Faith Tabernacle splintered off. A chunk of them came here."

"Are you their pastor?"

"I'm more of a spiritual leader."

"Was Aust—I mean Pastor James—the pastor here?" I asked.

"He tried to be. After . . . he, uh, came back." He breathed noisily through his nostrils. "But the congregation here wasn't . . . uhm . . . happy with him continuing, so he had moved on."

"Moved on to Everlasting Missionary Baptist Church?" Koby asked.

"I wouldn't think he would have been welcome there either," Brother Ron said. "But sometimes forgiveness frees those that need the forgiving as well as those that are doing the forgiving." He closed his eyes momentarily as if contemplating on his words. "That makes all the better for it."

Koby and I both raised an eyebrow.

That couldn't be Pastor Lee. He had allowed Austin James and Pete in his church, and I remembered him saying something about "all" were welcome at his church. But he quickly turned on Pete, seemingly not even giving him a chance to prove his innocence.

"But," Brother Ron said, "with the three of them, I don't think that would be the case."

Chapter Fourteen

I WOKE UP early Saturday morning to the smell of bacon and my Siamese curled up next to me licking her paws. At first, I thought I was dreaming, because where would Roo get bacon? Then I realized the smell was coming from my kitchen.

Koby.

I checked my bed for food. "Did your Uncle Koby give you food?"

She purred at me. No crumbs. She was just grooming. I turned and looked at the clock. It was just a couple minutes past six. The shop didn't open until ten. I had planned on sleeping until about eight.

"Change of plans," I said to Roo. "Koby is not going to let me have a lazy Saturday morning." I sat up and swung my legs out of the bed, stretching before I stood up.

I knew exactly what Koby wanted, why he was here. I shook my head as I padded down the hall to the bathroom, my cat jumping off the bed and following me. Yep, I knew, I just wasn't sure I was up to it today. We'd done a lot of investigating yesterday, but for the last two days spent not a lot of time in our shop.

The shop hadn't been open long, and while sales were okay on both sides, I knew if we were going to be able to continue our business, I was going to have to do more on the Books side.

More author events—signings, readings like the one coming up on Tuesday. It was a perfect venue for it. We had the space and a caterer that was right through an archway. And I wanted to plan a book fair.

It was hard running a business, just doing that was time-consuming and stressful, dealing with employees and customers, remembering to wear a smile no matter how frustrating they were or how the day was going. But throwing solving murders into the mix? All I could say was: Geesh!

Thursday's murder, I now knew, was going to halt all my planning of everything I had had in mind.

I squeezed toothpaste on my toothbrush and ran water over it. "Roo, seems like Koby would have been happier opening up some kind of PI office instead of Books & Biscuits."

"Eerroww."

"Yeah, I know. Don't give him any ideas."

I threw on a pair of drawstring sweatpants and a T-shirt and padded downstairs in my bare feet.

"How did you get into my house?" I asked. Spying a plate full of bacon, I swiped a piece.

"I climbed in the window." He glanced at me. "You hungry?"

"If you want to know the truth, eating this early hadn't crossed my mind."

"Until I showed up?" He had a grin on his face.

"Yep. And woke me up."

"Looks like someone appreciates me." His head nodded toward Roo. She had her head in her bowl.

I shook my head. "Where's Remy?" I took another piece of bacon.

"Out back."

"So glad you built that doghouse for him." My brother had worked over one weekend and erected the cutest doghouse painted the same cerulean blue as my house with white trim. We were trying to get permission to put one out back of the kitchen at Books & Biscuits, too. "But you might have to put one in for Roo. When you guys are here, she tries to chase him out." I turned and glanced out the window. "Remy likes having his feet on land, huh?"

"He loves the boat *and* the water."

I smiled. We both knew how much Remy loved running around in my backyard. There wasn't room like that at the marina. Remy wasn't cooped up there, but he was always happy to visit with me and Roo.

"What's in the skillet?"

"A frittata."

"What?" I went to stove and leaned in. "What's in it?" I sniffed.

"Not any stuff from your fridge."

"There's not much in my fridge."

"I know."

I looked over at my white retro refrigerator. "I've been meaning to go shopping." I looked down at Roo, still hovering over her bowl. "I have plenty of cat food."

"I put a can of that in."

"What!"

"Frittatas are filled with things you have in the kitchen. And all you had was the milk, eggs and cat food."

"Koby."

He grinned at me. "I brought leftovers from the boat." He lifted the cast iron skillet from the stove and sat it on a hot pad. "Grab some plates and silverware."

I did, as well as the plate of bacon.

"Did you put bacon in it?" Setting everything on the table, I slid into a chair.

"No. That was just to get you woke." He grabbed a glass pitcher of something fruity that was orange on the top and purple on the bottom out of the fridge and sat it on the table.

"That looks yummy." I popped back up and grabbed two glasses. I sat one in front of his place and one in front of me. "What's in it?"

"I had some leftover beets."

"Beets?" I pushed my glass back. "No thanks."

"When have you *not* liked something I made?"

I cocked my head to the side. Of course, I couldn't think of an instance. I loved everything my brother made.

"It's got orange juice, ginger, lemon, turmeric." He picked up the pitcher and poured himself a glass.

"And beets?" I just needed to make sure. "You did say *beets*?"

"Yep. Beets."

I pushed my glass over for him to fill up. "I'm sure a couple of those things are not meant to be drunk."

"How big of a slice of frittata do you want?" He picked up the large kitchen knife and looked at me.

I looked into the skillet. "Any beets in that?"

"None."

"Medium slice."

"I've got croissants, too," he said. "I picked them up at the bakery."

I saw, for the first time, a box on the counter. I glanced at the clock on the stove. "Where? It's just now six thirty."

"Bakers are early risers."

"So, it seems, is my brother."

"We have stuff to figure out. I know you can't think on an empty stomach."

"Yes, I can."

"Well, I can't."

He swiped the bakery box off the counter and pulled out his chair. "Dig in and let's get to work," he said. He took a forkful of the frittata. "Okay, so where do we start?"

"With what?"

"Don't play with me."

"Can't we eat first?"

"We can do both at the same time."

I exhaled—loudly—through my nose.

"You didn't think you were getting this awesome breakfast for free, did you?"

I grabbed bacon and put it on my plate. There were some delicious pieces of Italian sausage in the egg dish that popped with bursts of oregano and sage. It was peppery and maple-y. And the croissants were soft and buttery. But my brother knew how I loved bacon. I was a willing participant with the plate of bacon at my side.

"Looks like that random phone number we found in Rocko's security hut did turn out to have some significance."

Koby gave me a nod while chewing that said, "I told you so."

"We need to find out more about Hatton & Lyndale," I said. "None of those three—Austin James, Calvin Lee or Pete—are in jail. What happened?"

"What?" Koby cut another slice of the frittata. That boy inhaled food. "You want them to be in jail?"

"No. I'm not saying that." I frowned. That was a terrible thought. "I'm just wondering how they lost their jobs and got arrested—at least Pete—and then end up being pastors at churches. Big churches."

"Not Pete. He ended up homeless."

"Right," I said. I stretched my eyes at the realization. "He seemed to be the only one that fell on hard times."

"So, let's see what happened. Where's your phone?"

"My phone?" I asked.

"I'm eating," he said.

"I am, too." I crunched on another piece of bacon.

"You're better at multitasking than I am." He looked at me. "And reading."

I knew that wasn't true. I was a prolific reader, no doubt. It was the nature of a librarian. But my brother read just as much as I did.

"Which reminds me," he said. "Don't you have a book that goes with this case?"

Case . . .

Is that what it was? I stole a glance at Roo, who'd finished her bowl off and was cleaning herself, probably before she settled down for a nap. The two of us had just discussed—well, I talked, she listened—that Koby had chosen the wrong profession.

I swallowed the food I had in my mouth and nodded. "I had come up with one, Kathryn Dionne's first book in her Stevie Elliot series."

"What is that about?"

"A traveling chef. And in the first book, the chef goes back home to Quapaw, Mississippi, and cooks for the church's Holiday Bazaar."

"Ahh." Koby's eyebrows went up. "Like the potluck."

"Right."

"And the pastor ends up dead with a chicken leg in hand."

"And she's accused of murder by a poisoned chicken leg?"

"No, her assistant is." I took another bite of my egg dish.

"Pete!"

"No." I covered my mouth with my hand to talk with my mouth full. "His name was Milo."

"No. I mean *like Pete*. He was the assistant. Austin James had Mama Zola's peach cobbler in hand."

"Oh. Right."

"But the cobbler didn't kill Austin Janes." He sounded disappointed.

"And the chicken leg didn't kill the astor in her story. It was—"

He stretched out an open hand, palm nearly touching my nose. "No. Stop. Don't tell me. I want to read the book. You have a copy here?"

"Weren't you just talking about not being a good reader?"

"Did I say reader?" He smiled at me and wiped his mouth with a paper towel. "I meant researcher."

I shook my head and had to keep myself from rolling my eyes. "Yes. I have a copy here." My brother was quite familiar with the vastness of my home library. It stretched the entire front wall of the living room in my Craftsman. There was a little of everything on it. But mystery was my passion.

We'd finished eating by then, and for me, being the daughter—even though I was the *adopted* daughter—of a research librarian, I thought it better if we did research on my desktop.

I got up and put the plates and glasses in the sink.

"C'mon," I said. "I'll give you the book and we can do some research on the big computer."

"Sounds good," Koby said. "Let me get Remy. I'm sure he wants to play with Roo."

"She's sleeping." I let my eyes turn to her, curled up by her bowl, so his eyes would follow mine.

"Don't worry. He'll wake her up. Just like I did her mama."

Chapter Fifteen

ROO WAS CHASING Remy through the house. Koby had flopped down on the couch and I had sat down at the small desk I'd pushed up into a corner and fired up my Dell computer.

I'd found the book for Koby and he was flipping through the pages, his legs propped up on the coffee table while I Googled.

First thing was Hatton & Lyndale. It didn't take long to find articles on the embezzlement incident.

"Okay. The money came up missing six years ago."

Koby looked up at me from his reading. Didn't say anything and then went back to his book.

"But no one was accused of it until four years ago."

Koby looked up again, his eyes staying on me a little longer this time before he went back to reading.

"Let me see what happened," I said, mostly to myself. Koby was so engrossed in *Murder at the Holiday Bazaar*, he wasn't paying me much attention.

"Let's see . . . It says here that a VP, Mark Masters,

along with members of his team, had intentionally over-stated earnings in the company's books." I skimmed over what I'd already read, paraphrasing some of it. "People involved with him were going to be brought up on charges of fraud, money laundering and embezzlement. The guys they named were Hector Carreras, Peter J. Howers, Sandoval Greenstein and Austin James . . ."

I stopped reciting and looked up. "I never knew Pete's full name," I said. Koby took his eyes off the book and set them on me. "Did you?"

He shrugged. "He put it on his W-9."

"Why didn't you tell me?"

"Think about that question," Koby said and went back to reading.

I scratched my head. Okay. So it wasn't any kind of pertinent information that anyone would talk about or share.

"Do you have a middle name?" I asked, realizing I didn't know that about my brother either.

"Not sure," he said.

"How can you not be sure?"

"I was never told I had one. Not one on my birth certificate, but you have one so maybe I do, too."

"How do you know I have—" I didn't even finish that sentence. It was Koby I was talking to after all. "Maybe my parents gave it to me after I was adopted."

He glanced at me from the top of his book.

"I can ask," I said.

He shrugged and went back to the story he was reading.

He didn't seem too interested in whether they gave it to me or not. But now, of course, I was. Did my parents keep my first name and change my last name? Did they give me a middle name to make me seem more like their child? Was Keaton even really my first name?

"And our mother named you Keaton," Koby said. "In

case you're wondering. I found that out when I was looking for you."

Sometimes he could read my mind. Twin . . .

"Twin telepathy," he said, this time without even looking up. "I know that's what you were thinking. But that wasn't it. It figures you were wondering if Keaton was your real name after I talked about how our names were different."

I smiled. Because even though he used logic to know I was wondering about my name, he still knew I was thinking about twin telepathy.

"Now can we get back to our research?" he asked.

"Ha!" I said. "*Our* research."

"I'm helping," he said and held up the book. "Lots of useful information here."

I went back to the article I'd found.

"Hey," I said after rereading the part I'd just looked at. "It doesn't mention Pastor Lee. Didn't Brother Ron say that Calvin Lee worked there with them?"

"Uh-huh." He hadn't stopped reading, just muttered his answer.

"Let me check to see when he started pastoring at Everlasting."

"Wait," Koby said. He moved the book from in front of his face. "What happened at Hatton & Lyndale? To the people who were involved in overinflating." He laid the book open on his leg. "Don't go to something else yet."

"They overinflated and manipulated accounting records."

"You didn't say that before."

"What?"

"About manipulating accounting records."

"I didn't?"

"No. You didn't."

"Well, they did. At least somebody did."

"Did they manipulate them? And was it because they were skimming money off of them?"

"Yes."

"You didn't say that either."

I let my eyes roll up to the ceiling. I *had* read all that stuff. I guess I hadn't read it out loud.

"So that's fraud. Where did the money laundering and embezzlement come in at?"

My eyes got big. "What's the difference?"

"Embezzlement is taking funds that are placed in your trust, or your employer's money."

"Well. They stole from the company."

"Generally trading firms deal in other people's money."

"Oh," I said, just starting to process that when he gave out another definition.

"Money laundering is when you take ill-gotten gains and put them into a legal enterprise to cover up where the money came from."

"Let me look at another article."

I found several. One was about Austin James. I picked it and started reading it.

"Read it out loud," Koby said.

I started reading from where I'd left off. "It is believed that Austin James used money from client funds to start Abundant Faith, a megachurch on Seattle's Southside."

"Ahh," Koby said. "Money laundering." He nodded. "So that means thousands of people could've wanted him dead."

"I guess," I said. We'd never be able to figure out whodunit if that were true. I didn't say that to my brother, though.

"Now what about embezzlement?" he asked.

I searched with Pete's name and the word "embezzlement." I found an article, clicked on it and started reading it. Out loud.

"'Peter J. Howers, an accountant at Hatton & Lyndale and the trustee for the Martin H. Kenneth Trust, was arrested today and is expected to be charged with embezzlement. For two years during his tenure at the trading firm, Howers wrote checks to himself that should have been paid to charities and other expenses so designated by the trust fund he managed.'"

I looked up at my brother. He didn't say anything, just stared right back at me. Didn't he hear what I'd just said? I spelled it out for him.

"Pete stole money from a business he worked for."

"No he didn't." My brother shook his head and had that same look on his face that Pete had been sporting. The one where there *is* plenty evidence against him, and he acts as if *none* of it is true.

I pointed at the computer screen. "Yes, he did."

"Then why were the charges dropped?"

I got quiet. My mouth still opened, I shut it, looked at the monitor and then back at my brother. "Oh. Right." I looked back at the screen. "Oh no," I said.

"What?" Koby asked.

"It says that Pete had a wife and two children."

"Really?" Koby leaned forward.

"Yeah. Really. And that she left after he was arrested."

"Oh wow," Koby said. "I never knew that."

"What do we know about Pete?" I asked. "I mean really know?"

"I know he came here from Detroit. I know that his birthday is in May. I know his favorite food is lasagna and that he played baseball in high school."

I cocked my head to the side. "You know all that?"

"You would, too, if you talked to him."

"I do talk to him."

"I mean about stuff other than work."

I leaned back in my chair. "I mean. I would. I guess.

But he's always busy with the customers and then he's off on his own when it gets quiet."

"Did you know he was homeless?"

"Of course." I scrunched up my face. "Maybe I just thought he was. And I had been feeling bad about asking him where he lived."

"Did you?"

"No, because I couldn't offer a solution for him. I didn't have a place for him to stay."

"His whole life went down the drain."

"I know," I said, feeling pretty bad about it.

"When, according to his lawyer," Koby continued with what I'd been set to say, "all he did was get arrested."

"So then what happened?"

"Don't know," he said. "We'll have to find out. But right now"—he dropped his feet to the floor—"we have to get to the shop." Remy came right over. Seemed he knew Koby was ready to go. Koby ran a hand over his torn ear and under his jaw, then patted Remy on the head. "C'mon, boy, time to go." Koby snapped his leash on him and stood up. "I need to make biscuits and you have to help me."

"Help?" I pushed air into my cheeks and let it out. "Help cook?"

"Bake," he corrected me. "And yep. Mama Zola said she has something to do this morning."

"Is she feeling okay? She never doesn't come in."

He held out his hands. "She didn't say she was sick."

"Okay," I said. "But you know I don't know how to make biscuits from scratch."

He smiled at me. "You're going to learn today."

Chapter Sixteen

I LOVED HANGING out with my brother, but this was a bit much. I was covered in flour and we were just getting started.

"It's in your hair and all over your cheeks." Koby squinted and me and shook his head. "How did you do that?"

I swiped my cheek with the back of my hand.

"You just made it worse."

I had run back upstairs when he said he was ready to go to work at Books & Biscuits. I had to change into work clothes. Jeans wouldn't do for me.

I put on a baby blue mohair light knit sweater with puffy short sleeves and light gray pants. I slipped my feet into a pair of flats and twisted my hair into a top knot. Kissing my cat good-bye and making sure he had enough food and water for the remainder of the day, I headed out with Koby and Remy.

I often wondered if Roo minded that we took Koby's

dog to the shop and not her. She never said anything, but still . . .

We left the house and headed for our shop on foot. Timber Lake had a high walkability rate. My house to downtown, where our shop was, were only about a ten-minute walk. I didn't even own a car. If I had to leave my little town, I'd just take the light-rail and that took me anywhere in Seattle I wanted to go. To get whatever I needed to get.

As we walked, we passed the waterfront, where Koby had taken up residence. Butted up against clear waters that ran underneath bleached-out wooden docks. Always overhead were glaucous-winged gulls, with their gray wings, red spots and yellow bills. Then we'd taken the walking trail, carved out from decades of foot traffic that cut across the Timber Lake ravine for another seven or eight minutes before we stepped onto the paved road and headed into downtown.

But that was when it all went downhill for me. Even with an apron on that covered my entire torso and went down past my knees, I was a mess. I didn't know how I was going to work all day.

I even made a mess of cutting the butter into pats. And when the first batch of biscuits came out of the oven, they were all different heights.

"That's from not being consistent with rolling them out," Koby said. He smiled. "But those are pretty awesome."

I smiled back. Semi-proud of myself. He was probably only complimenting them because he was my brother.

"You'll do better on the next batch."

That made me frown. "Next batch?"

But before he could try to talk me into doing it again, we heard a *tap, tap, tap* on the window outside Biscuits.

"Who is that?" I asked. It was too early for customers. I knew the smell of biscuits, even ones made by me, was like the music of the Pied Piper, bringing all unwittingly to our doorstep. But they couldn't come in yet. I'd probably have to go home and change before I could let anyone see me.

I think I liked it better when he and Mama Zola didn't let me in the kitchen.

"Let me see," Koby said and clapped the small amount of flour off his hands. It would take a power vac to get me clean. "Stay here."

Of course, I didn't. I followed him out front. There was a murderer on the loose in Timber Lake and he, or she as the case may be, might think we were on their trail.

Koby peeked out of the window and smiled. "It's Maya," he said, pulling the curtain back so I could see. "I'll get the door," he said.

"Hi, Maya," I said with a smile when she came in. Maya had an aura to her, it seemed. Most times she had a sunny disposition and was an optimist. But don't get her heated. She didn't tolerate much.

"You and Koby having a food fight?" she asked. "Because I can see who's winning."

"She made biscuits," Koby said.

"Are they edible?" Maya asked.

"We're not sure about that," I said.

"They look good, though," Koby added.

We all laughed at that.

Maya's dark hair was pulled back and brushed flat on her head. She had on big hoop earrings and a gold-colored linen V-neck shirt with embroidery around the top and sleeves and a pair of hip-hugger jeans.

"What are you doing out and about so early?" I asked.

"I was out walking, just trying to clear my head, when I smelled the biscuits."

"Thought you'd come and get some?" Koby asked.

Maya smiled. "I had hoped I could sneak one."

Maya was there to see Koby. No way she would have

thought I was there that early. She would be a good match for Koby. She was relaxed. Laid back. But I had a feeling that Koby liked someone else.

"I'll get you a couple," Koby said and disappeared into the kitchen.

"Did the social media posts help with getting more people to RSVP for your book event?" Maya asked.

"I've had a couple more. The other two events we hosted weren't totally a bust, but I was hoping as we had more and more, more people would come."

"This is only your second one?"

"Third," I said.

"You're still new at this. It'll come around. You'll have big-time authors and crowds out the door," Maya said.

"I hope so."

"You hope what?" Koby came out of the back with two biscuits in a wax-paper-like bag. "Here you go," he said, then looked at me expectantly.

"Maya was just saying that after a while we'll have droves of people coming in for the book events we host."

"Are you worried?" Koby asked me. Now he had a worried look on his face.

"A little," I admitted.

"Fewer people are coming than the last two times?" Koby asked.

"Uhm . . ." I thought about it. "Maybe. But I know it's probably because she isn't a local author."

"What can I do to help?" Koby said. "You want me to invite people?"

"No. It's okay." I looked at the both of them. They had concerned looks. "I'm making more out of it than necessary. I know building up a customer base takes time. But this event will be fine." Both were staring at me without saying anything. "Spectacular. Especially with the wonderful flyers and social media shout-outs Maya had done for me."

"Okay," Koby said. "And yeah, Maya, great flyer. Thanks for helping Keaton."

"Happy to help," Maya said. "But I gotta go. I still have some walking and thinking to do." She held up the bag. "Thanks for the biscuits."

"Anytime," Koby said.

Maya took the biscuits and left, and we returned to the kitchen.

"You know she likes you," I said.

"Who? Maya?" Koby frowned.

"Yes, Maya. And why you say it like that?"

"I don't think Maya likes me." Koby took in a quick breath. "She is definitely out of my league."

"Is that what you think?" I asked. "Because she isn't. You could date anyone you wanted. Even Maya. Because she likes you." I leaned into him. "She's really nice."

"Change of subject," Koby announced. "Ready to make more biscuits?"

"No," I said.

He dragged me, literally, back to the kitchen.

"You ready to do this?" he asked like he was my high school track coach. Not that I ran track in high school. It was too far from the library, where I tended to hang out.

"If I said no again, would you listen this time?"

"No," he said. "But if you get started, I'll help by keeping you company."

"Thanks," I said, sarcasm in my voice.

"How about we finish talking about the murder?" he said.

"What about it?" I said, cutting up more butter.

"I think before Maya came, we were talking about Austin James."

"Mmm-hmm," I said. I had to concentrate on measuring my dry ingredients.

"And his megachurch."

I looked up at him. Distracted because I didn't want to mess up the biscuits but trying to figure out what he was talking about. "We didn't say anything about the church, did we?"

"No. But we should." He pulled out his phone and typed into it. "Okay. Looks like Abundant Faith Tabernacle started about five years ago," Koby said.

He'd started googling on his phone while I made up the next batch of biscuits. This one I was doing on my own. Wasn't sure if they were going to be edible.

"So that was after the illegal action started."

"Right," I said. "And before they got caught."

"How did they get caught?" Koby asked. "I don't remember you reading that."

"Someone reported their accounting practices to the SEC and they did an investigation."

Koby nodded.

"Google to see when Pastor Lee's church was established."

Koby's fingers scurried over his phone. "Eight years ago." He looked up at me.

"So that was before the illegal activity," I said.

"All good information," Koby said, "but this doesn't give Pete any motive to kill Austin James."

"True," I said. "But remember his lawyer said everything was circumstantial anyway."

"Circumstantial is enough to convict," Koby said.

"So where do we go from here?" I asked. I was quite pleased with how we'd dug up information and found out about Austin James. Koby evidently wasn't.

Koby shook his head, disappointment showing in his eyes. "I don't know." He scratched his chin and ran a hand over his cheek. "Who are our suspects?"

I'd been thinking the same thing. Ever since the day Austin James' murder was discovered. But Koby, asking the question—the word *suspect* actually materializing from his mouth, I got goose bumps. I had all kinds of ideas about who might have done the deed.

"Ray. Billy Ray. Or whatever his name is," I said, "is at the top of my list."

"Do we know his last name?"

I let my eyes roll up and to the left. I'd been kneading dough, my fingers were tired, so it was the perfect time to pause and think. It seemed to me that I had heard it spoken before. "Umm." I squinted one eye and tried to think. "Patton," I said. That's what Pastor Lee called him, right?" I nodded, remembering. "Brother Patton."

"Yeah." Koby nodded in agreement. "I do remember that."

"He knew about the coffeepot," I added. "Before the pastor told us."

"What about the pastor?" Koby said.

"I don't think he would do that," I said.

"Do what?" Koby smiled. "Kill someone?"

"Yes." A look of disbelief on my face. "That would be terrible."

"Terrible, yes. Impossible because he's a man of the cloth? No."

I rolled my eyes.

"He's on my list," Koby said.

"He had left Hatton & Lyndale by the time all the stuff happened. He didn't have a vendetta with Austin James. Not for getting him in trouble. Not for getting him fired."

"Maybe for stealing some of his church members," Koby said.

"Oh." I stopped my kneading again. "Hadn't thought about that." I picked up the rolling pin and dusted it with flour. I had learned my lesson with the last batch about dough-sticky surfaces. "Who else?" I asked.

"Rocko Jackson."

"Now, I can get on board with him," I said. "And I

think if he did do it, he did it with that Power Company guy."

"Looks like he had some kind of Abundant Faith connection, too."

"Why do you say that?" I asked.

"Because why would he call Brother Ron and let him know about Austin James?"

"True," I said. "But you don't think Brother Ron had anything to do with it, do you?"

Koby hunched his shoulders. "Not sure. But I think you're right about Power Company Guy. There's some kind of connection there. Maybe not intended to be murderous, but that was where it ended up."

"Who else?" I was cutting the biscuits and placing them on the cookie sheet. They were looking much better this time.

"I think the other two people on the video," Koby said. "We should look into them."

"How in the world can we find the 'mysterious woman in the hat'?" I did air quotation marks.

"I don't know," Koby said. "But tomorrow is Sunday. We know where we'd probably find the deacon."

"At church," I said.

"Yep." Koby nodded. "And maybe we could get another crack at talking to Pastor Lee."

That idea, I decided, was just as bad as my first batch of biscuits.

Chapter Seventeen

MY INTRODUCTION TO biscuit baking was the start of what turned out to be a busy day. The way I like to spend my Saturdays. Or really any day in the shop. There was a constant jangle from the bell that hung over the door of the Books side. And a constant smile that hung on my face.

Right before time to open, Pete and Georgie came into the kitchen together, laughing. Something that was rare for Pete, but Georgie was always in a good mood. I didn't ask what was funny or what was going on, because it's okay to be in a good mood and no one should be questioned about it.

Koby had put a makeshift bed for Pete in a storeroom near the back door as soon as we'd returned from our misadventures the day of the murder. We'd told the police that our shop was his home address—for now—and we were going to stick to our word.

"And we're going to have to help find him a place to live and pay him more money so he can afford it."

I had raised an eyebrow and sucked in a breath.

I honestly didn't mind paying Pete more money. He was an excellent employee, but if I was going to spend half my time solving homicides and chasing down murderers, I wasn't going to be able to turn as much revenue as I hoped I would.

But it wasn't long after that that something lucrative for the store came our way. Something big. Author events weren't the only thing I had come up with to get people interested in our shop.

Well, it hadn't just come, I had been working on the idea for a while, but today we got a break. So unexpected.

A friend of mine from college, Kevin Williams, had offered to set up the online store part of it for me. Only I, per him, just needed the "right" software. He was willing to pick one for me as I didn't know the right software from any other software. But I wanted to research it myself. So I did and found the one I thought to be the best for our little shop. Of course, it came with an expensive price tag.

I'd been watching different sites, hoping to catch a sale. My plan was to use it to sell books generally in the store, but also for a used books section I was planning on adding to Books. I didn't want to start it until I had enough books to fill it up. Which turned out to be a good thing once I found out how much the software, the creation of the website and the hosting were going to cost.

Still, I didn't stop shopping around for used books. I'd go to flea markets on Sundays, get books from the local library when they had book sales, and from the Timber Lake Community Center. People were always donating books there. I also wanted to create a loyalty program to get people to bring books in. Bring in a book, get a discount toward a new book. I'd use a punch card and allow users to stack up their discounts to 50 percent off.

And then there was the owner of the market at the corner of our street. For some reason he'd taken a liking to our bookstore and consistently, from the time we'd opened, had given me boxes of books.

But the part I hadn't expected was to find a used book that would—could—pay for it all.

And then the day took a turn and became potentially a really great day. And that smile that I'd worn all day for my customers turned into one that lit up the entire shop—both the Book and the Biscuits sides.

Second Street, where half of our shop was located, was in the heart of the downtown district. We'd been lucky to get a place and even luckier to get a corner store. On our block, all the shops were connected. And to one side we were anchored to The Attic, an antiques store. Next was the Mane Attraction, a hair salon. Neither one of those places had I frequented much. But I had spent much time in the last store on our block, the Second Street Farmers Market. It was where I was headed. It was an open-air market with fresh fruits and vegetables, artisan breads, fresh-cut flowers and a deli whose cases were filled with food that could make a person swoon. The sandwiches and sides of potato salad and antipasto salad were delicious, and I made it a habit, unknown to my brother, to have lunch there once a week, if not more. He sold fresh herbs in the back of the store, and I could have sworn I saw Mama Zola in there one day grabbing a few bunches of them. I didn't want to be seen, so I ducked out of her line of sight until she'd left.

But there was something else that gave me reason every week to visit and that was the box of books Mr. Al, the owner of the market, kept under his counter for me. I'd never asked him where he got them from, until today. Pete had helped me pull out the last two boxes of books that Mr. Al had had given me so I could go through them.

At the rate I was going, I remembered thinking as I ploughed through the first box, the used book section was going to outsize the new books pretty soon. But I dismissed any problems with that—once they were old, they were always old, so technically I could keep them in storage as long as I needed. Still, I liked to keep an inventory of everything I had. And that was when I saw it: a signed first edition of *A Lost Soul* by A. K. Hess.

The book, written in 1960, had been on the *New York Times* bestseller list for a record 290 weeks. It had sold over 100 million copies and had been translated into fifteen languages. But something had happened to the first run of books, only a handful had made it into circulation, and no one had seen a first edition in years. No one actually thought any existed. But here I was holding one in my hands. One with a signature by the author.

That was what really made the difference. It hadn't even been a week since I'd read in *Reader's News* that A. K. Hess had died. Nothing fishy or sinister like the deaths I seemed to constantly be dealing with. He was old and it had been reported his death was of natural causes. But because of that, this book was probably worth a fortune. Well, a big enough fortune that I could get my e-commerce set up.

I Googled it to make sure, and sure enough, it would get Books & Biscuits into the world of e-commerce.

But as I sat holding the book, I had second thoughts about that money being all mine to do what I wanted to do with it. I thought I had better let Mr. Al know.

Maybe he'd want the book back. I had heard that possession is nine tenths of the law, but I wasn't sure about that. Plus, it was only fair that I let him know.

I held up the book and called out to Pete. "I gotta run over to see Mr. Al."

He nodded. "I saw that book earlier," Pete said and walked over to me. "Might be worth something, huh?"

I smiled. If my brother had been standing there, he would have said, "See? No reason not to trust Pete."

And I did trust him. Even though the things I had found out about him were disquieting.

"I know," I said and smiled. "But I want to make sure he's okay with me making that much money off of it."

Pete nodded. "Everything will be good here until you get back."

I walked down to the end of the block, but before I could get into the store, the smell of fresh bread nearly lifted me off my feet and floated me the rest of the way in.

I loved their food.

No worries, though. The Second Street Market wasn't any competition for us. They served a different kind of food, had a different vibe. There were plenty of places in Seattle that had restaurants next to one another, and located on every block. Still, I always looked around whenever I went in to make sure no one saw me. I didn't want to give out the wrong impression.

"Keaton!" Mr. Al called out from behind the deli counter and waved. "How are you?"

"Hi, Mr. Al," I said, smiling. "I'm good. I was wondering if I could speak to you for a minute."

The store always had a steady stream of people going in, especially at this time of the day. Today was no different. In fact, it even seemed more crowded than usual. I thought I'd have to wait for him to have time for me. I glanced at my clock and then at all the people.

I might have to hang out for a minute . . .

Sure enough, he said, "Keaton, give me a second, okay?"

"No problem," I said.

I decided to check out what goodies Mr. Al had on hand. I ended up with a small basket of stuff I wanted to buy by the time he made it over to me.

"Do you want me to get you a bag for that?" Mr. Al said, winking. He'd caught up with me just as I put what

I had just promised myself was going to be the last thing I was going to buy in my basket.

"No. Thank you," I said and smiled. I certainly believed in supporting other small businesses.

"You sure? You're welcome to whatever you need."

I drew in a breath. *Just wait until you find out what I'm here about*, I thought. *You might just have a change of heart.*

"I wanted to talk to you about this," I said and held up the book.

"*A Lost Soul.*" He looked at the book and nodded. "Good book. Hope you'll find it a good home."

"You know the author just died, right?"

"No," he said, raising his eyebrows. "Sorry to hear that. Did you know him?"

"No." I shook my head. "But this is a signed first edition."

"I knew it was signed, but I didn't know it was a first edition."

"It's worth a little money," I said. "And I didn't want to take the book and . . . you know, all the money without letting you know."

"How much money?" His eyes got big.

"A lot."

"Enough to buy me a yacht?" he asked.

"Oh my goodness, no. Maybe a couple of anchors for a yacht."

"So then I couldn't use it to retire either?"

"Probably not," I said.

"Are you going to sell it?"

"Yep, but not without your permission."

"And what are you going to do with it?"

"I am going to buy software so that we can start selling books online."

"For your business, huh?"

I nodded.

"I gave it to you. It's yours. Do what you want to do with it."

"Are you sure?" I asked.

"I'm sure," he said. "You have enough stuff going on over there. I've wanted to think of a way I could help." He let his eyes meet mine. I knew he was talking about Pete.

"Thank you," I said and held up the book. "Thank you very much."

"No problem." He patted me on the shoulder. "Now give me that basket and let me get you bagged up."

"Oh no," I said. I really wasn't going to do that now. "I'm getting in line to check out." I smiled at him. "But thank you. For everything."

"Okay then," he said. "I've got to get back to the deli counter. That new guy doesn't know how to slice meat. He's giving away all my food!"

I went to get in line after he left, my mind on the book, its sale and Books & Biscuits moving into the twenty-first century.

I wonder what Mama Zola would have to say about that.

"Oh!" Lost in thought, I ran right into someone. "Excuse me," I said and looked at him to show my sincerity and make sure I hadn't caused any damage with my heavily filled basket.

"You're fine," he said and smiled at me.

I started to smile back, but something about him was familiar. And the wave of familiarity didn't bring good vibes.

Then I knew who he was. Chief Ross Franklin. Well *Acting* Chief Ross Franklin. The man who was determined to put Pete in jail for something Pete swore he hadn't done.

Chapter Eighteen

JUST STANDING IN line next to the chief of police made me nervous, whether he was actually a real one or not.

I was happy he didn't know who I was. And if I could just stop trembling like a leaf on a tree, I could get through the line and out the door unnoticed and possibly unscathed.

"Excuse me," I said again, trying to get out of his way. I started to step aside to the right, but he stepped the same way I did. And then we did that dance again. This time to the left. "Sorry." I shook my head in frustration. "I'm trying to get in line."

He extended his arm and gestured with his hand, telling me to go ahead.

I got in line, and of course, he got in line right behind me.

"Aren't you Keaton Rutledge," he said more than asked.

How did he know my name?

So much for him not knowing who I was.

I swiveled around, a fake, cordial-like smile on my face. "Yes. I am," I said. "And you're . . ." I acted as if I didn't know.

"Ross Franklin," he said and stuck out a hand. "I work for the Timber Lake Police Department."

I shook his hand, that stupid smile still stuck on my face. "Nice to meet you."

"You own Books & Biscuits?" He pointed.

I followed his finger, just for the sake of it. I certainly knew the direction our shop was in.

"Yes. With my brother. We own it together."

"I've heard about you two."

I crinkled my forehead, my brows knitted together. "Excuse me?"

"You and your brother, twin brother, right?"

I nodded.

"You two like to go around solving murders?"

That made me take a step backward. Where did he hear that from?

"I don't think that's true."

"No?"

"Not completely," I said. He looked at me as if I wasn't telling the truth and it made me feel like I wasn't.

"I don't *like* doing that."

"Ahh," he said and nodded. "And Books & Biscuits"— he cocked his head to the side—"isn't that where Peter Howers is staying?"

Was he trying to trick me?

And why was he calling him Peter?

Duh. Koby would have told me to think about that question.

"Yes," I said. Trying not to let my eyes show all the stuff that was going on in my head. "He's with us." I looked at him, and from somewhere inside, which I wasn't conscious of knowing was there, I got the nerve to say more. "And Pete didn't kill Austin James. He couldn't do anything like that."

"Austin James had taken a lot from him. His family. His job." The detective looked at me with what seemed like pity. Pity that I couldn't see that.

"And Austin James did, too. He lost things, too. His job. His church. His freedom. They were in the same boat. People don't kill people for that."

"Sure they do. Especially when they run into the person that made all that happen to them for the first time."

"Austin James caused Pete to have all that trouble?"

He gave a nod. "It's public record if you want to check it out. James and his cohorts used Mr. Howers, set him up as the fall guy. If it hadn't been for one guy turning on Mr. James and telling the truth, Mr. Howers could have lost a lot more."

Public record. Huh. I had looked up information on it, but I didn't find that.

So that was why Pete only got arrested and nothing more.

"Then why didn't Mr. James go to prison?"

"He did. For three years. But he got out on a technicality. Found on appeal. In fact, he'd only been out a couple of months when your employee got his revenge."

I snorted. "Everything you have is circumstantial."

He chuckled. A kind of chuckle that told me he had something more than what I thought. "Whoever killed Austin James had to leave a little bit of themselves at the scene. It won't be long before we get it processed. And we already have Mr. Howers in the system. It'll be an easy match-up."

DNA. I knew that was what he was talking about.

"And when we do," he continued, "we'll be issuing another arrest warrant for one Peter J. Howers and I won't mess anything up. He'll be gone for life and it will probably be a good thing that his family had already left him."

I turned up my mouth, turned sideways and scooted past him out of the line. I didn't even want to be near that man. He was vile. He just had his mind set on Pete being the killer.

And what was he talking about? *Leave a little bit of themselves.* People had been all over that place, including Pete. Was he going to take DNA wherever he found it that belonged to Pete and use it against him?

Oh! That man had made me mad.

I couldn't even think straight. I sat the basket on one of the display tables and left. I couldn't even stand to get into another line—I was too jittery. I just wanted to get back to the store and away from Acting Chief Ross.

I hurried back to the store and my mind was racing as fast as my feet were moving. I thought about all the places Pete had touched when we were there. He'd gone in with Rocko to get a cart, he'd helped Mama Zola put things up in the kitchen. She'd taken him to serve with her, so he'd been in the dining area where the potluck had taken place. Probably the restroom. And for some reason he'd gone to that door where the camera was located. Who knew what end of the building that was on, if it was anywhere near where Austin James had gone when he left the kitchen with Pastor Lee, or if Pete had touched or brushed against anything along the way. And what about if that was really the first time Pete had seen Austin James since everything had happened?

Ugh!

If so, maybe Pete confronted him. Pushed him. Spoke loudly to him and spewed spittle on him. All those things would transfer DNA.

This was making me so nervous.

At any time now, things were going to get turned upside down at Books & Biscuits. Pete would be dragged out of the shop. We'd be in the paper like Hatton & Lyndale had been when a scandal interrupted their business.

But after talking with Acting Chief Ross, I realized the thing that was going to bother me the most wasn't what would happen to the store, but what was going to happen to Pete.

His life had been snatched away from him once for something he hadn't done. He hadn't been turned loose on a technicality like Austin James. He was actually innocent. He had been used to cover up that man's wrongdoings.

And now that man—Austin James—even in death was trying to take Pete's life from him again.

Even though I wasn't sure how great a life he had. I knew how much it bothered Koby not to know our biological mother. A woman he'd never met. So I couldn't even fathom what Pete must've gone through losing his wife and children. Little ones that he'd probably spent every day with all of their lives.

No wonder he hit bottom. I wondered how long had he stayed there. But at least he was trying to pull himself back up. Working. Making friends.

But it all was making my world spin until I walked back into the store. Everything was normal. Pete was helping a customer. I could smell biscuits and wafts of green peppers and onions from the kitchen. People were browsing.

And I knew Koby was right. Even though he wouldn't have let me back out of whatever plans he had to help Pete, I now knew for sure I wanted in.

Pete looked up when the bell jingled over the door. I smiled at him and held up the book. He smiled.

I blew out a breath.

Yep, things around here were only going to get better. Books was expanding to being accessible to the world, we had good, reliable employees and our food would make anyone's mouth water, whether they had soul or not.

Before I could settle in behind the counter, Mama Zola and my mother came in like a gust of wind.

They were all smiles and giggles and laden with bags.

"Hello." I smiled at them.

"Hi," they said.

"So the two of you are playing hooky?"

My mother ran her own show. She had an office near the neighborhood I grew up in and a small but thriving practice. But Mama Zola was on our payroll, although I'd never reprimand her. I'd leave that to Koby. Still . . .

"No. Not hooky," Mama Zola said.

"We were out helping Books & Biscuits," my mother said.

"Helping us do what?"

They looked at each other, then at Pete and then back to me.

"We've been shopping for things for his room," Mama Zola said.

"You're planning on fixing up the storeroom?" I asked. I wondered what we'd do with all the stuff that was supposed to be in there.

"No. Of course not," she said. "His room at my house."

"What?"

"Zola is letting Pete come and stay with her." My mother wrapped an arm around Mama Zola's shoulder and gave a squeeze. "Isn't that just wonderful news!"

Chapter Nineteen

"SO, NOW WE have enough to get the software," I said, going through the open ledger on my lap. "Once it's up and running, I'll clear the area for the used books."

We were on Koby's houseboat having a business meeting. It was good to take care of store business and not the business of murder.

Koby's new abode had been a present. It came at a time when the once vibrant and busy marina was on a decline. A time when the slips began to be filled with fewer pleasure boats and with things more practical like houseboats. All sizes and shapes, the line of them dotted the shoreline. Koby's was a two-story canal boat with an uncovered deck, sparsely decorated. He hadn't done much with the motif. It looked almost the same as it did when the last owner had occupied it.

"That book was a good find." He turned from the counter, where he was dicing onions for the pot of chili he was making. "You've got a good eye." He smiled. "The best librarian I know."

That made me blush.

"So what's our ETA on getting the e-commerce store online? And what does the learning curve look like?"

"Kevin said it won't take him any time to install the program and that he could teach it to us in a day." I closed the ledger and put the cap back on the pen with a snap. "So, I'll call him right away and tell him to get started." I noted that task on my to-do list. "We're getting the top-of-the-line software—it has an accounting feature, generates invoices, does all the work for us."

Independent booksellers were making a comeback. In the last decade, around the country, the number of them had nearly doubled. And I remembered from my freshman year economics class that how you handle your business and what you have to offer makes a big difference when there is a lot of competition. I wanted to make ours able to go the distance even if we were off the well-beaten path. Running a business was hard, especially for two newcomers with an entrepreneurial spirit but not a lot of (or any) experience.

Being online was a good marketing ploy and so was selling used books, because they were cheap. Cheap books would bring in customers. We needed more customers. Once we got them in, I knew we offered enough good things, books, book events and food to keep them coming back. And with the loyalty program of people bringing in used books (not ones they'd bought at Books & Biscuits) and my own book-hunting endeavors, I hoped we'd always have a good supply of used books in stock.

"Will we be able to tie that into the one that came with our POS system?"

He was talking about the cash registers we'd had installed when we were setting up. I wasn't sure whether the two different software programs could sync.

"It's okay if it can't," he said, I think he could read that

I didn't have the answer to that question. "We'll figure it out."

He dipped up two bowls of piping hot chili and got out the saltines. "I have sweet tea," he said and grabbed a couple of glasses.

Setting my ledger aside, I got up and headed to the table right outside the kitchen area that took up half of one of the walls of the boat. I grabbed the pitcher of tea out of the fridge.

"What flavor is this?" I asked.

"Pomegranate." He sat the glasses on the table and I filled them up. "With a touch of lime." He watched me pick up the glass. "Top secret recipe. You're the first to try it." He clasped his hands together. "Let me know what you think."

I closed my eyes while I drank. I let the punch of the tart, sweet pomegranate roll over my tongue and slip down my throat. "Mmm," I said, and the freshness of the lime kicked it. I smacked my lips.

"You like it?"

"Mmm-hmm." I took another gulp. "That's good."

"I was thinking about introducing it at your next author event."

"The one on Tuesday?" I asked. "Nicole D. Miller and her book, *Stories for the (Urban) Soul*?" I hadn't had as much time to work on it as I thought I would after Pete, my best and only employee, was being accused of murder.

"Yep." He nodded. "Thought that might be a good way to pique people's interest."

I nodded, pulling my bowl in front of me. I realized I was hungry. I hadn't eaten since breakfast.

"Kind of worried about this one. Don't know how much traction we got with the flyers Maya made." I took in some chili, and, talking with my mouth full, I said, "I do need to get on that."

"I'm sure it'll be fine," he said. "But, if you want, I can help you brainstorm on some marketing ideas."

But before I could answer, Izzy, Koby's next-door neighbor, popped in unannounced and let herself in the side door.

She was the girl I thought Koby liked.

"You didn't get the lock fixed on that door?" I asked, leaning in and lowering my voice. I wasn't sure if she was the right girl for my brother. "That lock has been broken since you got the place."

"If I fixed it, how would Izzy get in?"

"Why do you want Izzy in whenever she wants to pop in?"

"Hi, Izzy," he said, greeting her and warning me, I guessed, that she was in earshot.

I gave a wave and a smile before stuffing a big spoonful of chili and smashing crackers into my mouth.

I wasn't so sure how I felt about her.

Isabella Ramirez lived in one of the floating homes on the marina. Some of them were fully seaworthy. Some, like Koby's, were rickety and probably wouldn't make it a mile out into the water. I had only been in Izzy's houseboat once. She'd been drunk, twisted her ankle and I had to help her get home. Hers was one of the nicer ones. Like the ones being used for Airbnbs, and like the one that sold cupcakes out of the moored bakery.

She'd come in bearing a half dozen or so as gifts.

She liked my brother. I was sure of that.

What I wasn't sure about was how he felt about her. He seemed to like the attention she gave and spending time with her.

And, it seemed, her popping in whenever she had the chance.

But it wasn't hard to see, if he did, why. Izzy was beautiful. She had long, dark hair, and every time I'd seen her, she'd had an even, perfect tan. I wasn't sure how she could get that tan in our rainy part of the world. She was always scantily clad, showing off her curves and a lot of skin. And that charming, engaging smile of hers was always beaming at my brother.

"Hi, twins," she said. "I brought dessert." She held up the box.

"You want a bowl of chili?" Koby asked and started to get up.

"Oh no," she said. "The beans make me gassy."

I lowered the spoon that was nearly to my mouth. For some reason I couldn't eat any more. I dropped it into my bowl. "Really, Izzy?" I said.

Koby laughed.

"I only stopped by for a minute," she said, ignoring my reaction to her inappropriate comment. "Did you guys know that detective from your last case is going to be Timber Lake's new chief of police?"

"He isn't our detective," I said.

"He should be," Izzy said. "He saved your life."

"With the help of my brother."

"Our hero," she said and smiled at Koby.

"They have to have the election," I said.

"Yeah. But no one is running against him." She pulled out the chair at the table and sat down. "But there is a mixer at Hemlock tomorrow night. Dollar Beer Night. You guys going?"

"I don't think I will," I said, and thinking maybe Izzy shouldn't either. She and liquor didn't mix well.

I knew Daniel Chow coming to our neck of the woods was inevitable. No matter how much I protested. Still I didn't like it.

"Maybe we'll stop by," Koby said. "Might be fun."

"What's going on with you, Izzy?" I asked, wanting to change the subject. I wasn't sure what Izzy did all day or where she worked, if she did, but anything had to be better than talking about Daniel Chow or getting Koby to understand I didn't want to be anywhere Chow was.

"Oh, nothing," she said. "I just wanted to get the tea."

I looked at the pitcher, then at my brother. Hadn't he just said I was the first to try it? How did she know about it? Not that I minded, just wondering why my brother would say that.

"The gossip," my brother said, explaining it to me. He must've have read my mind. "She wants the 411." He turned to Izzy. "How did you find out about the murder?"

"I heard it on the news."

"Why would you think we knew anything about it?" I asked, wiping my mouth with a paper towel.

"Because it was murder."

I looked at her as if to say, "And?"

"You and Koby are involved in murder."

I frowned.

"Have you figured out who done it yet?"

"No," Koby said. "But we're working on it."

"I knew it." Izzy was beaming. "I bet there are a lot of suspects. That man was trouble."

"Did you know him?" I asked.

"Everybody knew about him," she said and looked at me, perplexed. "You don't remember hearing about him on the news?" She put her hands on her lips. "They called him Pastor Socks because he always took off his shoes and walked around in his socks."

Koby and I looked at each other. Him taking off his shoes then was a well-known fact.

"I don't watch the news," I said. "I don't even own a television."

Izzy gave me another look. "No TV?" It seemed to be mixed with pity, disbelief and another one from my childhood—a look that called me a nerd. "I am so undone." She held up her hand, palm out, into my face. "Don't even tell me any more." She turned and looked at Koby. "Did you hear about him?"

"Not that I can remember." I knew he hadn't, because he didn't mention it the day we'd visited Grace Spirit Revival. "Because what happened?"

"He started that big megachurch. What was the name of it . . ." She sucked her tongue and snapped her fingers.

"Abundant Faith Tabernacle," I said.

"That's it," she said and looked at me out the corner of her eye. "Then boom!" She made a gesture with her two hands like something had exploded. "He got arrested and come to find out that he had not only stolen money from his accounting firm or hedge firm, or whatever it was"—she was all into the story, drawing the words out—"but he stole from the people in the church."

"Wow," I said. Surprised he'd done all of that and still was lurking around a church.

"He must've been a good preacher, though," she said, "because no one could take his place."

"What do you mean?" Koby asked.

"You know how you usually have an assistant pastor who takes over the church?" We nodded. "Well, instead, it splintered. Everybody left and started their own church. It was like four or five churches that started with the members of Abundant . . . whatever the name was."

"Abundant Faith Tabernacle," I said, but my mind was far away in thought. How were we ever going to solve this murder? Thousands of people could have been upset enough with him to kill him.

"He got like ninety years or something," Izzy said. "Definitely the only way he was coming out was on a gurney. And then, boom!" She did that hand explosion gesture again, and this time, it startled me. "He was out of prison!" She shook her head. "People were mad."

"We heard he got out on a technicality."

She shrugged. "Something about some bad fruit."

"Bad fruit?" I crunched up my face.

"Something in the Constitution about bad fruit."

"Ohhh," Koby said. "Fruit of the poisonous tree."

Then it clicked with me, too. "A Fourth Amendment violation."

"Right." She pointed a finger at me. "They didn't get evidence in the right way or something." She drew in a breath. "So they had to let him go. But"—she raised her eyebrows—"someone gave him a life sentence anyway."

Chapter Twenty

IT WAS A beautiful and sunny Sunday morning and we were at the Everlasting Missionary Baptist Church without Mama Zola. She had dug her heels in deep yesterday, moving in Pete to stay with her. Looked like she wasn't ever going to be welcomed back through these double doors, which worried me.

Mama Zola didn't like change. She'd lived in the same house for more than thirty years. And when she found Everlasting Missionary Baptist Church, she'd said she couldn't feel more at home.

She'd shopped for Pete's room and was making a big deal over it. She hadn't wanted a big place when she and Koby decided to move her here. So Koby found her the first-floor unit of a two-family house. There was an older gentleman who had lived on the second floor for years, so the landlord told them. Mama Zola got permission to plant flowers in the yard and paint the inside in whatever color she pleased. She had picked warm tones and made the house feel cozy. And the second bedroom—the one that Pete was now going to occupy—was going to be her second closet.

She was going to repaint it in "a more manly color," she had said.

"All colors are for everyone," Koby had told her. "I'm sure he'll be happy with the walls and the roof over his head. "But are you okay?"

"I don't need all those clothes and things anyway," Mama Zola had said about giving up her extra bedroom. "Not when Pete is sleeping outdoors."

But I think her fussing over everything was to cover up how she was really feeling. I knew she was sad about not being able to go back to Everlasting Missionary Baptist Church if she helped Pete. And of course, she was going to do that. It was in her nature to help. She had taken in more foster kids probably than anyone in the city of Seattle. She'd asked me several times since that day, what exactly did Pastor Lee say. I hoped when all of this murder business was over, she might be able to go back.

Mama Zola had left her apartment in Seattle so she could come work at Books & Biscuits. She lived too far, and was too old, to make the trek back and forth in her car every day with the crazy traffic that was Seattle. Or at least those were Koby's thought on the matter.

Just like a child taking care of his mom. Whether they were related by blood or not.

So Koby had found her a first-floor unit of a two-story house, with two bedrooms, living and dining rooms and an eat-in kitchen halfway between our shop and his houseboat. She had beamed for days. And shopped for days. She wanted to outfit her new place with all new things. Koby put her things in storage just in case she had a change of mind and wanted some of them later on.

And now she was going to have a roommate.

At least until all this murder mess blew over.

My mother totally surprised me. I couldn't believe she

was on board in having a *malefactor*—as she liked to call them—around. But she seemed almost giddy, even taking off the day to help Mama Zola get things ready for Pete.

And it was because of Pete that we were once again at church. The only day Books & Biscuits was closed and yet we were still on the job.

At least, according to Koby, that's what our snooping was. He'd said, "Let's get to work." He emphasized that we needed to find, as Izzy put it, who gave Austin James the time which basically amounted to a life sentence the courts hadn't been able to uphold.

"Can I help you?" It was Rocko, the parking lot attendant slash security guard for the church. He'd stepped out of his booth when he saw us pull up and stretched out both of his arms and waved them as if he were flagging down a plane flying overhead.

"We're going to church," Koby said.

Rocko peeked into the car and surveilled our outfits.

"Aren't you banned from this church?"

That made me nervous. Were we not allowed in the church? Not even in the parking lot? What had we done? I scratched my head and remembered how we'd snooped through his booth the day of the murder. And how we'd called the Grace Spirit Revival.

Koby looked like he did any other day. Jeans. Boat shoes. At least he wore a button-down shirt. But I put on a dress. Empire style. Sweetheart neckline. Bolero jacket. It was dark beige and fit clingier than anything I was used to wearing. I even wore my hair down and put on dangly hoop earrings.

But I didn't know how fresh or churchy I'd look by the time we actually did attend service. Koby had gotten us there extra early so we could surveil the outside of the building.

"Are we going to walk the *entire* perimeter?" I asked and looked down at my feet. I wasn't ever in the habit of wearing heels, but these were a nicer pair of shoes than what I'd wear to work. I scanned the ground where I stood, then into the distance as it wound around the building. Gravel. Dirt. Some concrete, a little grass but not enough to allay my fears of ruining my shoes. "What exactly are we looking for?"

"Camera. Points of entry. Footprints."

"Footprints? What in the world would we do with a footprint we'd find?"

"We'll determine that once we find one."

I could only hope we didn't. I could see us in Koby's kitchen trying to make plaster of Paris from flour and water or something, to pour in the imprint to make a mold.

I'd had enough of flour.

Reflexively, I brushed a hand down my cheek.

"Look." Koby pointed above the first door we passed. "No camera."

I noted it, for what reason I wasn't sure, and we moved on.

"Here's another door," Koby said and tried to pull it open. "No camera."

"Yep. And nothing to see." I looked around. A small concrete pad held a couple of small dumpsters. I figured we must be near the kitchen because it was where they'd put trash and I saw no other reason to have a door there. Beyond there was grass and woods. I tried the door handle. "And locked."

"You need a key for this one." He stood back and looked at it. "Probably easy to get into."

I widened my eyes. That was a thought that wouldn't ever cross my mind. I looked back from where we'd come. I was glad he hadn't tried that at the last door and, fingers crossed, he wouldn't try anything more with the next one we happened upon.

"Why would they do that?" he asked as he kept walking. "Have a camera only at one door."

"We haven't checked all the doors yet."

"And then the one they do have doesn't even work."

I didn't think he'd heard what I said. We were in the back of the building and there seemed to be a door at every corner. I was expecting at least three more.

After another door, we came out on the other side. The door opened to a parking lot.

"That has a code to it," I said, noticing the numbers on the keypad.

"And it's the one with a camera." He stood and looked at it for a long while. "I wonder will it show me on it."

"Why wouldn't it?" I asked.

He hunched his shoulders. "I don't know. I mean that video we saw in the lawyer's office was so . . . different."

"How?"

"It only showed each person once. Didn't they go in and come out?"

"Maybe they just shared the video where people were going in. Didn't need to show the other part."

"No." He scratched his head. "That doesn't make sense." He turned and looked at me. "Wouldn't they want to know how long he was in there? If he had time to commit a murder."

I hunched my shoulders. "Maybe he didn't come back out that way," I said. "None of them did."

"I hope we can find that deacon," Koby said. "See if we can't get some answers."

HIS NAME WAS Deacon Brown. At least that was what the nameplate he had pinned on him read. Standing next to a table by one of the entry ways to the sanctuary, there were about ten paperback books on display. They were written by one Moses Brown. I hadn't ever heard of the author or the title. Next to the books were programs for today's service and hand fans. He had a few of each in his hands to pass out as people entered the chapel.

Not that there was anyone else there.

We were the first to arrive, seeing we'd come so early for our reconnaissance mission. I didn't know what Koby gleaned from it, but I learned that security on the building was inconsistent and whoever designed the church liked doors—there were so many of them.

It was a good thing that no one was around because Koby had a few questions for Deacon Brown.

Deacon Brown had dark skin and curly salt-and-pepper hair. He wore it cut low and his mustache was neatly trimmed. Medium height and build, he had on a deep red jacket, black pants and shirt and a tie that had diamond shapes in red, white, and black. He looked as if he was going onstage with a sixties R & B group.

"Good morning. Welcome," Deacon Brown said to us as we walked in. "Sunday school will be ending in about ten minutes. Then you can go in for church service."

I smiled. Nervous about what my brother was going to say and whether it would get us kicked out of the church before service even started. I'd seen the pastor's car in the parking lot. I'd remembered it from when we followed it the day of the murder. We'd just finished our perimeter search for doors when I spotted it. I didn't want the deacon to sic the pastor on us.

"Good morning," Koby said. "We were wondering if we could speak with you."

I hated it when he included me in his machinations.

The deacon placed a hand on his chest. "Me?"

"Yes." Koby nodded. "About what happened here Thursday."

"I didn't hear you." He took a step closer to us and turned an ear.

"We wanted to find out what happened here Thursday." Koby leaned in and spoke a little louder.

"Oh." Deacon Brown gave a small smile. "I don't know a thing about it." He squinted his eyes at us. "You mean Mr. James dying?"

"Yes," Koby said and nodded. I guessed just in case the deacon hadn't heard him.

"You were on the video," Koby said.

"The video?"

"Yes." Koby raised his voice a little louder. "You. Were. On. It."

"So I heard."

"We were thinking maybe you left the door open and that's how the killer got in?"

He shook his head. He'd heard us that time. "That door locks on its own."

That made sense. We'd seen that it had a punched code on it. I knew that was the one he'd gone in because it had been the only one with a camera perched above it.

"So how did the other people get in behind you?"

"Who did what?"

"Other people came in behind you. Got into the building."

He shook his head again. "No one got in behind me."

"How do you know?"

"Because I went into an office that's right by the door. I would have seen them."

Oh no, I thought. Were we going to have to add Deacon Brown to our list of suspects?

"The video shows—"

"I don't care what that video shows," Deacon Brown said, no need for Koby to repeat it. "No one else got in here. And what nobody seems to understand is that camera hardly ever works. Got some kind of short in it, what you might call a glitch or something."

"Did you tell the police that?"

"What police?"

"The ones investigating Mr. James' death."

"No one's asked me anything."

"I don't understand," I said. Although I hadn't been part of the conversation as yet, I had been following along.

"You say you don't understand?"

"Yes. How did those people get on the camera if they didn't come in?"

"Those other people could have come to the door, it captured their image and then shut off."

"Oh," I said and realized just what had been on the film we'd seen. "It doesn't show them going in."

"Say what?" The deacon looked at me and furrowed his brow.

"The other two people. It only shows them coming to the door."

"Right. Because they couldn't have gotten in. Not without the code and not without me seeing them."

"What time did you come in?" Koby asked.

"About ten o'clock."

Koby looked at me. We both looked at him.

"In the morning?" I asked.

"Sure wasn't ten o'clock at night."

Well, that conversation didn't help and I told Koby that after we left speaking with Deacon Brown. We had to stand off in one corner of the lobby because Sunday school was still going on and we couldn't interrupt it by going into the sanctuary.

"That didn't help."

"It helped me."

"It did?"

"Yeah because all this time I was thinking that showed Pete going into the building, but it didn't."

"It only showed him going to the door."

"Right. And the same thing with the other woman. The one in the hat."

"So why did they go to the door?"

"Good question."

"Pete has the answer," I said. "But he isn't sharing."

"I think he's kind of traumatized. He acts like nothing has happened. Like he isn't in any trouble and everything is the same as it always is."

"Maybe he should talk to my mother," I said.

"Might be a good idea." Koby dug his hands down into his pants pocket. "But I'll talk to him again anyway. Something or someone made two people go to the door."

"And why hasn't that police officer talked to the deacon?" I asked. "I knew when I talked to him yesterday that he didn't care about doing anything but pinning it on Pete."

"Wait." Koby narrowed his eyes at me. "You talked to who yesterday?"

"Acting Chief Ross."

"You did not tell me that."

"Oh," I said and flinched. "I meant to."

"Keaton." His palm went up to his forehead. "Really." Then he held that hand out to me.

"He had me so frustrated," I said in explanation. "I saw him when I went over to the Second Street Market."

"Why did you go over there?"

"Mr. Al gave me a book that was worth a lot of money. I wanted to check and make sure if it was okay to keep it."

He leaned into me and opened his eyes wide. "Alright to keep it? You didn't give it back, did you? Because a gift can't be rescinded or revoked."

"Why do you always know something about the law?"

"I grew up in the system. A system made up of laws."

I didn't have anything to say to that.

"So back to the chief, what did he say?"

"That Austin James went to jail but was released on a technicality."

"What technicality?"

"I don't know." I let my head sway. "Maybe that's a question for Pete's lawyer."

"Yeah. Maybe so. What else did he say?"

"That Pete was guilty. He did it as an act of revenge because Austin James caused him to lose his job and his family. It was the first time Pete had seen him since his release and he just snapped. And that once they find Pete's DNA in this church, it's a wrap."

"A wrap? He said that?"

"Basically."

Koby bit down on his bottom lip. "I don't get that. Of course Pete's DNA is going to be here. He was here."

I made a face that said I agreed with him.

"All of this because Pete's face was on a video?"

"I guess," I said. "And now we know the camera was faulty and that Pete never went in that door."

"Yeah, but it seems only me, you and the deacon are the ones who know that," Koby said.

"Seems like they're just railroading Pete."

"I know."

"Is that where Austin James was? Down that hallway? The hallway by that door with the camera?"

"Why you asking me? I don't know."

Koby was staring right past me. He was thinking hard. "Because why else make such a big deal about getting in that door?"

"Which hallway does that door lead into?"

And as soon as the words left my lips, I knew I shouldn't have said them. Koby's eyes lit up and he said, "Let's go see."

Chapter Twenty-One

I WAS BACK to wandering the hallways of Everlasting Missionary Baptist Church. I wasn't sure how we'd even find which door went to the one that had the keypad, but it looked like we were going to give it our best try.

"We'll just open each door we get to and see what's on the outside. A regular lock or the keypad."

"What about if the door is locked from the inside?"

"Then that can't be it because why would you need a passcode to get in it but a key to get out?"

"True."

We had to leave and go one way from the chapel and then double back to go to the other side to check out those hallways, but we finally found the door. Down a hallway I hadn't been down before. I was sure of that because there was yellow crime tape across one of the office doors down that corridor. I would have remembered seeing that.

"Look at that," Koby said. He acted as if I could miss the crisscross mess guarding entry through that door.

"I see it."

"We should probably go in there."

I frowned, panic rising up into my throat. "No we shouldn't. Why we would we go in there?"

"To see if there are any clues."

"I'm sure the police got all the clues."

"Just in case . . ." Koby turned the knob, his eyes on me. I knew if I said anything to try and stop him, it probably wouldn't work.

I stood back and crossed my arms.

"Come on," he said, ducking down. He stepped through one of the gaps in the tape. "If someone sees you standing out there, we'll both be in trouble." He held out a hand.

Trouble.

I was never one to be in trouble.

I smacked his hand away and held on to the frame of the door to help me balance as I stepped through.

"Look at that."

He was already snooping. I turned and closed the door before I took a gander at what he was pointing out.

"His shoes," I said. "Those are the ones he had on that day."

"He took them off," Koby said. "Just like they do at that Grace church."

"What is that about?" I looked next to the shoes. There were no prayer rugs like there'd been at Grace. "Was he just in the habit of taking off his shoes?"

"And did the person who killed him know that?" Koby had gone over to the desk that was in the room, and he was bent over a big brown spot on the carpet. "That's a coffee stain. And in the middle of it is a burn."

I bent over next to Koby to get a closer look. "Is coffee a good conductor of electricity?" I asked, pulling out my phone and standing up.

Koby hunched his shoulders, but Siri and I were already on it. I clicked on a couple of links. "Seems like it might be," I said, "but it's made with tap water."

"Which is filled with ions." Koby got the connection.

"Yep," I said. "So what? He spilled the coffee and stepped in it?"

"No." Koby was shaking his head slowly from side to side. "I don't think so. I think that the spill was under the desk." He put his foot next to a disruption in the carpet. "I think this desk used to be right here. I think somebody moved it."

"Probably the police," I said. "To see what happened."

"What happened . . ." Koby repeated what I said. It seemed involuntarily. He was processing the scene, too.

"So when he sat down, in his sock feet"—Koby looked at me and nodded—"they got wet."

"Yeah, and the murderer ran the broken and frayed extension cord across here." He pointed to the burnt spot and let his finger trace a path to the outlet. "And plugged it in."

"The current came out with the exposed wires." I was in awe, but not in a good way. "Somebody really went through an elaborate scheme to get him."

"They did. And he wouldn't have ever noticed."

Then I remembered something Ray Patton had said the day of the murder. "Did you see a coffeemaker in the kitchen the day we were here for the potluck?"

"No." Koby was certain in his answer. "There was no coffeepot there that day."

"Do you think that someone moved it in here that day? Knowing Austin James was going to make a cup?"

"That had to be what happened."

"Ray Patton said that he knew coffee was going to be what got him in the end."

"I remember that," Koby said. "What time did Austin James die?"

"I don't know," I said.

Why would he think I would know that?

"Deacon Brown came in at ten."

"I know. I heard him say that. But"—I took in a breath—"lots of people were in here before then."

"So was Austin James already dead before that? Because if he was, then only the early people could have done it. People like Pastor Lee"—he rocked his head—"Pete. Ray Patton. Emerald Shoes Lady. Rocko." He filled his cheeks up with air. "But if he wasn't dead by the time that Deacon Brown got here, then we'd have to add him to the list along with the lady in the hat."

I decided just to let Koby have this conversation by himself, because everything he was asking was premised on a question he knew I didn't have the answer to.

"Or did he die even later than that? What time did Mama Zola call me?" He touched my arm. "You know what else? I don't know who found him, do you?" He tilted his head to the side. "And if he did die after ten, why didn't Deacon Brown hear him? Didn't he call out for help or something?"

I did know the answer to that one.

"Deacon Brown is hard of hearing."

"Oh yeah. He is. He probably wouldn't—couldn't—have been able to hear anything."

"Including someone coming in that door," I said. "So he might not have been truthful with us."

"But he didn't say he would have *heard* them. He said he would have *seen* them." Koby turned around and looked.

"C'mon, let's go," I said.

"Okay," Koby said and took one more look around the room. "I didn't check the drawers," He hesitated as if he were about to.

"No!" I said. I went behind him and pushed him toward the door. "Fingerprints."

"They already dusted."

"They may dust again, and," anticipating what he was

going to say, "even though it's after the fact, they'd get us for tampering with evidence."

We got back out in the hallway, and I was ready to move on. Koby wasn't finished yet. He walked over to the first office door in the hallway.

"That one is the closest to the exit." He looked at me.

"Yeah?"

"That must've been where Deacon Brown was." Koby reached for the doorknob. I got to him just in time and moved his hand way. "I wonder what he was doing in there."

"Maybe just sitting there? Staring out into the hallway?"

Koby chuckled. "I guess so."

"Okay," I said. "Can we go now?"

"Yeah. We can go. But now it's possible we may have had a witness to the murder."

A witness who probably didn't hear anything and definitely one who wasn't saying anything. Why wouldn't he go and talk to the police? That was the craziest thing I ever heard. I decided maybe it wasn't a witness we'd happened upon, but the murderer. I was adding Deacon Brown to my suspect list.

AS WE MADE our way back, I realized that I was just as bad as Acting Chief Franklin Ross—adding people to my list of bad guys without a real reason why.

Because Deacon Brown was sitting in a room near the decedent (I had decided to adopt Attorney Jenkins' word), I had him pegged as a possible killer.

Just like Ross had done to Pete.

The only difference was that I hadn't homed in on only one person with dogged determination. I actually had several people I thought were good suspects, if there was such a thing as a "good" bad person.

I turned the corner to head back toward the chapel, but my brother didn't.

"Hey," I said. "This way." Seemed like I was finding my way around the maze of the church.

"The light is on in the pastor's office." He pointed.

"And?"

"Maybe he's in there."

"So?"

"So we can talk to him."

"I don't think that's a good idea."

"Why?"

Now he was the one with the one-word question.

"Because," I said and tugged his arm, "that didn't work out so well for us last time. Plus, he's getting ready to deliver this morning's sermon. He's probably meditating or praying or something."

"Good." Koby wiggled out of my grasp. "If he's doing that, maybe he'll be nicer."

I sighed. Loudly.

"You can go back to the chapel."

"I'll go with you," I said. "Help you stay out of trouble."

"Or is it because you want to talk to him, too."

"That's not it."

That made Koby laugh.

But it wasn't the pastor we found in the office. It was the woman who'd been there the other day. Crying. Today she was dry-eyed.

"Hi," Koby said.

I stopped in my tracks. I wasn't going to go past the threshold. I tried to peek through the crack of the door to see if that Voice Behind the Door was going to come out swinging at Koby.

"Hello," she said. "May I help you?"

"I was looking for Pastor Lee."

"He's teaching Sunday school." I saw her glance past Koby at the wall behind him. I figured there must be a clock there. "Oh. That's over now. Church is getting ready to start."

"I'm sorry to interrupt," he said. "I'm Koby and this is my twin, Keaton."

There he went again, dragging me into stuff.

She looked my way. I waved.

"What's your name?" he asked.

But we already knew that. Mama Zola had told us. She was Lacey Bell and her mother was Mother Tyson.

"I'm Lacey," she said.

I turned an ear for a minute, trying to detect another person's presence. It didn't seem as if anyone else was in the room, so I stepped inside.

Lacey was thin with pale skin, light freckles and thick brown hair. She had a crime fiction book on the desk next to her, *All Her Little Secrets* by Wanda Morris. Her open palm was resting on the book.

I could relate to a person having a book with them. I used to carry one with me at all time, too. I still did, only it was an ebook instead of a physical copy. Wanda Morris' book was on my TBR list, but with Lacey reading it, and curious as to what kind of person sits and cries at her desk, I decided to move it up.

But Koby had noticed something else on her desk. A Rolodex of cards. You didn't see that much anymore. He pointed to it.

"The other day Pastor Lee got a card from one of the power company guys. I needed to get his number."

"You needed the number?" She seemed to tense.

"Yeah. Off the card." Koby smiled. "I can just take a picture of it." He pulled out his phone and held it up.

She glanced at the Rolodex. Then back up at Koby.

"Sorry you were feeling so bad the other day." His voice softened. "I know that was hard. All that stuff that was going on the other day."

"Yeah, it was hard." Her shoulders seemed to relax. "I

used to attend Abundant Faith and . . . you know . . . even after all the stuff that happened . . ." She tugged on her bottom lip with her teeth. Koby waited for her to start talking again. "He was still my pastor."

"I get it," Koby said. I wasn't sure if he really understood or just generally. I knew he understood the concept of loss.

"But then," she started talking again without any prompting, "she came in here saying all that stuff to me. It was just too much."

Koby stole a glance at me. I knew what he was thinking. *Who is "she"?* I hunched my shoulders. I had no idea.

"Some people have no sense of empathy."

"Or sympathy," I said, chiming in.

She nodded and put her head down. I hoped she wasn't going to start crying again.

"What did she say?"

My question would have been who she was. Leave it to Koby to keep going like he knew just what Lacey was talking about.

"That I better watch out. I could be next."

"What?" Koby seemed surprised.

I was certainly surprised, and I didn't know the backstory, but I couldn't resist anymore.

"Who was she?" I asked.

"Kim." She must've realized we didn't know who that was. "Brother Austin's ex-wife."

"Austin's ex-wife?"

She nodded. "She had it in her head that he and I . . . you know." She dipped her head and got quiet.

"And whoever came after him was going to come after you?"

"Exactly. But there was nothing between the two of us. Then I started thinking, what if it were her."

Koby was nodding like he was on track with everything she was saying.

"Her?" I asked.

"Yeah. That killed Brother Austin."

"Oh." I lifted my eyebrows and nodded.

Lacey became a little bolder and animated. "She came in here looking like the Wicked Witch of the East with her emerald shoes."

I laughed. "Those were ruby shoes that Dorothy wore in *The Wizard of Oz*," I said. "They were going to the *Emerald* City."

She laughed, too. "That was what my grandmother said. Guess I didn't watch that show as closely as she did."

"Your grandmother?" Koby said.

He was still on that, but that observation got me to thinking. "Kim" was the woman that I'd seen talking to Pastor Lee the morning of the potluck. The one outside the kitchen door that morning. The one that Koby said it looked like the pastor had a business relationship with.

Kim was Austin James' wife. Or ex-wife.

"Yes," Lacey said to Koby's question. "Remember, my grandmother was here the other day?"

"Oh," I said and looked at Koby. The one who wasn't tolerating his intrusiveness. I was thinking he should change the subject.

"Mother Tyson is your grandmother?" he asked.

Okay, this time he wasn't thinking the same thing I was.

"Yep. She raised me, though. Lots of people think she's my mother." She smiled. "Technically she is." She glanced down at her hands. "I think of her that way."

"I was raised in foster care," Koby said. "Don't remember my mother."

"I'm sorry," she said and looked at me.

"Oh." Koby looked at me and then back at her. "She was adopted."

She looked back at Koby. A painful look in her eyes. "I'm sorry."

"But he found me," I said. "And we're back together."

I knew Koby was being sincere when he talked about our upbringing. He might weave a yarn of a story to get the things he needed, but when it came to what happened to us, he didn't try to play on people's emotion or manipulate them with it. But it worked anyway.

"I remember that guy said he could do some electrical work around here if we needed it."

"I don't know if we'd ever use him. My cousin is an electrician and he's a deacon here." She pulled the card out and handed it to Koby. "He takes care of stuff like that around here."

"Oh." Koby took the card and kept talking in an off-handed way. "Who's your cousin?"

"Moses Brown." She watched Koby take the picture and then took the card back. "Deacon Brown. You probably saw him this morning."

"We did," I said.

So he was the author of that book . . .

I wished I had looked at it more closely.

"His office is right down that way, isn't it?" Koby asked.

"He doesn't have an office." She put the card back in the Rolodex. "All the deacons share a room."

"He's a sharp dresser," Koby said.

She chuckled. "I always tease him that he looks like one of the Temptations."

"Can he sing like them?" Koby asked.

"Pitch perfect. And he can play any song on the piano just by listening to it once."

I opened my mouth. I wanted to say something about it being too bad he was losing his hearing, but Koby stopped me.

"Okay. Thank you, Lacey." He held up his phone. "We don't want to miss service."

"Me either," she said and glanced at her cell phone.

"Oh my goodness. I can't be late." She stood up, "I have to read the announcements."

"We look forward to hearing them," Koby said. "There is so much going on at this church."

She waved us out the door and locked it behind her before scurrying down the hallway toward the chapel.

I was happy she didn't seem to notice that my brother was being facetious. She seemed like such a nice girl.

Chapter Twenty-Two

"THIS MURDER IS nothing like that book you gave me," Koby said.

"*Murder at the Holiday Bazaar*?" I asked, surprised that that was the first thing he had to say. We had just learned a lot of stuff from Miss Lacey Bell. I would've thought his mind had landed on something other than that. "What makes you say that?" I went along with his conversation.

"I finished the book."

I chuckled. Koby was always falling for the girls. "We still don't know who the killer is, so don't go jumping to conclusions. That book might be right on the money."

"I doubt it," he said.

I switched gears on him. "How about we talk about the deacon, then?"

"Deacon Brown?"

"Yes." I gave him a punch. "The electrician."

"And the author." We started walking toward the chapel. "Those were his books on the table."

"Is that the first thing you can think to say about him? After all the stuff we just heard?"

Hadn't he listened to what Lacey had told us?

"No," he said, a thoughtful look on his face. "I got that Austin James' wife was in the building the day he died. Giving her the opportunity to be the cause of his demise."

I blew out a breath. Noisily.

He'd shifted people. Suspects. I wanted to talk about Deacon Brown. Now not feeling so bad that I'd zoned in on him and moved him up to the top of my list. But now Koby wanted to talk about the Emerald Shoes Lady.

"Don't tell me you think *she* did it?" I said.

"Maybe."

"She wouldn't be my first guess."

"Don't tell me." Koby smiled at me. "Deacon Brown, right?"

"Yes," I said. Emphatically.

"Seems like the deacon lied," Koby said.

"Exactly," I said, happy to have the conversation come back to who I wanted to talk about. "He doesn't have an office."

"Did he say he had one?"

"Yes. He said he went into his office."

"Or did he say he went into *an* office."

I stopped walking. After Koby realized I had, he stopped, too. I tilted my head to the side and thought about that. I couldn't remember exactly what he'd said. Maybe he hadn't called it *his* office.

I took back to walking. Koby followed beside me. "What about acting like he was hard of hearing?" I asked. I know I wasn't confused about that.

"Now that was more of a lie, although he never said he was."

"He gave us the impression that he was," I said. "I think Lacey would have mentioned it, said something if he was. She was talking about singing and playing the piano, all about his hearing."

"Right." Then Koby asked the question that had been swimming around in my head. "And why would he do that?"

"Because he killed Austin James."

"Or because he didn't want to talk about the murder."

"At first, when Lacey first mentioned he was a musician, I felt bad for him. You know," I said, "not being able to hear well anymore."

"Yeah. Well, don't feel bad for him. He put on an act for us today."

"Yeah. Now I know. And I don't." Smirk on my face. "I don't feel sorry for him the least little bit. I'm kind of scared of him."

"Why?" Koby asked. We'd made it to the foyer of the chapel.

"Because he knows about electrical stuff." I lowered my voice and looked around. I was sure Deacon Brown was somewhere close around. His books and the fans were still cluttering up the table.

"Yeah, he does. We already established that." Koby nodded.

"So him coming in the back way, being related to Lacey, who used to go to his church, and knowing about electrical stuff makes him the prime suspect."

"Ah. Related to Lacey, who was wronged by Austin James."

"Exactly," I said.

"So now can we talk about Mrs. James?"

I saw how he'd turned the conversation right back around. Steering it in the direction he wanted to go.

"The ex–Mrs. James," I said. Correction, I knew, was not a good stalling tactic when it came to my brother.

"Yes."

"With the emerald shoes?"

"Yes." Koby nodded. "She needs to go on our suspect list."

"What has she done suspicious?"

"She's the spouse."

"No she isn't." I frowned.

"Spouse. Former spouse. All the same." Koby gave me a "trust me" look. "And the significant other is always the prime suspect."

"She seemed nice enough."

"You're just saying that because you liked her shoes." I scrunched up my face. "I never said that."

"But you can't deny it, can you?"

"I don't base my opinion of things on clothes."

"You notice them, though." He smiled at me. "You'd probably fall over if you tried to wear those things. They were so high."

"Yes, high but pretty," I said. My brother knew me too well.

IT WAS EASY to notice her. She and Mother Tyson were the only ones donning one.

The woman in the hat.

Everlasting Missionary Baptist Church looked like most churches I'd been in. The pews were a light wood, the carpet red, which matched the banners and upholstery on the king throne chairs that surrounded the two-step-up elevated altar and pulpit.

The church wasn't packed, but it was full. A growing church, Mama Zola had told me, because there were lots of young people. They even had a children's choir, she'd noted. Not everyone was dressed in their Sunday Best, making Koby in his outfit right at home. They all did don smiles, though, seemingly everyone happy to be there even though a murder had taken place only a few days earlier and right down the hall.

After Koby and I got settled in, he disappeared for a moment, so I let my eyes scan the congregation to see if there were any familiar faces. I certainly expected to see Ray Patton, but he was nowhere in sight.

That was when I saw her.

The only person left for us to talk to who had gone into the church early the day of the potluck. I hadn't expected to see her there. In fact, after we left the pastor's office, I was ready to go. We had learned a lot and we'd have to wait until church was over—which might be three or four more hours—to speak with the pastor. But Koby insisted we stay. "Just in case," he'd said. And he'd been right. We discovered something else.

The hat she was wearing today was bright pink.

She'd come in after Lacey, who turned out to be more of an extrovert than I expected, had read the announcements. She slid into her seat just as they announced the last of the Sick and Shut-Ins. And Mother Tyson led what seemed to be an impromptu song from her seat, "The Old Rugged Cross." It wasn't on the program, but everyone happily sang along. Me included, after I found it in the hymnal on the back of the pew in front of me.

Miss Pink Hat hadn't joined in. She sat in the second row of pews, right up front. Right on the end. Facing forward, she didn't seem to worry about what was going on around her. Seemingly not a care as to whether she was being watched. She didn't try to act inconspicuously—not in the least. Her bright pop of color hat was a testament to that. And her obvious phone in hand—who has a phone out in church?

"There she is," I said and nudged Koby. I pointed with my head. "The woman in the hat."

"Who is she?" he asked.

"The woman in the hat."

"Yes, Keaton, I see that, but why are you telling me about her?"

"Not that she has a hat on today—"

"Which she does."

"Yes. No." I shook my head. "She's the one who had on the hat the day of the murder."

"Ohhh." He drew the word out and took another look her way. "Are you sure?"

"Positive."

"She likes hats, huh?"

"I guess so," I said.

"And taking pictures."

"Pictures?"

Koby nodded. "With her phone."

I leaned forward and over to have a better look. "Is that why she has that phone out?" I turned back to look at my brother. "What is she taking a picture of?"

He hunched his shoulders. "I have no idea."

I tried to think of a reason that she would take pictures in the sanctuary on a Sunday morning. She'd been in the church on Thursday, she could have taken pictures then, although, after thinking about it, I didn't know whether she had or not. I did know now, thanks to Deacon Brown, that she'd been there at least after ten o'clock. Early enough that morning that no one coming to the potluck, other than those that were helping set up, would have been there. She could have taken pictures of the church then. Sight unseen. Because if she was a real photographer, she wouldn't sneak in to take them now and she wouldn't be doing it with her phone.

"So you want to talk to her?" Koby asked.

"No," I said and shook my head hard enough to move my hoop earrings from side to side. I leaned over and in a strained whisper said, "Why is it that you want to talk to *everybody*?"

"You want to find out what really happened, don't you?"

I held my breath and looked at him out the corner of my eye.

"Help Pete get out of all this trouble." He nudged me with his elbow. "Be the Watson to my Holmes."

I blew out my breath and shook my head. I didn't want to laugh out loud in church.

"We are not Holmes and Watson and we could get in a lot of trouble. Didn't I tell you the part where Acting Chief Ross told me that we needed to keep our noses out of this?"

"He said that?"

I nodded.

"Well, he's only 'acting' the part, I'm not sure if that gives him the authority to really tell us what to do."

"I think it does. And I don't want to use the money I made off that book yesterday to go toward bail money."

"You get your bond money back if they find you not guilty."

"You just know too much about that stuff." I turned my attention from him and noticed the choir had stopped singing. Pastor Lee was walking over to the pulpit.

"Today's sermon," Pastor Lee announced, "is about smiling faces."

"Smiling faces?" Koby leaned over and said to me, a frown on his face.

"Yes," I said. "People who smile at you, like you're their friend, but really they associate with you because they have an ulterior motive. Most times not a good one."

"How is that the kind of thing he should be talking about? That makes no sense." He looked around the church. "We should go."

"Shh!" I told my brother and held on to his arm. "You probably need to hear this." Then I leaned in and whispered, "It's how I feel sometimes about you."

Chapter Twenty-Three

I WAS ABLE to keep my brother from going over to shake the pastor's hand after service, only because I suggested we talk to the woman in the pink hat.

He laughed and asked me what happened to not wanting to talk to her. I told him I realized we'd lucked up catching her here, and if we didn't speak with her, we might never be able to find her again.

That worked. Of course. He was all about interrogating people.

Still, I wasn't too keen or happy about how he was so dead set on talking to Pastor Lee. Hadn't that gotten us into enough trouble? Well, at least it had gotten Mama Zola into trouble—she'd lost her church home.

"Excuse me." Koby was already on our new mission. "Hi," he said to the lady in the pink hat. "Can we talk to you for a minute?"

She turned to us. The smile on her face seemed pleasant enough. She had been talking to Mother Tyson when we walked up, and had just given her a hug before Mother Tyson waddled off. Pink Hat Lady had a pretty face, one that didn't show any sign that she'd been up to something devious. Nor did it give a clue that she was back at the scene of a crime she'd committed.

"Sure," she said. "How can I help you?"

"We"—he wagged a finger between the two of us—"saw you taking pictures during the service."

Well, he just dove right in there, and pulled me right in with him. No need to be surprised. That was my brother's usual.

"Oh." She blushed, seemingly surprised we had noticed her. But it hadn't seemed to me that she cared about being seen. She reached down in her purse and pulled out a business card. "I'm a reporter."

"For the *Gazette*?" I asked. Timber Lake's newspaper was more like a newsletter. Nothing ever happened here. Well, it used to be nothing much ever happened here. Things were changing—one murder at a time.

"No, I work for an independent paper." Her eyes went from me to Koby. "Are you two the amateur sleuths?"

I frowned. *Where were people getting this from?*

"We're just trying to help our friend."

"I'm Katy Erickson." She stuck out a hand. An introduction that we should have started out the conversation with.

"I'm Koby Hill, and this is my twin sister, Keaton Rutledge."

"I know who you are." She gave a sly smile before leaning in and lowering her voice. "I completely understand about going after a good story. This article started out about Austin James trying to make a comeback with the sheep he'd led astray. But I am not letting a good murder story get by me."

"No murder is good," I said.

"You know what I mean." She gave me a smile like we were old girlfriends and had some secret understanding of things between us.

"And who were you taking pictures of?" Koby asked. "Pastor Lee?"

"Calvin Lee had no reason to let Mr. James anywhere near his church." She gave a knowing nod. "He must have wanted James here for some reason. Murder seemed like as good a reason as any to me."

"Pastor Lee wasn't involved in any of the criminal activity," I said. "He left the trading firm long before that."

"So, you know about that." I saw a glimmer in her eye. "But did you know that Calvin Lee was fired because of a discrepancy in his accounts? An account that he and Austin James worked on together."

"And Austin didn't lose his job then?"

"No," she said, letting her voice trail off. "He was a slippery guy. You see he got out of what amounted to a life sentence."

"How did he do that?" Koby asked.

"That's all public record, if you read the transcripts, you can see. Fourth Amendment violation," she said clucking her tongue. "But I know something else. Something new." She winked at us—or me—not sure.

"Meet me at the Hemlock tonight," she said. "The new chief of police is going to be there and I wanted him to hear what I have to say first." She smiled like she was proud of herself. "But I don't mind letting you two in on it. Maybe the three of us can get this solved."

She was calling Detective Daniel Chow the new chief of police. I knew who she meant because she didn't refer to him as the "acting chief." And she seemed to want to impress him by being instrumental in solving the crime.

But I wondered why she wanted to get involved. She didn't seem to care about Austin James or think very highly of him. Maybe her dislike of Pastor Lee was stronger. But why?

"Before you go." Koby stopped her as she started to walk away. "Why were you trying to get in the door of the church the day of the murder?"

"This is my first time here."

Koby looked at me. I know he wasn't wavering on believing I'd picked out the right person on the video.

"You were," I said. "You were wearing a hat just like today."

She narrowed her eyes at me. I guess the "girlfriends" phase was coming to an end.

"I don't know what you mean," she said.

"The police have you on video," I said.

She studied me for a long while. I could tell she was trying to determine if I was telling the truth or not.

"My sister isn't one for lying." He gave her an unsmiling face. "We've seen the video."

"Oh shoot," she said and blew out a breath. "I completely missed that camera."

"It's okay. It's the only one on the property, and from what we've learned, it doesn't work very well."

"But it caught me?"

We both nodded.

"I wanted to get in the back and snoop around to see if I could find out what Austin James was up to."

"Why didn't you just go to the potluck and get in with all the other people?"

"The potluck hadn't started yet," Katy said.

"What time was it?"

"About nine thirty."

Koby and I looked at each other. According to the video, Deacon Brown had been the first one of the day to enter that door, and when we had talked to him, he said he hadn't gone in until ten.

"Are you sure?" Koby asked. "About the time."

"Of course I am. I was taking notes on a recording app on my phone. It's time stamped."

"You had the code for the keypad?"

"The what?"

"To get in that door. It has a keypad."

"Oh. Yes. I know. But no." She shook her head. "I didn't have the code."

"So why were you there?"

"There was a sign on the first door I tried to get into, the one where the security guy had told me to enter through."

"The security guard told you just to go on in?" Koby asked.

She pursed her lips and nodded. "Not a very good security guard if you ask me. He didn't know me from Adam, and like I said, the potluck hadn't started. I could have been anyone."

"Like the killer," I said.

She shrugged and smiled.

"Was it a handwritten sign?" Koby asked.

"No." She shook her head. "Printed on a computer. Like a hot pink or fuchsia color. You would notice it a mile away."

"So?" I said. "What did the sign on the door read?"

"It had an arrow pointing to another door. I guess where the video camera was if you say there's only one on the property. All caps. The words were something like 'USE NEXT DOOR.' Or 'GO TO NEXT DOOR.' Or something like that."

"Taped on the door?" Koby asked.

"I suppose," she said. "I didn't check, but it was stuck there. Evidently someone wanted me to go to that door."

"Didn't that seem weird?" Koby asked. "Seeing that you couldn't get into that door."

"Very suspicious," she said, nodding. "Especially when I saw a light flickering in the room that I later discovered was the room where James was found. Dead."

* * *

IT WAS STILL sunny when we left the church and our lat-
est interrogation ended. I was glad to be outside, out of
that church. I'm sure Mama Zola would scold me about
saying such a thing and lecture me on what I needed for
my eternal soul. But when we went in there, every time,
there was always so much information coming our way.
My mind was always thinking and, to be honest, accusing. It couldn't be such a good thing to have so many bad
thoughts about people attending church.

"Who put that sign on the door?" Koby wondered
aloud.

I hunched my shoulders. "No camera on the door where
the sign was."

"That's what I'm saying. I'm thinking whoever put it
there knew that there was camera on the door where the
sign pointed. They wanted them to go in that door. So
they could be seen by the camera."

"And by the police."

"Exactly." Koby thought about that. "And then who
took it down?"

I hunched my shoulders again.

"And when did they take it down?"

"When people stopped going through the door." I
looked at Koby. "You think the killer put that sign there?"

"I don't know. It's a possibility."

"Then it couldn't be Deacon Brown," I said.

"Why not?"

"Because he was on the video."

"Yeah. But he said he went in later than he really had,"
Koby said. "Maybe he already knew the camera had
picked up other people and they would be his alibi."

"He could point the finger at them."

"Katy said she saw flickering. At nine something."

"Nine thirty."

"So now we have a time of death." I waggled my head. "Approximately."

"If she was telling the truth."

"You don't think she was?"

"I mean if she's writing an article, why is she snooping around? Why not just walk up to Austin James and ask your questions?"

"Like you would do?"

"I'd love to talk to him," Koby said. "If only it was possible." He smiled at me, then tugged on my arm. "C'mon."

Finally, I thought. *We're leaving.* I was glad to be heading home. Change into some jeans and put my nose into a book.

Only, it didn't seem that was where we were headed. Now the parking lot was behind us. And so was Koby's car.

"Where are we going now?" Koby had gone back to walking the perimeter of the building. I tramped behind him.

"To see if there is a window by the door that Hat Lady could have seen flickering from."

"Katy." I blew out a breath and trotted to catch up with him. "Was there a window in the room?" I asked, looking down at my feet, worrying again about my shoes in all the grass on the rocky gravel.

"I don't remember," Koby said. "You didn't give me time to look around."

"I had nothing to do with that. You could've looked."

It was true, I had been nervous snooping around the room for sure, but I gave in and it did turn out to be good that we went in. If we were going to do this thing, and we were—even though I had bouts of "What the heck am I doing!"—we needed all the info we could get our hands on. Even if some of it made me jittery. And like today, I didn't want to hang out in a place we weren't meant to be in for long.

"Did you notice a window?" he asked.

I stopped to ponder the question.

He'd got a few steps ahead of me and realized I wasn't walking anymore.

"C'mon." He backtracked and tugged on my arm. "Don't have to stop and think, we're going to go and verify."

I followed behind him, and sure enough, before we even got to the door, we could see the window.

"I know this is it," Koby said, cupping his hands. He turned and looked at me. "Do you think she knows more? Is that what she wants to tell Detective Chow?"

"He'll soon be Chief Chow."

"Not now, though. He has no jurisdiction here now, so why is she wanting to tell him?"

I shrugged. He'd started asking questions again that I didn't have an answer to.

WE WERE FINALLY headed to the parking lot. Koby's car was in my line of sight, when we got pulled away again.

"Are you two lurking around again?"

I knew that voice.

Mother Tyson.

She was standing next to the longest car I'd ever seen. It was a green color, I think, no color I'd seen on a car before. I thought maybe she had a custom paint job. And she was dressed in purple. The two of them looked regal.

Her purple hat, perched on her head, matched perfectly with the sheath dress she wore. She had on gloves and a pashmina around her shoulder.

The pout on her face did seem genuine, and a smile did follow, but I just couldn't imagine why she was being nice. I hadn't ever encountered her close up, but I knew my brother had caused her some anguish.

I glanced down at her purse. At least it wasn't swinging like a pendulum.

"Hi, Mother Tyson." Koby greeted her like they were old friends. "You know my twin, Keaton?"

"Hi," I said.

"I didn't know you had a twin. She's cute." She smiled at me. "If you ever need to talk about having such an obnoxious brother, I'm here to help."

The two of us laughed. I don't think Koby even cracked a smile.

"Where's Mother Jackson?" she asked. She was talking about Mama Zola, only she wasn't a mother of the church. Heck, she wasn't even a member anymore. "I expected her and Ray to be somewhere exchanging recipes. They were the hit of the day on Thursday."

Yeah, I thought, before the murder took the spotlight and Mama Zola got kicked out.

"She can't come back here," Koby said.

"What do you mean?" This time the frown on her face looked real. "Can't come where?"

"To the church," Koby said. "Pastor Lee said that if she was going to help Pete, she wasn't welcome back."

"Who is Pete?" she asked.

"The man who helped her that day at the potluck," Koby said.

"Oh. My. Lord," she said. She waved a dismissive hand at the church. "I know who you're talking about." She sucked her tongue. "We don't act like that around here. He, of all people, should know that. Even if that young man had killed Brother James, he still would need forgiveness. And where else are you going to get that?"

"Than at church," I said, finishing her sentiment.

"That's right." She nodded as if she was making up her mind about something. "We are a close-knit group here. All family. He had no business telling her that. The man is innocent until proven guilty." She clicked the fob to her car. "Follow me," she said.

"To where?" Koby asked.

"We're going to Pastor Lee's house and have a talk with that man. Shame on him."

Oh no, I thought. That was all my brother needed to hear. He'd been trying to talk to that man since day one. I wondered if any of us would be able to return to Everlasting Missionary Baptist Church after this little interrogation trip.

Chapter Twenty-Four

I HAD WONDERED, too, why Ray Patton hadn't come to Sunday morning service. I had looked for him among the congregants, evidently, just as Mother Tyson had.

So on the way over to Pastor Lee's my mind went from Deacon Moses Brown to Brother Billy Ray Patton.

Brown was a liar and an electrician, things that paired well with the murder of Austin James.

Ray Patton knew things about the murder before the police had reported it. And there'd seemed to be some animosity between the two of them.

And I had an inordinate amount of time to think because Mother Tyson drove like a turtle. Every now and then, she'd poke her hand out of that green car, like a turtle pokes its head out, and waved at us like she was saying to keep up. We could have put the car in neutral and coasted and probably still have passed her.

It wasn't the first time I'd been to Pastor Lee's house. But this time I wasn't stalking. I was going inside like a normal person. All courtesy of Lydia Tyson. She wasn't worried in the least about walking up on the pastor unannounced and at his home, something I would have never had the nerve to do. Mostly because I would have been standing next to my brother, who doesn't mind getting personal with strangers if he thinks they can answer the string of questions I'm sure he'd spew.

Mother Tyson parked in front of the gray-painted bungalow. The stained-glass window gleamed in the sunshine. The refraction of light through the reds, blues and yellows created a sparking, dancing light. Today, I noticed the red and white geraniums that were ruffled with the light breeze.

She got of the car with a grunt. Koby went over to give a helping hand like Pastor Lee had. She waved his hand away and heaved herself out of the car.

She tugged on her clothes to straighten them out and corrected the tilt on her hat.

"Let me do the talking," she said.

For that I was grateful.

I worried what my brother would come up with to say.

Mother Tyson waddled up the walkway to the house and we followed her like dutiful little ducklings.

"Calvin," she started calling out to him at the same time she started knocking on the door. "Calvin, I need to talk to you."

Her voice was loud enough to carry through the wooden door, but she didn't give him time to get there and open it.

"Mother Tyson." He appeared at the door with a look of surprise, which was accompanied by a smile until he noticed Koby and me. "What's going on?" he said. "Everything alright?"

"Are you going to invite us in?" she asked.

"I just walked in the door," he said. "And I'm expecting another church member."

Koby nudged me and pointed to his feet. The pastor didn't have on any shoes, wearing only his socks.

I nodded. Noting, as he wanted me to, the similarity between him and Austin James. And the members of the small storefront we'd visited.

But I didn't know how it meant anything. Lots of people walked around in their sock feet. Koby evidently thought differently.

"Can you only have one church member at a time?" Mother Tyson said and stepped inside, not waiting for the invite. "C'mon." She waved us in behind her.

"Hello," I said as I walked past him into the house. By then, he had stepped back and pulled the door all the way open, a gesture, I thought, of welcome.

"Nice to see you two at church," Pastor Lee said to me and Koby. "That was a first, I believe?"

"I came once before," I said.

Koby hadn't said anything since we'd gotten to the house. And he still wasn't talking. Fingers crossed, at least for me, he kept that up.

"Probably won't see them again, seeing that you threw their grandmother out of the church." Mother Tyson was obviously upset with her pastor.

I looked at Koby. Thinking he'd correct her, letting them know we weren't related to Mama Zola. But he didn't say anything and he even gave me a slight shaking of his head, telling me not to say anything either.

"I only meant . . ." He shook his head. "I didn't . . . say . . ."

"Oh, stop sputtering," Mother Tyson said. "Zola Jackson is a wonderful addition to our church. Why would you want to kick her out?"

"I didn't kick her out." His words were defiant.

Both the reverend and Mother Tyson turned a glance our way.

"Pete." Koby said only the one thing and kept his gaze on Mother Tyson.

"Right," she said and nodded, like she'd just remembered the rest. "Mr. Howers." She turned back to the preacher. "You treating that young man Pete like the woman the scribes wanted to stone."

"I have not." He frowned. "And what do you care about him? He isn't even a member."

"The man, until the courts say otherwise and whether he's a member or not, ain't done a thing, yet you want to cast the first stone. It ain't like you ain't never been in any trouble."

Pastor Lee puffed out his chest and raised his chin. He seemed ready to argue the point, but he must have made a sudden realization because he became deflated. "None of us are without sin, Mother Tyson."

"Amen," she said. "Now. I suggest you tell her grandchildren right here and now, you made a mistake."

"I think maybe you are missing a thing or two about the situation," Pastor Lee said.

"I don't think I'm missing anything." She leaned into the reverend. "He was at it again and you didn't do anything to stop him. "

Pastor Lee's face seemed to freeze. I could see him swallow hard.

"Let God see to Pete or whoever it was," Mother Tyson continued, not giving him time to speak. "I've had been praying long and hard over this." She gave him a nod.

And just like that he turned to us. "I'm sorry," Pastor Lee said. "My decision and words were harsh and not well thought through. I hope you understand," he said. "Austin had been a colleague and friend for a long time and I was just distraught."

"So can Mrs. Jackson come back to church?" Koby asked.

"Yes. Certainly." He took in a breath. "I didn't mean she couldn't, I just meant—"

"That you didn't want Pete there," Koby finished his sentence. Although I wasn't sure Pastor Lee would have said that with Mother Tyson standing there.

"It's over and done," Mother Tyson said. "How about we forget about it and you give me glass of something cool to drink before I go."

She hadn't included Koby and me in that offer of hospitality, so I took it that our part of the business was over with.

"Why would you just assume that Pete killed Mr. James in the first place?" Koby asked. "Hadn't he wronged you, too?"

Oh my goodness . . .

I knew Koby wasn't going to be able to resist.

"I don't know what you mean, son," the pastor said.

"Austin James seemed to ruin a lot of people's lives," Koby said.

"We don't speak ill of the dead," Mother Tyson said. "Time for people to start healing. What's done is done. We'll let that man's maker sort that out."

"We're just trying to help Pete," Koby said.

"Help Pete?" Mother Tyson asked, looking confused.

"Clear his name," I said.

"And find the killer," Koby said.

Just then there was a knock on the door.

"Excuse me," Pastor Lee said, walking through our little group. We'd only made it as far as the front entryway. Crowded there, we were in his path.

"That must be the church member," Mother Tyson said. "We'll leave so you can take—"

But she stopped midsentence.

"She ain't no church member of mine." Mother Tyson spat her words out. "What is *she* doing here?" She flung her finger at the woman standing at the door.

It was the woman who had worn the emerald green shoes.

Only today her shoes *were* ruby.

I smiled and thought of Lacey, the church's secretary. She hadn't gotten it right. But then again, the movie didn't depict the right color either. The shoes that L. Frank Baum wrote Dorothy wore were silver.

"Mother Tyson, please," Pastor Lee said.

"Why is she here?' Mother Tyson may have been the role model and confidant for women of the church, but she did not appear to like *that* woman.

"She's here to make arrangements for Austin's funeral."

"Not at Everlasting." Mother Tyson's eyebrows shot up.

"I know you aren't still holding a grudge," the woman said.

I still hadn't learned her name. All I knew was that she was Austin James' ex-wife and that she'd made Lacey cry. And that while he wasn't fond of wearing shoes, she had a wide variety of them.

"He's dead. We just need to let everything go," the woman said.

"I have," Mother Tyson said. "But that doesn't mean I want his memory lingering on. They're not good thoughts at all."

What happened to not speaking ill of the dead . . .

"But you seem to be holding it against me," Pastor Lee said, seemingly genuinely concerned about Mother Tyson's thoughts of him. "I've tried to help repair the wrongs."

"Didn't work."

"I did my best," the pastor said, his look sincere.

"Well, your best wasn't good enough," Mother Tyson said. Then she turned to Austin James' ex. "And if you knew how to keep up with your husband, be a good wife, so he'd stay put, maybe this wouldn't have happened."

"Maybe that's true," Austin's ex spoke up. "And maybe you don't think what Calvin's done was enough."

"I just said I don't." Mother Tyson didn't seem interested in what the woman had to say.

"It wasn't enough," Austin's ex said, squaring her shoulders, "but you can't deny, I've made it right."

Chapter Twenty-Five

THIS DAY JUST kept going and going. And I, as my brother didn't seem to get, was not an Energizer bunny. But as I was learning, he was.

For me the day just seemed like it wouldn't end. We only had one day out of the week when Books & Biscuits was closed. Days were long there, not always because we had a store full of customers, but because there was a lot of back office work to do, which somehow I didn't anticipate.

I knew when we started there'd be ledgers to keep, books to order, and stuff, but I didn't realize it was so time-consuming. I couldn't imagine how much back office stuff went into the restaurant side. And even though Koby had two workers to my one, I knew he put in a lot of work and he spent most of his time in a hot kitchen.

And it wasn't often that either one of us had time to help each other out, even though Koby was convinced we needed to learn the business of each side. I wasn't averse to that idea, it was just that the learning curve on my side was pretty big and I was still trudging through. I loved books as much as he loved cooking and baking, but after making biscuits, I was good staying on my side awhile longer.

Running your own business is satisfying, no doubt, especially when you're young. But, speaking for myself and not having a lot of life experience before I jumped in made it, in my opinion, even more of a challenge.

So on Sundays I liked to chill. Hang out with my Siamese, Roo, and lounge on the couch surrounded by books.

But instead, after getting in from a day wondering if church members were actually capable of murder and stalking the pastor of the church's house, I was getting dressed to go to a bar.

I wasn't a bar kind of girl.

Those were my thoughts as I twisted and turned in my dress, standing in front of my cheval mirror. It was the only pseudo-going-out kind of outfit I had. I mean it kind of met the criteria.

It was black. Check. It was clingy. Check. But it had a high neckline and long sleeves. I could hear the loud, red, blinking "Fail" buzzer going off in my head.

I looked at my reflection full on, ran my fingers through the curls I'd put into my hair and sighed.

What did I care? I was going there to see a man I did not like. One Daniel Chow. Detective of the Seattle Police Department and, it seemed, new resident of Timber Lake and, to make matters worse, its soon-to-be chief of police.

I hadn't ever had any run-ins with the police before Reef's murder, unlike my brother, who had a former law enforcement officer on speed dial. Avery Moran had turned out not only to be the policeman who tasked Koby enough to keep him from getting into trouble but a good friend.

My twin would have definitely been one of the kids that my mother would not have let me play with growing up. But now, he was my best friend. And that was exactly why I was going to do it.

I had to admit, although I tried not to outwardly show it, I didn't mind sleuthing so much. And I seemed to be getting the hang of it. Probably thanks to all of my reading of mystery books. But Koby had actual experience out in the world, dealing with all kinds of people, unlike me. Not a bad thing, or a down thing about me. But an observation on how we ticked differently. But with my reluctance, I think it made for a better investigation. I questioned things and it made us think harder and dig deeper.

I just hoped that this was the last murder we'd have to solve.

I grabbed my black beaded purse with the long gold chain strap and slung it over my head and stuck one arm through so it rested on my hip. Smacked my lips one last time to even out the pink frosted gloss. Before I headed out of the door, I put out some food for Roo.

"I'm gone, girl," I said, pulling and locking the door behind me. I was going to walk over to the Hemlock.

Although I don't go out much, I had been to this particular jazz club once before. I was supposed to meet Reef Jeffries there, Koby's foster brother, for a date of sorts (practically a first for me) and to hear him play his saxophone. But before that could happen, he was killed and I ended up going there only to attend his memorial.

I stepped off my porch, down the steps and toward the marina. Koby had wanted to pick me up in his car and drive us there. I couldn't understand why.

The Hemlock Jazz Club, my guess being named after our state tree, was on the other side of the marina, past Koby's boathouse and the small beach area. Located on the boardwalk with a few other bars and restaurants, it was a short walk. I saw no reason for him to come get me and then backtrack. I actually saw no reason to take a car at all. To anywhere.

Timber Lake's high walkability meant that I could

stroll to just about any place in our little town. So, I did. I told Koby I'd just meet him there.

It took all of fifteen minutes for me to get there. I enjoyed the fresh air and the sounds of the seagulls as they flew over the lake, taking my time, just strolling along.

I'd worn flats but took them off when I got to the sandy area. The outside seating area on the patio was already filled with people. They were congregated on the steps that led down to the beach, which had people milling about as well.

I opened the bar's wooden door and stepped inside. The bar was one big room. In the front was an elevated platform for a band, where there was a band already setting up. Hung on the wall behind the platform was a big white banner with cheery red lettering that read: WELCOME, CHIEF CHOW.

I guess the people gathered here didn't need to wait for the election.

On an adjacent wall there was a bar that ran nearly the entire length of it. Stools in front of it were littered with people, and the bartender seemed quite busy. The music was loud, which made me glance back at the band. I guess there was a DJ somewhere.

I squinted to adjust my eyes from the brightness of the outside to the dim, sparse uncovered bulbs that hung low and cast a cloudy glow. The place had a smoky atmosphere—not from cigarettes, they, of course, were not allowed—and reminded me of the kind in the old black-and-white movies.

The inside wasn't as crowded as it had been outside of the bar. I guess there weren't many civic-minded people in Timber Lake.

I saw a couple of people I'd met at the bar last time I was there. Then I spotted Maya. I started to go and speak to her, but I saw Izzy come up to her and thought I'd wait until later. Last time I'd seen the two of them together,

Maya was ready to choke Izzy. She'd thought Izzy a liar who was trying to play on Koby's emotions.

Maya was the one I'd choose for Koby, at least over Izzy. For the time being, I was glad I'd gotten to know her. And I appreciated all the help she was giving me with my upcoming author event.

Continuing my scan of the room, I spotted Katy Erickson. She wasn't wearing a hat today and it made me almost not recognize her. She wandered over and stood with Maya and Izzy.

Does she know them?

No paper to jot down notes. No recorder that I could see. I'd force myself to stomach Izzy to find out what Reporter Katy was up to. She just might have found out something useful. She did say she had something to share with the new chief of police—Daniel Chow.

"Big story." Was the first thing I heard when I walked up.

"Hi, Maya. Izzy," I said. "Katy, hello again. Here for your big announcement?"

"What announcement?" Izzy asked. "I thought you said you were a reporter."

"Isn't that why you came over to us?" Maya asked. "I thought a story on the election?"

"I never said it was about the election." Katy frowned. "I am here on a story, though," she said. "Like I just was saying, something big." She turned to me. Put her finger up to her lips. "Shhh. I don't think I'm ready to spill the beans just yet."

Maya raised an eyebrow, holding her drink up to her mouth. She looked at me over the rim of her glass.

I couldn't see why Katy was shushing me. She was the one walking around talking to random people, telling them what was going on with her.

I wondered if she had anything to tell that Koby and I

hadn't found out already. And most of what we knew was from the newspaper. Anyone who read it would have the same information as us.

Unless she wanted to let Chow know what she'd seen that day. And then I realized maybe she hadn't relayed that tidbit of information to anyone other than Koby and me. I didn't think that the police knew who the woman was that was in that video. Was she just sitting on the information? Was she hiding her identity from the police?

"Did you talk to Acting Chief Ross about the light you saw flickering?"

"Who?" she asked.

"The police," I said, figuring I'd break it down for her.

"I'm working on a story. They don't like to cooperate with me."

"You are supposed to cooperate with them," I said, making up my mind that I would let him know. Even though he'd warned me not to play amateur sleuth. Which reminded me . . .

"Why did you call my brother and me 'amateur sleuths'? Who told you that?"

"Someone from the church," she said. "I can't divulge my sources, but I'll say that much so you know it came from someone reputable." She pursed her lips. "And because you stopped to question me. Why else would you do that?"

I wasn't sure I would equate "reputable" with the members of Everlasting Missionary Baptist Church. After all, probably one of them was a murderer.

"They said your grandmother told them about the two of you solving another murder here in Timber Lake."

"Oh yes," Izzy said. "That was terrible. Keaton almost died."

"Probably not as terrible as this one," Katy said, her eyes lighting up. "This one is front-page news."

"There's nothing big and exciting," Maya said, speaking for the first time. "This isn't anything we want to have here. You can take your front-page news elsewhere."

"This is where it happened," Katy said. "And at the church."

"Leave it alone," Maya said. "It can be dangerous." She glanced my way. I certainly could attest to that.

"I like danger," Katy said. "And I'm becoming fond of being involved with murder."

Chapter Twenty-Six

I CAUGHT A glimpse of my brother standing near the bar. Glass of something in his hand, already chatting it up with Detective Chow, who also was nursing a drink. I blew out a breath and headed over to delve into a conversation I wasn't sure I wanted to have.

"Congratulations," I said to Chow, stopping and standing next to my brother. I smiled. "And welcome to Timber Lake."

"Well, hello there, Keaton," Detective Chow said. He smiled back. "How are you doing?" Concern in his eyes. He'd been there the time I almost died. But I also knew it was something more.

He looked nearly the same as when I saw him the last time. Dressed in mostly black, even trading in that tan trench coat of his for a black one. Like his pants, shoes, belt. But his shirt was powder blue.

He rubbed his hands together and I saw he still wore that pinky ring. And bit his nails.

My mother, the clinical psychologist that she is, would

say it had to do with stress. Probably from his job. But he always seemed quite confident in it to me. Doggedly determined. Like my brother.

"I'm doing good," I said. "Just here to welcome a new neighbor. A new town official."

"I'm not either one of those yet. But," he said, glancing toward the banner that differed in that opinion, "when I am in my new position, I want the two of you to know that I will be the only one solving crimes. You remember what happened last time?" His words were directed toward me.

"I haven't forgotten," I said.

"I won't let anything happen to my sister," Koby said. "Not again."

"This guy wasn't a joke," Detective Chow said, continuing without acknowledging Koby's comment. "This Austin James. He was pretty ruthless even if his crimes were considered white collar."

"Yeah. We've *heard*"—Koby emphasized the word—"that he was good at getting into trouble and good at getting out of it."

Koby had said "heard" as if it hadn't been *us* who were the ones out looking for information on the man.

"Seems like the two of you are the same way."

"Who?" we said practically in unison.

He didn't answer that question, but added: "As well as the people you associate yourself with." He raised an eyebrow. "People like Zola Jackson."

That threw me for a loop. Why would he bring Mama Zola's name up? He'd met her during the investigation of Reef's death. But only in passing.

And then I remembered—at the police station. When we went to pick up Pete. The officer who'd brought him from the back had asked her who could vouch for her. Like she needed an alibi.

Maybe even then they had been considering her?

"What about Mama Zola?" Koby asked.

"I've heard that the thinking is that she might have helped in the planning of the murder."

I saw Koby's shoulders straighten and he spread his feet apart. "That is not true," he said and crossed his arms over his chest. I could see the anger rising in the color of his face.

"Didn't say it was," Chow said, his temperament not changing at all. "Just that the consensus has started to form."

"What consensus?" I asked. "What are *they*"—I did air quotes—"saying?"

"That Pete brought Mrs. Jackson along to help facilitate his plan. She sent him off on fake errands in the church so that he'd have time to set up the murder."

"Ugh!" A guttural groan of disbelief came out of Koby. He stepped away from us and I could hear his breathing.

"Calm down, Koby," Chow said. "I'm not saying I believe any of that."

"But you're not in charge of the case," I said.

"Doesn't mean I don't have any sway." He weighed his words. "Ross might be trying to wrap it up before the election, take all the credit for solving the murder. But by the time it went to trial—"

"They're trying to put Mama Zola on trial?"

This time I knew exactly who "they" were: Acting Chief Franklin Ross.

"I don't think it'll go that far," Chow said.

"We have to stop this," Koby said. Something I was surprised he said out loud in front of Daniel Chow. He'd warned us before about butting into police business when we wanted to find Reef's killer. And just now when he reminded me how dangerous it was. "We already have a couple of leads."

We do?

I knew we had people we thought may have committed the crime, but I wasn't sure if that was the same thing.

"You might want to stay away from the people Austin James knew," Chow said.

"Oh my. That's half of Seattle," I said, hoping Chow wouldn't think I was admitting to following leads. "He was the pastor of a megachurch. And it would be all the people at Everlasting."

"We found out that one of those people works for us," Koby said. It seemed like he was fishing for information on Pete. I guessed since they were implicating Mama Zola, Koby wanted all the info he could get.

Chow gave us a look. "I've also heard that Ross thinks convicting your guy is a slam dunk."

"What do you think?" Koby asked, anxiousness in his voice. From what we'd learned, if Pete was going down, then maybe so was Mama Zola.

"Can't be sure. And I'm just speculating here." He looked at the two of us, saying, it seemed, that what he was about to share shouldn't go any farther. "Some of the church members at Everlasting had reason to kill him, so I've learned. They were members at his megachurch."

"Where he probably stole money from them," Koby said.

"And the people he worked at Hatton & Lyndale with." Chow seemed to be mentally going down his list.

"So that's why Pete is the guy," Koby said. He seemed to be exasperated at the turn in subject matter.

But, "Pete's not the only one. At least not for me," Chow told us, which made both our ears perk up. "There's Calvin Lee."

"Pastor Lee?" I said. I was sure I remembered reading in the article I'd found that Pastor Lee wasn't there at the time although I remembered Koby thinking he should be a suspect and I said so. "But he'd already left the trading firm when all the illegal activity had started. Hadn't he?"

"He wasn't there when everyone got caught, true. But he was there when it started."

For a man who hadn't won the election yet, Daniel Chow sure was up on all the things that were going on with the case.

And then I thought about Pastor Lee. He could hardly stand up to Mother Tyson. Could he be a killer? And what about Ms. Ruby Slippers? (I was going to have to find out her name. She kept changing shoes and I couldn't keep changing how I referred to her.) Were they in it together? Mother Tyson also said she couldn't control her husband. Maybe that's how she got him to stop.

But stop doing what exactly?

Then I wondered if Chow thought the same thing about me and Koby. That we were somehow involved. That we knew a lot about something we shouldn't know anything about.

No. That was last time. The last murder. He accused us of being involved. Looked like this time it was only our employees.

"And then there's the guy who was in prison with Austin James," Chow continued. "The one who wouldn't testify against him, but told everyone outside the courtroom all the things Mr. James had done."

"Oh. He liked to gossip."

"Yep. In everybody's business," Chow said, "but he did not cooperate with the people who could handle James." Chow took a sip of his drink. "Stoking the fire for people wanting to get back at Mr. James."

"If the guy didn't testify against Austin, even if he was willing to gossip about it to other folks, that doesn't seem like a reason for him to kill Mr. James."

"No. But although this guy wouldn't testify against James, Austin James testified against him."

"He did?" Koby said. I could tell his interest was piqued.

"He did. Lied right on the witness stand. Mr. James sent the man to jail for nearly two years."

"Oh," I said. "That would make someone mad enough to kill. You don't tell on someone but then they tell on you? Geesh."

"That's what I'm thinking," Koby said.

"Who was that guy?" I asked.

"His name is William Patton. But I think he goes by 'Ray.'"

Chapter Twenty-Seven

KOBY WALKED ME home, stopping at his houseboat to pick up Remy. The Lab ran out the door and up the dock, already knowing which way to head. Remy was always excited to visit the doghouse at my place.

We didn't talk most of the way there. So the fresh night air and the soothing sounds coming from the whisper of a breeze had helped me to unwind some. I needed that. It had been a long day.

But once we were on my porch, Koby wound me back up.

"What do you think about that Ray Patton?" He had to hold on to Remy's leash. The Lab was trying to get to the backyard.

"I think we should talk about it tomorrow." I patted Remy on the head to try and get him settled. Although Koby and Remy visited often and did their own thing while over, I wanted to just fall across the bed and not have to worry about anything, including company.

It wasn't actually what I thought he'd get out of the

conversation with Chow. True enough, it was the last thing we talked about before Chow had to go up on the stage and make his speech. After that the live band, all set up, was too loud for anyone to talk over.

I would have thought Koby would want to talk about what Chow said about Mama Zola.

But if he wasn't bringing it up, neither was I.

"Just wondering what you thought," Koby said. "Although I think I can guess."

I chuckled. "Go ahead and guess."

"That you always thought Ray Patton a good suspect."

"Right." I smiled. Probably didn't take twin telepathy to figure that out. "Now my turn," I said.

"Your turn to do what?"

"Guess what you're thinking."

"Okay." A grin on his face. "Go ahead."

"That we should go and talk to Ray."

His grin got bigger.

"But not tonight, Koby," I said. I knew there was no discussing the subject. And even though he hadn't mentioned it, I knew now he was probably that much more determined. Now that there may be a chance that the police were interested in Mama Zola.

"No. Not tonight. I didn't mean tonight," he said. "Plus, where are we going to find him? We'd have to figure that out first."

"Yeah." I sighed. "I don't know where we'd find him. He didn't come to church today, which could mean nothing."

"Or it could mean he's left town because he just killed a man."

I certainly could agree with that.

We'll figure it out," I said. "Tomorrow."

I leaned down and planted a kiss on the top of Remy's head and stroked him down along his back.

"See you guys tomorrow."

Koby threw up a hand as he stepped off the porch and headed down the walkway home.

When I opened the door, Roo was sitting there like she'd been waiting for me to come in.

"Did you wonder why Remy was here and you didn't see him?" I asked her, still standing in the doorway.

"Eeerrow."

"Aww." I stooped down. "I'm sorry. I should have let you say hi to your cousin Remy and Uncle Koby." I held out my arms to pick her up. Wasn't sure she'd let me. She was already picky and now, being upset with me, she might ignore me altogether.

"What a cute cat."

A voice came from behind me. It made me jump. I turned around and found Katy Erickson at my door.

"Oh my goodness!" I said, grasping the area over my heart. "You scared me. Why didn't you knock?"

She pointed. "The door is open."

I stood up and grabbed the door, thinking about shutting it then, but that would have been rude.

"What are you doing here?" I looked past her to see if I could still see Koby and Remy. She must have passed them. I hadn't even had time to get inside the house.

"Looks like I just missed your brother." She turned and looked behind her, seeming to know what I was thinking. "But that's okay, we can fill him in later."

"Fill him in on what?"

"Our next sleuthing move."

I rolled my eyes. "I have to go," I said and started pushing the door shut.

"Are you inviting me in?" she asked.

"No," I said.

She sure was pushy. But I guessed that was the nature of being a reporter. And she smelled like alcohol. Guess she took her fill of the dollar beer.

"I think we have to look at everyone involved with the

trading firm," she said, putting her hand on the door so I wouldn't shut it. "Start there, you know."

"I thought you already started. Had something big to announce." I raised my eyebrows at her.

She lowered her head and looked up at me with what I think she thought were innocent-looking eyes. "I really don't have anything to announce. It was a ploy to get information."

"I'm thinking it didn't work?"

"Not yet. But I've heard details about you and your brother."

There she went again talking about us.

"Yep. I know. From reputable people at the Everlasting. Although, I'm not sure why they'd speak to you."

"Not at the church. My source there had no details, just that you've been asking questions. I heard the *details* from Isabella."

"Izzy?" I said.

"Yes. At Hemlock."

"What kind of details?"

"How you solved a murder."

Mouth closed tightly, I pulled in a breath through my nose.

"And I heard how you almost died."

"I have to go," I said and pushed on the door.

"Wait!" She put her hand on my arm to stop me from shutting her out. "I can give you an exclusive in my story."

"I think that goes the other way around." I narrowed my eyes at her. "And I don't want to discuss any of this with you." I started shutting the door. "But I would like to put on record that neither my brother nor I are amateur sleuths. And we, unlike you, are not fond of murder."

I was able to get the door shut, but I wasn't sure if I hit the tip of her nose, that was how close she was. I locked it tight, and while checking the lock on the window, I peeked out to see what she was doing.

She stood in my yard for longer than I thought appropriate. Looking up and down the street, she acted as if she was trying to decide what to do. Then she walked over to a white Range Rover and got in.

"Mighty expensive car to drive on a reporter's salary," I said to Roo, who'd come over to be nosy with me. "And she didn't seem to understand the concept of an exclusive story."

I watched as she drove away.

"C'mon, Roo," I said, leaving the window. "Let's see what Miss Journalist is really all about."

I sat down at my desktop in the living room, and after firing it up, Googled "Timber Lake the *Gazette*." She'd said she worked for our local newspaper. I opened up their website, but after clicking on several tabs and links, there was nothing by her or about her. So, I deleted the words "Timber Lake" and searched again for "the *Gazette*." I got nothing but a Japanese band. I added "newspaper" to my search. And while there were a slew of papers named that, I couldn't seem to find another one local. I typed "Seattle" to the end of my search string. I counted thirteen newspapers in Seattle, not one named the *Gazette*.

Huh." I sat back in my chair and stared at the screen. "So you're not a reporter at our *Gazette*, and seeing there is no paper nearby called the *Gazette*, I'm thinking maybe you don't work there." I bit my bottom lip. *"Are you a reporter anywhere?"*

I started a new search, typing in "Katy Erickson." There were a few links to Instagram accounts and LinkedIn profiles, but nothing I could see that matched her or any of the information she'd given me. I did find a Facebook page that I thought might be her, but it was quite innocuous and didn't have one post about reporting anything. And then there was a blog, written by someone with the same name, but no picture for me to verify. It was all about heartbreak and lost love and—I took a gulp—abuse. I inhaled sharply and leaned in to read. It hadn't been physical abuse the author of this post had suffered, but mental. One no better than the other. I clicked off and hoped that wasn't the Katy I'd met. I hated that it happened to any Katy, though.

I leaned back in the chair. Nothing. At least anything concrete that would connect the Katy I'd met to anything that was going on now. Not any of the churches Austin James had been associated with. Not the trading firm James, Pastor Lee and Pete had worked for. Not even the newspaper she said she worked for.

Maybe everything she'd told me had been a lie.

One thing did strike me odd. If she'd heard about Koby and me from a church member, why hadn't whatever person from Everlasting who had watched the footage recognized her on the video? Or had they, and already ruled her out. Perhaps that was why she seemed unperturbed at church. She knew people there and she had nothing to hide. I remembered she spoke with Mother Tyson and even gave her a hug. But it didn't seem she was a member. But if she knew Mother Tyson, maybe she knew Moses Brown.

Maybe she was in on it with Deacon Brown . . .

A simpler answer to everything that had happened with her was that she was there for the potluck. She was nothing out of the ordinary. Not a suspect. Not a reporter.

And who at the church could have told her we were there trying to solve the murder? That we were amateur sleuths. We didn't know anyone that attended the church other than Mama Zola, although we'd made a few acquaintances (or enemies) through the questioning during our investigation.

Hmmm . . . our *investigation* . . .

I placed my fingers back over the keyboard and typed in "definition of an amateur sleuth."

I clicked on the first link I got to and, leaning in close to the screen, I read the definition out loud. "'A protagonist who, having no professional direct ties to the police, stumbles upon and sets out to solve or help solve crimes . . .'"

Okay. I agreed. I wasn't a stranger to what the term meant.

But considering what Katy said . . . well, I just never associated . . .

Katy made me think about it in a different way.

And she was right. According to this link, that sure did sound like what my brother and I were doing. Being amateur sleuths. And Katy hadn't been the only one to make reference to us being that. Others hadn't said the exact words, but still . . . We'd been warned, by more than one person, not to go sticking our noses in the solving of this murder.

But evidently, if we suspected Katy, who seemed to be nothing more than a liar, we weren't very good ones.

And yet we weren't listening. To anyone. And were making Katy's words true. Tomorrow we were all set to go and find out how to find and interrogate William Ray Patton.

I shook my head and kept reading. "The crimes, most notably," it said, "are murder."

And it continued: "Amateur sleuths are most often seen in the sub-genre cozy mystery."

"Huh," I said again, leaning back in the chair, I crossed my arms. "Koby and I are living in a cozy mystery."

Chapter Twenty-Eight

I WOKE UP sleepy.

Sunday had been a full day and I guessed I didn't have time to wind down from the week. It was going to be a long day.

I stroked my cat, who was curled up next to me. "Time to get up," I said. "Start our week." She didn't budge. "Fine. I'll greet the day all by myself."

I glanced over at the clock. There was no more time to sleep. I blew out a breath and threw the covers off me. But as soon as I hit the floor, a whiff of it smacked me in the face.

Bacon.

Koby was here.

"Bacon or no bacon," I muttered, "that boy is not dragging me all around today." Yawning, I went down the hall to the bathroom. "I have an author's event to get together."

Although there wasn't anything to it. The area on the Books side I had relegated to events was mostly ready. I'd have to pull the podium out of the storage closet and set the folding chairs up and the table with the books for Nicole, my traveling author, to sign. And knowing Pete, even with criminal charges possibly looming over his head, he'd have it all done hours before we needed it.

And anyway, that wasn't happening until tomorrow.

Still . . .

While brushing my teeth, I decided I was going to be firm with my brother. No murder stuff today or tomorrow. We—at least I—needed to concentrate on Books & Biscuits business.

I dressed with resolve and promised myself no matter how good that bacon looked, I wasn't going to take one piece of it or listen to one thing that Koby had to say about Austin James.

"We can't let Mama Zola go to jail."

Okay, that, along with the look of desperation in my twin brother's eyes, melted most of my resolve. Almost instantly.

But with the little I had left, I said, in no uncertain terms, "I'm not eating that bacon."

"I just thought if you were feeling as bad as me about what Chow said about Mama Zola, you'd need a pick-me-up."

"You know I have an author's event tomorrow, right?"

Change of subject, steering things where they needed to go, might help build back up determination.

"Of course I remember," he said. "I'm making pomegranate and lime sweet tea."

"And other stuff, too, right?"

"Yes. Lots of stuff." He tilted his head. "How many people are coming?"

"Our online reservations say seven."

"Seven."

Him repeating my number made me feel uneasy. "My author isn't from around here and she's just starting out as a self-published author."

"I wasn't saying 'seven' like it was a bad thing." He picked up the plate of bacon and, standing in front of me, extended his arms. He'd pushed them right under my nose. "I was thinking that maybe we should cancel and use tomorrow night to do more—"

I didn't let him finish his sentence. I knew what he was going to say.

I stepped back from the bacon.

"We are not canceling."

"What about Mama Zola?"

"I think she will be fine." His face showed that he didn't agree with me. "We are already working on getting Pete off. Right?" He didn't nod, grunt or say a word, so I continued. "So, if we help find out that Pete isn't the culprit, then that would mean Mama Zola would get out from under any scrutiny as well."

"I couldn't sleep last night, Keaton." He sat the plate on the table and rubbed a hand across his head. "I kept thinking about them railroading Pete, and Mama Zola getting drawn up in the middle. I couldn't take it if something happened to her."

"Nothing is going to happen to her," I said. "We just keep doing what we're doing."

"Because you really think we can find out who did it?"

I thought about what he'd asked me. I wasn't sure if we could. We had figured out the last murderer but not until it was almost too late for me. And like Chow had said, it wasn't our job. And we could get in trouble doing it.

"If Pete didn't do it," I said, "and we agree on that, right?"

Again Koby didn't even nod.

"If he didn't do it, then she couldn't have helped him. We'll figure this out."

"Okay," he said. "I just need to get this done. Find out what happened."

"We will get this done," I said.

"Yep." Koby drew in a deep breath and pushed it back out. "But how about we go see Mama Zola. We'll wrap this bacon up and take it over to her."

"I thought that was my bacon."

"You said you didn't want it."

I had said that. Because I didn't want him to use it as leverage against me to talk murder when we should be talking shop.

"Okay. We can go," I said, reluctantly giving up ownership of the bacon. "But when we get there and until my seven-audience author event has ended, no more murder talk."

"MAMA ZOLA, YOU have to tell us everything that happened the morning of the potluck. The day Austin James was killed. Every time Pete left you and where he went."

Koby walked in the painted blue front door of the two-family house Mama Zola lived in, asking questions about the murder. Definitely not sticking to the plan. Although he'd said later, when I asked him what happened to that agreement, that he hadn't actually agreed to it. "If you recall," he had said, "I didn't answer at all."

And he hadn't.

We soon learned Mama Zola didn't want to talk about it either.

"What?" Mama Zola said. "You want to talk about that first thing in the morning?"

"I asked him not to," I said.

"I brought bacon," Koby said. He took the foil cover off the plate and stretched out his arms, offering her some as he'd done me.

"He tried to bribe me with bacon, too," I said.

Mama Zola eyed me. "Did it work?"

"No," I said. "Then he tried enlisting my help by guilting me into cooperating."

"About what?" Mama Zola said.

And I paused, mouth open, about to speak, when I realized I didn't want to be the one to tell her what Daniel Chow, the soon-to-be chief of police, had to say about her. I reached over, took a slice of bacon and stuffed it into my mouth.

"What's going on?" Mama Zola eyed me suspiciously.

"We're just trying to help Pete," Koby said.

"I know," Mama Zola said, "but you've never come asking *me* questions. And now you're here at my house with bacon." She tilted her head. "Why are you doing that now? Did something happen? Did someone say something?"

I hadn't wanted to talk murder, but maybe it was a good thing Koby came to see Mama Zola. I would want to know if someone was looking at me sideways. Thinking I'd be capable of doing something so heinous. Even if it was just clearing the path for Pete, helping cover up something he'd thought of and executed all on his own, I think I would need to know that people, especially people like law enforcement, were talking about my involvement.

Only, like I said, I wouldn't want to be the one to tell her. I took another piece of bacon from the plate.

"You remember Detective Chow?" Koby asked. He sat the plate down on the kitchen table and pulled out a seat.

"Of course I remember him," Mama Zola said. She pulled out a chair next to Koby and sat down. "He arrested Reef's killer. I went to court every time it was in session until they put that monster in jail. Chow was there, too."

"Well, you know he's running for police chief."

"Not much of a race when there isn't anyone running against you." She got up from the chair and went over to the sink.

Koby nodded.

I was impressed. Mama Zola had just moved to Timber Lake and she was more current on happenings around here than I was. Until Pete had to go and talk to the police, I hadn't ever paid much attention to the law in the place where I lived. I was civic minded and voted, but with this one being a special election and our business trying to grow some momentum, it had gone right over my head.

"We saw him, Detective Chow, at the Hemlock last night."

"And?" Mama Zola turned to Koby and put her hands on her hips.

"He thinks that Acting Chief Ross thinks that you may have had a hand in helping Pete."

"He thinks. That *he* thinks. That's a whole lot of speculation to have and still get the story wrong."

"I know it's wrong, but Detective Chow says that Ross might be trying to make a name for himself before he has to leave the position."

"By catching the wrong killer?"

"Why was Pete back outside and trying to go into a wrong door? The door by the office where Austin James was in?"

"I don't know."

"Did you send him somewhere looking for something for you?"

"I may have."

"Mama Zola." Koby seemed exasperated.

"Pete didn't kill that man," Mama Zola said and turned back to the sink. Maybe she thought turning her back to Koby was going to stop him. But Koby wasn't letting Mama Zola back out of answering his questions.

"How many times did he leave? How many times do you *think* he may have gone to do something for you?"

She turned around. "What difference does it make?"

"Because that's exactly what the police are thinking.

They think you sent him for something and that's his alibi."

"He doesn't need an alibi."

"You can't be his alibi." Koby's voice was stern. "So you need to tell me what happened that day."

"I can tell you this." Mama Zola pointed a finger at Koby. "No child I helped raise is going to speak to me in that tone."

Contrition washed over Koby's face. He got up from the chair and walked over to her, taking her hands. "I just can't lose another mother." He let go of her hands and put his arms around her shoulders. "I don't want to lose another mother."

"They won't put me in jail." Mama Zola hugged him and patted him on the back. "Everything is going to be okay."

"Innocent people spend years in prison, Mama Zola. Some get executed even before the truth comes out."

"You think that's what's going to happen to me and Pete?"

"No." Koby shook his head. "I wouldn't let that happen to you. But you have to help me." He hugged her tight. "You have to tell me what happened."

"Don't you worry none about it," Mama Zola said. She unwrapped herself from him and put her hands on his cheeks. "That man has nothing on me or Pete. And when I see him again, I'm going to tell him what I think of his shoddy police work. Talking about a dog barking up the wrong tree." She shook her head. "That man isn't even in the right part of the woods."

Chapter Twenty-Nine

WE MADE IT to the shop late. At least, late for Koby, because he needed to bake and do prep. I again had to help him because before we left Mama Zola's, she informed us that she'd be late herself.

No biscuits, though. I made sure that wasn't on my list of tasks. And thank goodness Mama Zola made it in plenty of time to finish up. Even Georgie got there earlier than usual.

I excused myself and went over to the Books side. I figured I could get a little work done on the ledgers. Check some inventory and check emails. I also wanted to scour the Internet for other shops that offered online purchasing of used books. I didn't need to reinvent to wheel to set up our e-commerce site. I could get ideas from other bookshops. I'd already given Kevin, our newly hired webmaster, the go-ahead to start after Koby and I had our last board meeting.

And before I could get behind the desk, I noticed Pete already in the store working.

"Morning," I said. "What are you doing here so early?"

He hadn't moved in with Mama Zola yet. His room was there waiting, but he told her he needed to take care of something else first. She'd seemed so disappointed the day she told us.

Not so homeless, I guess, because Mama Zola said he was still sleeping in the storage room in the back of our store. Only he hadn't been there when we'd gotten in.

"Working," he said. He'd taken books off one of the smaller bookcases and was dusting.

Pete wasn't much for words, and I wondered if he'd always been like that now that I knew all the things he'd been through.

"You know we have an author event tomorrow."

"I know," he said.

"And did you know it's only seven people who've RSVP'd?"

"Seven is a good number. It's the number of completeness."

"Not such a good number when you have an author who wants to sell books."

He didn't have anything to say to that so I went over to the counter to do some busywork.

And that was the way our morning went. Smells from the Biscuits side made me wish I'd eaten more of that bacon.

Customers wandered in, not so many buying books, some drawn to the other side to find out what smelled so good, others back out of the door, but I greeted each one with the same smile. Luckily, we were getting more sales in books each week we'd been open, and I could only hope a larger online presence would bring in more revenue and that definitely made me happy.

But I lost the smile and the favorable disposition when Acting Chief Franklin Ross walked in the door.

"Keaton," he said with a familiarity that was disturbing. It felt as if he thought he had some authority over me.

He came in on a mission, his jaw set in determination.

There hadn't even been time to warn Pete, as I was sure he didn't want to confront the man who'd practically arrested him. I turned to see Pete's reaction but he wasn't there. I looked around. He wasn't anywhere.

Good for Pete.

"How may I help you?" I turned back to the intruder.

"One way you can help is to stay out of my investigation." He had an attitude walking in the door. I didn't know what he wanted, but I was thinking it wasn't to buy a book. Or a biscuit.

I scratched the side of my forehead. I had to try and not let Acting Chief Ross upset me. But I had a feeling that it wouldn't be too long before Koby would make an entrance and I wouldn't have to tolerate him all alone.

"I am not involved in your investigation," I said, scraping up more bravado than I thought I could. "Other than the concern I have for my employee."

That was true. I didn't think his investigation had taken the same turns ours had because he seemed to be concentrating on one person. At least we were looking at different people. Different angles. Although I think that his investigation and ours were both focusing on the same motive—revenge.

"We sell books and food here." It was Koby. He'd come over and was standing in the archway. "Unless you want to buy either one of those, you are loitering."

"I'm here on official business," Ross said, even though he hadn't moved from the door.

"And what would that be?" Koby asked. He walked farther into the bookstore.

"Zola Jackson," Ross said. I think he knew he'd get a reaction with that, because he paused before he said anything else. "I need to talk to her."

"About what?" Koby said. He'd moved all the way into the room and was no more than ten feet from Ross. This confrontation made me nervous.

"Is she here?" Ross asked, ignoring Koby's question.

"She is, but her lawyer is not," Koby said. "Unless you have a warrant?" My brother posed the last part as a question, but I knew it was a statement for him. He seemed to know enough about the law.

"How about if we let her tell me that."

"How about if we don't."

"I can speak for myself." Mama Zola came and stood in the archway. "I came to see what all the commotion was about, and Lordy, it's about me."

"Mama Zola, you shouldn't say anything to him without a lawyer."

"I don't need a lawyer," she said. "Because like Mr. Pete Howers, I haven't done anything wrong." She pursed her lips. "And if you were any kind of detective, you would know that."

"Did you help him cover up the murder of Austin James?" Ross asked.

"No. I did not. Why would I?"

"It seems that you didn't like the things that Mr. James was doing at your church and Mr. Howers didn't like the things he'd done to him previously."

"Who told you that?" Mama Zola asked.

"Is it true?" Ross asked.

"I don't know what you're talking about." Mama Zola looked at Koby. Koby, knowing full well what the law officer was alluding to, at least in Pete's case, hunched his shoulders as if he had no idea.

"You and Mr. Howers cooked up a scheme to get rid of Mr. James at the potluck, making what happened premeditated murder."

"The only thing we cooked up was peach cobbler." She scrunched up her face. "And God is teaching me a lesson with it about my vanity." She shook her head. I lifted my eyebrows. She'd made a fuss about the cobbler, but I wasn't sure it amounted to vanity or the wrath of God's ire. "But someone is going to get away with, as you say, premeditated murder, if you don't start looking at the right people."

"And who do you think that is?" Ross asked.

"I hate to say it, but the church members."

"Aren't you a church member?"

"I'm not one of the church members who had their life savings stolen by Austin James." She pointed her finger at him. "I didn't even know him until the day he died. But you best believe, there were members of that church who had it out for him. Knew he was coming there and where he'd be. That wouldn't be me or Pete."

"Pete was seen trying to get back in the building through the door closest to where we found Mr. James."

"He'd gone out to throw something in the dumpster for me," Mama Zola said. Making it look like she was supplying Pete with an alibi. But it was what I saw that upset me. There was a mix of guilt and remorse that crawled across her face with her words.

Koby must have noticed it, too. "What is it, Mama Zola?"

She shook her head in disgust. "I dropped a pan of cobbler." She paused and let out a groan. "I didn't want anyone to see my cobbler in the trash, so I had Pete take it out to the dumpster." Her voice cracked. "That's the only reason he was out there." She looked at Ross. "Not because he was killing anyone." She wanted to make that clear. "And then," she continued, "he couldn't get back in the same door. It locked behind him."

"Is that what he told you?" Chief Ross asked.

"Yes. And I know that's what happened. I know he didn't kill anyone. And if you had any sense, you'd know it, too."

Koby walked to Mama Zola and placed a hand on her arm. I know he wanted her to be nice.

I interjected. I wanted Ross to know that what Mama

Zola was saying about the door was true. "Pete had to use that door, the one with the video camera, because there was a sign on the other door that said to use it," I said. "Didn't you know that?"

"A sign?"

"Yes," Koby said. "With instructions."

Ross paused for a moment as if he were taking in all the information we had supplied. "How do you know that?" he asked, looking at each of us in turn.

"Katy Erickson," I said, speaking up before Mama Zola could. I could tell she was ready to say something else. "We know about the sign because of her. She was the woman in the hat on the video."

"I know who she is," he said.

"The reporter?" I said, testing to see if I could get some truthful information on her.

"Reporter?" He posed the question back to me with a furrowed brow. I think my research had put me on the right track about her.

"Never mind," I said. "But anyway, you should know about the sign."

He noisily took in a breath. "Why were you questioning her?" He looked from me to Koby, but it was Mama Zola who answered.

"Because it seems you don't know the right questions to ask to *anyone*." She put her hands on her hips and cocked her head to one side. "No wonder Timber Lake is electing a new chief of police. The acting one doesn't even know how to act!"

Chapter Thirty

RAY'S HOUSE WAS a ranch-style, L-shaped house. Nothing like most of the houses in Timber Lake. They were like storybook houses, as my father—adopted father—liked to say. Cottages painted in pretty colors with window pots overflowing with flowers and blooming trees out front.

It was Monday afternoon. Koby and I had taken lunch together, found out the address we needed from Mama Zola and driven over to the west side of Timber Lake. We were going to talk to Ray Patton. And on the way over, Koby noticed a car following us, or so he thought.

"It's a white SUV," he said.

"A Range Rover?" I asked and turned around to look.

"Yep. How did you know?" He glanced at me.

"It's Katy."

"The reporter from church?"

"She's not a reporter," I said. "I Googled her." And then I told him what I had found out. He shook his head in disbelief throughout the whole conversation.

"So we should cross her off our list," I said.

"Why?" Koby asked. "Felons are liars."

"I don't know how true that is, but okay. You could be right. If she committed the murder, she might be lying. Agreed."

"So she stays on the list."

"Yes." I sighed. "Still, what would be her reason for doing it? I couldn't find a connection between her and Austin James. She would need a reason to kill."

"Remember?" He glanced over at me. "Our conversation at the church? She didn't act as if she liked Austin James or Pastor Lee."

"Yeah, that's true," I said. "But is not liking a person a good enough reason? To kill them?"

"Is any reason good enough to take a life?"

"Yeah." I nodded. "You're right."

I turned and took another glance. She'd gotten a few cars behind, but when I looked in the side mirror, I saw that she was still there.

Maybe she was the killer. And maybe she thought because, so she believed, Koby and I were amateur sleuths who might just find out what she'd done, she needed to ingratiate herself with us so she could keep an eye on our progress. And when I didn't let that happen, she resorted to stalking.

Definitely not good.

And a bit scary.

I mentally moved her up on my suspect list. Then, wanting to not think about any harm she may cause us, I focused on the one we were going to see now.

I had suspected Ray from the time he'd said he knew coffee was going to kill Austin James and no one, at the time, knew his death had anything to do with coffee. Or a coffeemaker. That was another thing. Ray called the coffeemaker old. On its last legs. Anyone would go along with it giving out or malfunctioning and not think anything of it. It was a way he could get away with murder.

Then Mother Tyson wondering where Ray was on Sunday sent up a red flag for me, too. He'd taken part in the potluck dinner and seemed familiar enough (Koby thought too familiar) with Mama Zola. I thought he was an active member of the church. And missing one Sunday doesn't make one lose their soul, but it might be a sign about what kind of soul he had. Maybe Ray Patton didn't want to return to the scene of the crime he'd committed.

And it was easy for anyone to see that when Austin James was alive, the two of them didn't seem to like each other.

This time I took the ride that Koby offered. Ray lived in walking distance, for sure. But I'd learned my lesson about being close to killers. They weren't averse to killing again. And between Deacon Brown and Ray Patton, I was certain one of them was the killer. For once I wasn't against going to talk to someone we suspected. I was all ready to talk and had a slew of questions in my head, when Koby got me all flustered.

"So, I guess I should tell you."

"Tell me what?" Koby had sounded hesitant. It made me worry. "What's happened?"

He scrunched his eyes. "Don't be mad at me."

"What, Koby?" I looked out the window to see where the white Range Rover was, then turned back to my brother. "What?"

"You know how the other day when Maya dropped by and got biscuits?"

"Yeah."

"You said you wanted more people to come to your author event."

"Yeah."

"So I invited another author. A local one that I think may bring in more people."

"Is that what you wanted to tell me?" I let out the breath I didn't know I was holding. I gave him a push.

"Why you say it like that? Scaring me." I sucked my teeth. "Why would I be mad about that?"

"You don't mind?"

"No. It would have been nice if they had been on the flyer. But a surprise guest author couldn't be anything but good."

"Good," he said and cut the car off. "I was hoping you wouldn't be upset."

"Why would I be upset?"

Koby opened the car door, and on his way out, he said, "Because it's Deacon Brown."

He shut the car door and left me sitting there with my mouth open.

It took me a minute to process that, but once I did, I wanted to yell at him. Ask him if he was crazy, inviting that possible murderer to my book event.

When did he even do it?

We'd just found out the day before that Moses Brown was an author. Then I remembered that Koby had disappeared for a few moments when we were ready to go into the chapel for the Sunday morning service.

That must've have been when . . .

Geesh!

I glared out the window at Koby. Not that he saw me. He had his back to me as he made his way up the driveway.

And what in the world was Deacon Brown's book about? I again wished I had looked at it better. Then I slapped my thigh. Why was I even worried about that? I didn't want the man there.

But of course, I couldn't ask any of that to my brother, or express (scream) my concerns. Ray was standing outside his house in his wide concrete driveway and Koby had already approached him by the time I'd gotten out of the car.

Ray had khaki-colored shorts on, a Seahawks T-shirt,

a pair of sandals on his feet. He was watching something going on down the street. Well, it seemed that way. It made me turn and look.

"They haven't been at that house in a month," Ray was saying by the time I got to where the two of them were standing. "Then last night I saw a truck pull up."

"Who is *they*?" I asked, turning my gaze in the same direction as his.

"The people down there." He pointed toward a house that sat on the next corner. "I was thinking they had moved."

"Were *they* planning on moving?" Koby seemed to have adopted Ray's description of whomever it was he was talking about.

"I have no idea," he said. "But with a truck coming over, after dark, made me think they were up to something."

I had my first Koby moment. I knew something about this man by his actions and conversation—he was a nosy neighbor.

I guess that went along with being a gossiper . . .

"Maybe they didn't want other people in their business?" I suggested.

"Because they had something to hide," Ray said.

That was the exact reason I had taken time off from work and was standing in his driveway. People with things to hide. In this instance, him.

"See that house down there." He pointed.

"No," I said.

"You don't see that house."

There was a block full of them. "Which one?"

"The beige one with the cranberry-colored shutters."

"With the dogwood tree in the front yard?"

"Yeah," he said.

"Yep," I said. "I see it."

"Austin James used to own that house."

Well, how about that? He was bringing up the conversation we wanted to have without either one of us saying a word about it.

"Is that how you knew him?" Koby asked, already knowing the answer.

"Who?"

"Austin James."

"Oh no," he said. "I didn't move here until a couple of years ago."

"When did he live there?" I asked. Wasn't sure why I needed to know, though.

"Maybe ten years ago."

"How did you know him?" Koby asked. I wondered, did Koby think Ray would admit to it all? Admit to being a member of Austin's church? Admit to having to go to prison because of him?

"I knew him from when he pastored that megachurch," Ray said.

"Abundant Faith Tabernacle?"

Ray nodded.

"Were you a member?"

"Not a fan of being around a lot of people."

I took that to mean he wasn't a member, but that wasn't what Detective Chow had told us.

"But you know," Ray continued. "They paid the mortgage off on that church building, forty-five hundred square feet, mind you, within a year."

"It was a big church," I said. "Lots of members."

"And lots of money floating through it," Ray said.

Koby tilted his head to the side. "That's when you first met him?"

"Yep."

Seemed as if Ray didn't mind not telling the truth.

"So," Koby said, "do you think he was killed because of something that happened with the church?"

"They told me that he had his hands in lots of stuff. Real estate. Coffee shops. Barber shops."

"A businessman."

"That's what they say. But I guess it was to launder money."

"Who is *they*?" I asked, wondering again who he was talking about. He mentioned often that he got information from them.

"People."

"Oh," I said. Still didn't know. Maybe he was vague because he was involved. "Did these people tell you anything else?"

"Yeah." Ray changed his focus from the house down the street to us. "I heard that he was trying to take over Pastor Lee's church."

"Everlasting Missionary Baptist Church?" Koby said. I didn't know why he felt compelled to say the entire name.

"One and the same," Ray said. "Wanted to make it as big as Abundant Faith. I heard he'd already had some of the members who used to attend say they were willing to come back." He sucked his teeth. "But for the most part, that didn't sit well with Pastor Lee's members."

"Including you?" Koby asked.

"Me. Zola. The Deacon Board. Lots of people."

Koby glanced over at me when Ray mentioned Mama Zola's name. I hoped he wouldn't get sidetracked. So I spoke up.

"But you say some people were willing to follow him even after everything he'd done?" I asked.

"They were going to follow him blindly. Not one lesson learned." Ray shook his head and licked his lips as if the dislike of the thought made him ill. "And then, even former members who had gone to other churches were starting to change their membership to Everlasting."

That didn't sound right to me. Brother Ron sounded as if other members didn't want to come back. They had all split up. And Mother Tyson said he was a troublemaker.

"So, he was just going to take over Pastor Lee's church?" I asked.

"Coup."

"What?" Koby said.

"They call it a *coup*," Ray said.

"You think Pastor Lee would have let that happen?" Koby asked.

"Don't know if Calvin could have stopped it from happening. If he even had it in him, he wouldn't have let that man back in the door. Good Samaritan ideals or not." Ray shook his head, it seemed in disgust. "That Austin James was a force to be reckoned with." But then a small smile appeared on his face. Just crept right up. I don't know if Ray meant for us to see it, but it was definitely there right before he said, "But no worries, he's been stopped."

Chapter Thirty-One

"IS KATY STILL following us?" I asked as I glanced in my passenger side mirror. We were headed back to the shop.

"Yep," Koby said. "Two cars back." He adjusted his rearview mirror. His eyes averting to it and then back to the road.

"Can't you lose her?"

"Uhm, no." He looked at me, a smirk on his face. "My lose-cars-that-are-driving-behind-me-and-doing-nothing thingy is broken." He pointed at the dashboard.

I sucked my teeth.

We'd spent the last twenty minutes with Ray Patton and being watched by Katy Erickson, and I wasn't any more or less sure if either of them were involved. Although I still thought Ray Patton knew an awful lot, and although it was obvious, he had even admitted a dislike for the dead man.

I had no idea what was up with Katy.

Austin James, it seemed, was trying to bring change to

Everlasting Missionary Baptist Church. Ray confirmed what Acting Chief Ross had insinuated. James was trying to create another Abundant Faith Tabernacle.

And those kinds of things—changes—didn't sit well with Mama Zola. No change did. Not that the police could have known that specifically about Mama Zola. And I'd guess that Ray hadn't shared with Chief Ross what he'd said to us about Mama Zola being unhappy about it.

I heard once, the older a person got, the less tolerant they were of change. I didn't know if that was true or not, but right now it was what had Acting Chief Ross including Mama Zola in Pete's scheme to kill James Austin.

Although, if I had to say so myself, she'd stood up to him well. I only hoped she wouldn't have to go through the same ordeal as Pete. Being hauled down to the police station for questioning.

It did seem like a long stretch that Pete and Mama Zola had discovered their mutual hate for Austin James. Concocted a plan to disrupt his pacemaker by rigging a coffeemaker and pulled it off when there was a church full of people there or a least coming soon.

And if they were able to do that, they surely wouldn't be careless enough to send Pete out a door he couldn't get back in. Or to one where there was a camera.

Unless they didn't know there was a camera there.

That didn't matter. No one without the code could get in that door anyway. And the only person who had the code to that door that the camera caught that day was Deacon Brown.

Oh yeah. Deacon Brown.

I punched my brother in his arm.

"Ouch!" He rubbed his arm. "What was that for?"

"Why would you invite Deacon Brown to my book signing?"

"He's an author."

"Who commits murder."

"We don't know that, but this would be a good way to find out."

"Don't you know what happens when you invite a vampire in your home?"

"A vampire?" He scrunched up his eyes. "Where did that come from?"

"They kill you!" I answered the question myself.

"Oh. You're saying Deacon Brown is just like a vampire." He made a face that said my logic made no sense.

"That's not what I'm saying." I threw up my hands. "It's just that seeing we think he may have been responsible for Austin James' death, we—*you*—should have thought twice about signing him up to come to our shop."

"It'll be okay," Koby said.

"You don't know that," I said. "And you don't know what it's like to face a murderer."

"You've already 'faced' him once." Koby glanced at me and shook his head. "Nothing happened."

"I faced the last murderer a few times before they tried to kill me." I let my neck roll back and let out a groan. "If something happens to me, you'll be sorry."

"And if something does happen to you, I'll tell you 'I'm sorry.'"

"Fat lot of good that will do then."

"And if *nothing* happens, and everything goes smoothly, as I know it will, then you'll have to tell *me* 'Sorry.'"

"Whatever."

"Aw, c'mon." He pushed my arm. "Just think how many people are going to come."

"You mean the church members who Mama Zola said should be the prime suspects for the murder?" My voice had gone up to a few octaves. I had to keep myself from squealing.

"There will be lots of sales, probably on both sides of the store."

"Ugh!"

"I think maybe you shouldn't be the Watson to my Holmes," Koby said, giving me a pitying look. "You get too nervous about stuff."

I USED THAT nervous energy to go over the inventory of every single book in Books, order two more bookcases for the used books area and research how to sync our current POS system with the new one. I couldn't figure that out, so I called Kevin. He said he'd handle it. And I kept an eye out for that white Range Rover. It seemed to me that it passed by our window a couple of times. But it all made for busywork and helped me work over some of the anxiety I was feeling.

For lunch I went and bought food from the Second Street Market. I was still "acting" upset with Koby about his author guest and wasn't going to eat with him, although I was worried about running into Acting Chief Ross again.

Instead, brown paper bag in hand and stomach rumbling, I walked back into Books & Biscuits and right into Deacon Moses Brown.

Ugh.

Standing there smiling at me, my brother standing next to him, it seemed they were just waiting for me.

"Hello," he said. "I didn't know you owned a bookstore." His eyes scanned the room. "A nice one, too."

I tried to give Koby the stank eye without Deacon Brown seeing it before I answered. "Thank you," I said. "We've only been open a few months."

"And it was so nice for your brother to invite me as a featured author in tomorrow's event."

Featured author? I wanted to mouth that to Koby. To let him know he wasn't funny. But, since I couldn't without Deacon Moses seeing me, I made a real effort to send it telepathically to him.

What had he told that man?

But before I could answer, Lacey walked from behind one the bookshelves with an armful of books.

"You have great books here," she said, beaming.

"Hi," I said. I almost asked what she was doing there, but of course, any customer was welcome. Then I remembered she'd said she and Moses were cousins.

"We just stopped by to see where the author event was going to be and if we needed to do anything special." Lacey, unlike my twin, seemed to know just what I was thinking.

"Oh." I started to put a brown bag on the counter. "I can show you," I said.

"Your brother already did," Lacey said.

"Now he's going to show me some of what he's got cooking next door," Deacon Brown said. "I don't know how anyone stays on this side to buy a book."

I frowned and Koby hustled Deacon Brown out of the room.

Before they left, Deacon Brown turned to his cousin. "You coming?"

"No," she said and smiled at me. "I'd rather look at books."

I smiled back. "You need any help?" I asked.

"I have enough," she said, looking down at the small bundle in her arms. "I really can't afford all of this. And I haven't finished Wanda Morris' *All Her Little Secrets* yet."

"You haven't?" Last I saw her with the book, she was more than three quarters the way through.

"Nope," she said and shook her head. "It's so good, I don't want it to end."

I laughed. I knew just what she meant. Good books are meant to be savored.

"Let's see what you got," I said and walked behind the counter so I could check her out.

"I think I got carried away," she said, dumping her pile on the counter. "I am so excited about Moses having an actual author event."

"You know there's another author, too, right?"

"Oh yes. Koby told us." She started arranging the books into piles. "But it's more than he's ever done. He's been pushing his books on people for years. Now people are going to actually come to him."

"So far," I said, "only seven have responded saying they were coming."

She waved a dismissive hand. "When my momma got wind of it, she invited the entire county, I think. You'll have a crowd."

"You think so?" I guess Koby had been right about church members coming.

"You must have never seen her in action."

"I have," I said. "Mother Tyson reminds me of Mama Zola. She doesn't let anyone get away with anything."

Lacey laughed. "I heard she got on the pastor for putting Mama Zola out of church."

"She did," I said. "No offense. I don't want to talk about your pastor, but what happened to 'innocent until proven guilty'?"

"That's what Momma said." With her words, Lacey pushed five of the seven books she picked across the counter toward me. "I'll get these."

"Okay," I said and put the two throwaways under the counter. I'd reshelve them later. "I'll make sure we keep a copy of each of the ones you're not getting today until you're able to come back and get them."

"Thank you," Lacey said. "I love books. Always have. You'd think I'd be the one to grow up and write books."

"What do you do?"

"Other than be the secretary at the church?"

"Yeah."

"I teach GED classes to adults."

"Reading?"

"Reading. Civics. Math."

"Oh wow," I said.

"I love teaching," she said. "Took after my grandmother."

"Mother Tyson is a teacher?"

"Was. She became diabetic and was really sick for a while."

"Oh, I'm sorry to hear that," I said.

"She's much better now. Still has to take her insulin and I can't keep her away from the sweets." Lacey shook her head. "But although she's no longer in the school system, she still helps everyone. Not just the women in the church and the community, but everybody. And she encourages everyone to follow their dream. That's why Moses wrote that book."

"That was his dream."

"Yes. It was all he talked about. 'I should write a book. All the things I can do. I should tell people.'"

I laughed at her imitating his gruff voice.

"He's an electrician, right?"

"Yep. I told you that, didn't I?"

"Yes. You did."

"And a musician," Lacey said, a proud smile on her face. "An awesome musician seeing that he's hard of hearing."

"Oh, he really is hard of hearing?"

"Really is?" She frowned disappointedly. "Did you think he wasn't?"

"I was thinking since he couldn't hear, that he couldn't . . ."

Lacey sucked her tongue. "Disabilities shouldn't stop anyone from doing what they want to do. If they can manage it."

"I totally agree," I said. "Bad of me to assume otherwise."

"Momma encouraged him to pursue music, but she told him in case that fell through, he should take up something practical."

"A trade?" I knew exactly what that "something practical" was. It was the reason he was at the top of my suspect list. "As an electrician."

"Yep. She helped him study for that certification. Had all of us helping him. We knew just as much about it as he did by the time he was finished."

"He didn't do anything with his music?" I asked, trying not to make it obvious that I wanted to know more about how he could rig wires to kill.

"He tried," Lacey said. But her face changed as she thought about it. "At the last church he was working as the musical director until that pastor found out he was hearing impaired."

"He fired him?"

"In front of everyone." She shook her head. "It was humiliating. My uncle was so hurt. And mad. Said that that pastor was going to be sorry they fired him."

"Oh. That's terrible. And what church was that?"

"Abundant Faith Tabernacle."

SO THE AUTHOR my brother invited to our nearly new establishment had, previous to Austin James being murdered, threatened to kill him. He'd been a member of the deceased man's church.

He was an electrician.

And he knew the code to the door closest to the office where the body was found.

That was means, motive and opportunity.

Ding. Ding. Ding. Ding.

I thought the dings were in my head and it was my inner sleuth giving credence to my revelation like the ones on *Jeopardy!* when the contestant got the right answer.

But it was the bell over the door.

Customers came in and I got distracted, it seemed, until Lacey and her cousin Moses Brown showed back up in front of my counter as I was ringing out the last customer.

"That food was so good, Keaton," Lacey said, that now familiar wide smile on her face. She rubbed her stomach. "Your brother said he cooked it."

"He did," I said. "He's a great cook."

"I won't be able to eat again until next week," Deacon Brown said. "I ate almost until I was about to burst."

"Oh my," I said, that visual popping up in my head.

"I can't wait until tomorrow." Deacon Brown's smile was almost as wide as his cousin's. "I hope I have enough books."

"I'm sorry we couldn't order them. I usually have them here for the authors."

"Oh, that's okay. I print my own anyway."

"You print them?" I said, confused.

"No." He chuckled. "Not like I have a printer in my basement or anything. I order at a printer's in Seattle and go and pick them up."

"Oh." I nodded. "I see."

"I'm so excited," he said and pumped his fist. "I just know it's going to be a *killer* night."

With those words, all I could do was let out a moan.

Chapter Thirty-Two

I WOKE UP Tuesday morning and drew in a big sniff of air. No smell of bacon. Or biscuits. No sounds of cabinets or drawers opening and closing underneath me.

That meant no Koby doing a takeover of my kitchen and pitching his sleuthing ideas to me.

I let out a sigh of relief and looked for Roo. She was usually curled up right beside me. But she was up and nowhere in sight. Rolling out of bed, I felt a chill that was over the house. I shivered.

"Did I leave a window open?" I muttered as I slipped into my house shoes and wrapped my bathrobe around me. I checked the windows in my room and the spare bedroom across the hall. Nothing. So I headed downstairs.

I looked around the kitchen and out the window into the backyard. Remy's doghouse stood still and empty. Nothing looked out of place except there still was no sign of my cat.

"Roo," I called out and headed toward the front of the house. I stood in the middle of the living room floor and looked around me. "Where are you, baby?" My voice sweet and low. I looked out the front windows, not that she could get out of the house, but I didn't know where else to look. She wasn't one for hiding. Naps were her thing.

As I turned to head back down the hallway to the steps, Roo came flying off the top shelf onto my head with a snarl.

"Oh my!" I fumbled to grab ahold of her without her yanking out my hair. She was frenzied. "What's wrong, baby? What's wrong?" I tried to hold her in my arms but she tumbled out with one big leap and scurried up the stairs.

I turned around in the middle of the floor. I couldn't figure out what could have spooked her. And then I looked out the window again. It seemed that I caught the tail end of a white car passing my window.

"Was that . . ."

I walked over to the window and looked up and down my street. Only car in sight was a blue Honda Civic parked two houses down.

I scratched my head. *Couldn't be.* Not Katy again lurking around. Had she come up on the porch, peeked in the window?

I turned and glanced toward the steps that Roo had just bustled up, and I scrunched up my face. That wouldn't have frightened her like that. She'd seen Katy before. The last time she'd intruded into my space.

"Oh well." I shook my head as I headed up the stairs behind my cat. "Let's just hope the rest of the day goes better."

TUESDAY SEEMED TO fly by. To my chagrin. I wasn't ready to have Deacon Brown in my shop putting on an event. I had been tempted all day to call Acting Chief

Franklin Ross and give him a rundown of all the things I knew. None of which pointed to Pete. But I didn't.

I did call Detective Chow, though.

I knew better than to confront a killer on my own. I had learned my lesson.

"Not my job yet," he told me in our short conversation. I had spilled out what was going on and my fear all in one breath.

"But I don't know if we'll be safe here."

"Why do you think he'd want to hurt you?" he asked.

I took a moment to collect my thoughts. He hadn't ever given me a reason to be afraid of him. He hadn't done anything that I knew of *for sure*. But, I almost pleaded with Chow, what about circumstantial evidence?

I remembered Koby's explanation of it. Add no snow on the ground when you go to bed to snow when you get up and it equals a sure bet that it snowed overnight. Using that logic, it was a blizzard of a snowstorm when it came to Moses Brown being the murderer.

With what I knew, Chow didn't even want to bring out the snow trucks. All roads seemed clear to him.

He did promise to stop by.

After hanging up the phone with him, I only felt a little better.

"Hey. What's wrong?" Koby was standing there looking at me. Then at the phone. "Who was that? Something happen?"

My brother always fussed at me about wanting to call the police with information we'd gather during a murder investigation. (Okay, so we'd only been involved in one other one, but at every stage I was ready to spill the beans to the law, so he had fussed a lot.) I didn't want to tell him what I'd done. But it was so hard to keep things to myself when it came to him.

"I called Detective Chow."

"Why?"

I was already answering, talking over his response. "Because we are going to be doing this event tonight with a murderer in our midst."

"That was the reason I invited him. So we could find out about him. Ask questions. See if he might be the murderer."

"We spoke with him at the church."

"I know. But look how many people are going to be here tonight. People that knew Austin James. Who didn't like Austin James. People who may have been involved with his murder."

"Other than Moses Brown?"

"Exactly," Koby said. "It's a good opportunity."

"What makes you think that?"

"I heard how Mother Tyson invited people." He nodded. "And if she hadn't, that had been my plan all along."

I shook my head. "Your plan was to question people about the murder at the author event?"

"*Before* and *after* the event." He looked at me wide-eyed. "I wouldn't ever think of messing up your event."

"Okay," I said.

"You know," Koby continued. "When people are mingling about. Waiting in line to get their books signed." He shrugged. "And, you'd be safe the whole time with so many people around."

"Why didn't you tell me that?" I said. "That this was your plan."

"I thought you knew."

"I just knew I was scared. Nervous about Deacon Brown being here."

"So why didn't *you* tell me that?"

"I did." I blew out a breath. "At least I thought I made it clear."

"I told you, I'll always try my best to protect you."

"Yeah. Right. And how are you going to protect me?" I said. He seemed to not realize he was the one I was thinking who had put me in mortal danger.

"I can protect you," he said. He stood real still. His mouth slightly opened before he drew his lips tight. "Or you could have called Capt'n Hook." He shook his head at me, seemingly in disbelief. Or disappointment. "If you wanted a police officer."

"Oh yeah," I said.

Koby rolled his eyes up to the ceiling. His look told me he didn't approve of what I'd done and what I didn't do, and I think, who I didn't trust.

It made me feel bad and kind of like I was overreacting. Still . . .

I went on the defensive. "You weren't the one who almost died last time," I said.

Koby's eyes lowered to look at me. "And what did Chow say?"

"He said he thought everything would be okay, but he would stop by."

"Did that make you feel better?"

"A little."

"Okay." He gave me a reassuring smile. "And next time I invite a potential murderer to do an author event, I'll ask you first."

I sucked my tongue and gave him an evil eye.

But there was no time to fuss about it with my brother. I had an author event to set up for and hopefully lots of customers coming.

I'd gotten in twenty-five copies of Nicole D. Miller's book. I hoped I hadn't gotten too many or too few. I was in a panic either way.

Deacon Brown had dropped off a trunk-load of books while I was on a lunch break. One where I hadn't eaten lunch. (I'd inhaled a turkey and baby Swiss sandwich with lettuce, tomatoes and lots of black pepper that I'd gotten from Second Street Market while sitting behind the counter in between customers.) Instead, I had made a run to the bank to make sure I had enough money to make change for the book sales I was anticipating—hoping for.

Pete and I started setting up around five. Pete wanted to get an early start and get finished. Like Mama Zola, he didn't plan on attending the event.

I completely understood that.

I was starting to get excited about tonight even with the addition of Deacon Brown. And whatever Koby was cooking for the author event ramped up my excitement. My stomach grumbled as the sweet and savory smells streaming from the kitchen made me salivate.

Nicole, our featured author, arrived looking pretty with her frosty light pink lips contrasted with her dark skin and big, wide smile. She had on a mint green sweater and a multi-strand of white bobbles around her neck.

And opening the door and coming in behind her was Avery Moran—Koby's Capt'n Hook.

I smiled. Koby must have invited him. Involuntarily, I blew out a sigh of relief when my eyes fell on him.

"Hi," Nicole said. Seemingly just as happy at being in our little bookstore on the other side of the country from where she lived as I was to have her.

"Hi," I said back, beaming.

She'd walked in the door and stood there, her eyes roaming around the room as if it were her first time there. "I love your store."

"Thank you," I said, coming around the corner. Avery had wandered to the back of the store and pitched right in, helping Pete finish setting up chairs. He grinned from ear to ear when he saw Avery. "And we love having you here."

She walked over to the counter and inhaled. "What is your brother cooking? It smells so good."

"It's for the event tonight. He wouldn't tell me what he's making." I inhaled as well. "But he's definitely got biscuits baking and I'm sure he's filled our signature soul rolls with something delicious." I smiled. "I do know that he concocted a new sweet tea flavor, though."

"I love sweet tea," she said. "Can't wait to try it." She glanced back at the door and then at me. "How many people are we expecting tonight?"

People were already trickling in. I glanced over her shoulder and saw two women come in, read the poster-board I'd placed on a tripod near the door announcing the event and point in the direction of the event room.

Then I thought about what Lacey had told me. Her grandmother had spread the word and lots of people would come to support Deacon Brown. My own count had gone up to twelve, but I didn't want to disappoint Nicole with low numbers or get her too excited about high ones as I had no idea how the evening would pan out.

"Let's just see," I said, and moved on to the topic at hand. "Are you prepared for your reading? You need me to get anything for you?"

"All set," she said and held up a copy of her book, *Stories for the (Urban) Soul*. "Do you have any bottled water?" She licked her lips. "I'd like to have something to drink while I speak."

"Sure do. No problem," I said. "I'll get you one." I came from around the counter. "Let me walk you in the back and show you how we've got everything set up. I'll have Pete, my assistant, get you some water."

Before I gave her a rundown on how I planned for the evening to go, Koby rolled in with a cart of food, and like the Pied Piper of the kitchen he was, brought people in. The front door opened again. It seemed as if it was the draw of the food and not the author event that drew them near, but I didn't care. I was happy to have attendees. That was, until I saw Katy Erickson.

She slithered in and wandered around the bookshelves.

And just as I kept my eye on her once she arrived, she kept her eye on me.

What did she want? Following us around in her car and now she was here in the store.

"What is that?" Nicole was standing next to the food table watching Koby put the food out. "Strawberry shortcake?"

"It's more like a cassata cake made with biscuits."

"Oh," she said, her eyes lighting up. "It looks delicious."

When Koby looked up at her to smile his appreciation at her complimenting his food, I caught his eye and pointed to the stacks behind him. He turned, looked that way, then back at me. "Katy," he mouthed.

I nodded. Someone else we might get more information from later tonight.

Taking them from the bottom of the cart, he put out the mason jars we served our sweet tea in. When he'd finished up at the table, he rolled himself and his empty cart back toward me. "What does she want," he said, nodding his head toward our stalker guest.

It wasn't a question, but I answered it anyway. "I have no idea," I said.

"Well, maybe we should find out." He looked at me. "You want me to go over and talk to her?"

"No, I will," I said, getting up the nerve to confront her without giving it a second thought. As I approached her, another jangle came from the bell over the front door. It was Daniel Chow. His presence gave me more courage.

She had turned to see Chow come in just as I stepped into her personal space. She turned back to look me in the face.

"Hi, Keaton," she said. She was back to acting as if we were friends. "I see you invited backup." She nodded her head toward Detective Chow.

"Backup?" I frowned. "What are you planning to do?"

"Me?" She raised her eyebrows and put her hand on her chest. "I came to the author event. To buy books." She pointed to one on the shelf.

"Really?" The disbelief showed on my face.

"Well, you know." She gave a smirk. "And to see if the killer was going to show up."

"And you'll know the killer when you see them?" I said, letting my eyes meet hers.

"You never know," she said and tilted her head. She never let her gaze leave mine. "You could, at any time, come face-to-face with them. And it's only when they come after you that you realize who they are."

Chapter Thirty-Three

DEACON BROWN ARRIVED later than we had arranged for him to come. Good thing Pete had already gotten everything for him set up and ready to go. The sun had already gone down for the day and there was a nice, cozy warm glow around the store.

Moses came in followed by an entourage—Lacey, Mother Tyson (in a Sunday-go-to-meeting hat) and a few others I didn't recognize. They burst in with a lot of ruckus, wide smiles and eyes. And while he went straight to the table to check on his book display, Lacey, Mother Tyson and one other woman who'd come in with them lingered around the bookshelves. The others in the group that arrived with him hovered near the archway, eyeing the Biscuits side of our shop and licking their lips.

"Hi," I said, walking over to Lacey and her grandmother. "Did you come back for your books?"

Lacey blushed and glanced at her grandmother from under lowered eyelids. "Not in my budget today. I'm just here to support my cousin."

"That girl devours books," Mother Tyson said. "She doesn't finish the stack she has before she's off buying more."

I smiled. "I heard you had a lot to do with that."

Now it was Mother Tyson who blushed. "Yes, I try to guide women around me in the right direction. Getting lost in books is better than getting lost in other things." She gave Lacey a look. If I was left to interpret what "other things" she meant by her look, I would guess that Mother Tyson was referring to men. That made me remember that Lacey had been accused of seeing Austin James. "And I did spend a lot of time reading and talking with this one," Mother Tyson continued, pointing to Lacey.

Lacey shook her head and gave a small smile before eyeing a book on one of the shelves.

"Oh," she said, leaving our conversation. "I've been meaning to read this one." She headed off.

"Don't buy anything," Mother Tyson said. Then she turned and smiled at me. "You know," she said, "this was so nice of you to have my nephew come in as a featured author."

I smiled and nodded. He wasn't the featured author. Seemed like she'd gotten that wrong, too.

"I give teas for some of the women's groups at church," Mother Tyson continued. "You'll have to come to one sometime. Especially now. You know, to thank you for helping out Moses."

"Oh," I said, and grappled for my next words. I didn't want to say, "My pleasure," because I'd not been happy when Koby invited him. But I didn't want to be rude. "That isn't necessary."

"I know. I want to." She took my hand in hers. "He *thinks* he can write and him being here just means the world to him. I like seeing him happy."

I glanced over at him and he was that. Happy. He was

working the room, a big grin on his face, shaking every-one's hand.

"I spend most of my time helping the women in the church and often forget about him." She winked at me. "I just want to show my appreciation. So, the next time I plan something."

"Okay," I said. "That's nice of you."

"And Lacey will be so happy to have you there. She's always the youngest one there."

I laughed.

"Meanwhile," Mother Tyson said. "I'd like to ask a favor."

"Sure," I said.

"Lacey." She cut her eyes over to look at her grand-daughter. "Seems like Lacey has found her happy place here, so whenever you do see her, I was wondering . . ."

"Is there something wrong?" I asked.

"Well, ever since the day that"—she closed her eyes and blew out a huff—"that man died, she's been off. You know. Not herself."

I glanced over at Lacey. She was reading the inside flap of a book. She seemed fine to me, but I hadn't known her before Austin James' murder.

"Actually," Mother Tyson said. "She seemed troubled even before that. He did a number on her, you know."

"No. I didn't know," I said.

"I asked the pastor not to let him through the church doors, but he didn't listen."

Evidently.

"And you see how that turned out." She gave a firm nod. I raised my eyebrows. "I knew it wouldn't cause any-thing but trouble," she continued her assessment. "And look, it has." She pointed over to Lacey, who now had a couple of books cradled in the crook of her arm. "How can someone be so distraught over someone one day, boohooing with tears that wouldn't stop, and all smiles after that?"

Hmmmm . . .

"Something's not right with her."

I nodded. "So, what's the favor?"

"I was thinking you could talk to her. See if she's okay." She patted my arm. "You're such a nice girl. Seem to have it all together." She glanced around the store, then back at me. "Maybe you can see if something is bothering her. She won't talk to me."

"She won't?"

"No. Thinks I'm old. I don't understand." She ticked off the reasons. "I already had my mind made up about him."

"Him?"

"You know." She leaned in and lowered her voice. "Dead guy. Never mind I've helped so many other women."

"Oh," I said.

"I just want her to get past it. Him. And be happy." She looked past me. "Like Moses." She chuckled. "I better go over there with him. He's grinning so hard his face might crack."

I smiled as she left, making a pit stop, then she went over and spoke to Katy. They hugged just like they did in church.

What was that about?

They spoke for a moment and then they both turned and looked at me. Well, I felt like they were looking at me. I did glance behind me to see if that look could have been for anyone else. When I turned back, though, they were ending their conversation and Mother Tyson was headed over to speak with her nephew.

But, even without the image of them staring at me without reason, my mind was spinning. I glanced over at Lacey. I wanted to see if I could notice anything off about her. It *was* weird to be so distraught and then turn around and be all smiles.

I shook it off. It wasn't time to snoop. That time would come later. Afterward. I had an author event to put on. But my curiosity had been piqued. Koby and I hadn't ever followed up on Lacey crying the day Austin James was murdered. All we were ever told was that his wife had said something to her. But was that true? And what could she have said?

And then I cocked my head to the side. Come to think of it, we hadn't ever looked into Mr. James' ex-wife. Kim. A woman with the power to make Lacey cry. Over Kim's husband, it seems. Could Kim be a strong-enough catalyst to make Lacey commit murder, too?

Hmmmm . . .

My eyes searched the room for my brother. He had quickly dismissed Lacey as a suspect, saying that Kathryn Dionne's book, *Murder at the Holiday Bazaar*, wasn't anything like our real-life murder.

Maybe he had dismissed Lacey too quickly.

Maybe we needed to talk to Kim.

Then I cocked my head to the other side.

Maybe they were in it together. Two scorned women. I mean Kim must be scorned, right? She was the "ex" and evidently still bitter if she went after Lacey.

But maybe that was all a ploy. Make Lacey and her seem at odds so no one would suspect them. That might account for Lacey's demeanor. She only pretended to be distraught . . .

And then, Koby and I hadn't even discussed the conversation we witnessed at the pastor's house where Kim had said she'd "made it right."

What had that meant?

With that thought in my head, my eyes met with Koby's. He gave me a slight nod. He couldn't have known what I was thinking about. Still, I squinted my eyes and tried to send him a message, telepathically, telling Koby that we were going to have to look into Mrs. Kim James. Give her a ranking on our suspect list with a higher priority. Maybe even pairing her with Lacey . . .

And right with that thought, I heard a jingle over the door, and wouldn't you know, Kim walked in.

Looked like my telepathy skills were stronger than I thought.

Chapter Thirty-Four

KIM JAMES HAD on a pair of cobalt blue Mary Jane–style shoes that were almost an exact match to the blue in her skirt set. They had four-inch heels but she walked as if she were gliding over water. She wore a wide smile on her face, her lips painted a crimson red, her eyelids covered with a smoky shade of gray.

And right behind her came Pastor Lee.

And then, Rocko Jackson.

And right behind him was Brother Ron. The guy from Grace Spirit Revival.

I'd almost forgotten about him.

I leaned my head to the side. Hadn't he told me and Koby that he didn't know Rocko? That he'd only gotten a phone call from him?

I hadn't ever given a thought to questioning why Rocko had been the one to inform Brother Ron and why.

But it was Kim that got the majority of my attention. Only because she'd just come up in conversation.

Seeing her come to my bookstore made me even more

curious. Mother Tyson wasn't too keen on Kim and it made me wonder why she would be here for Deacon Brown—Mother Tyson's nephew.

I tried to watch to see if Lacey and Kim made eye contact, but I couldn't tell if they had. So I left my eyes on Kim.

She stood and waited for Pastor Lee while he spoke to someone I'd seen at the church.

Were they together? Why was she always with Pastor Lee?

I knew that Pastor Lee was married, although I hadn't ever formally met—or seen—his wife. I also knew that he and Austin James were good friends. Well, at least *had* been good friends. Austin, it appeared, was a womanizer. Was Pastor Lee like that, too?

Sometimes birds of a feather flock together.

But then I decided against that notion. Mother Tyson had gotten upset and had had a falling-out with Austin when they'd attended his church. The man even went so far as trying to date Lacey. I didn't think that Mother Tyson would attend a church of a man who was doing the same thing.

Maybe that was just Kim's cover. A way to get in. Get to Lacey, her possible partner in crime. Lacey, after all, was Pastor Lee's secretary. If Kim went to see the pastor, she'd have to run into Lacey and then they could talk. Make plans. Kill the man who had hurt them both.

I felt like I was in a plot from one of the books I sold . . .

"PUT AWAY YOUR cell phones and give an ear," I said, standing in front of the podium after giving my welcome speech. I was happy to be in the business I enjoyed and right now I was not going to let my mind get overrun with murder. I probably wouldn't have—no, I knew I wouldn't have—let my mind even wander to murder tonight if Koby hadn't told me that that had been his plan.

That was all I needed. First, I'd been obsessed with Katy waltzing in and then I conjured some conspiracy theory about Lacey and Kim.

I had shaken that off and was all smiles now as I spoke to the crowd.

"We want to take pictures," someone from the audience said.

"There will be plenty of time to take pictures later," I said.

While my brother and I snoop around to see if any of you were involved with murder . . .

"We just want you," I continued, "to enjoy our authors and their readings." I almost lost my smile when Ray Patton walked into the room. What did he want? He looked around before taking a seat all by himself. Had he been thinking that Mama Zola would be there? She wasn't going to come. After she heard the church members would be there, she'd bowed out.

Geesh, I thought. The entire crew from the night of the murder is here. I glanced around and looked for Pete. He was standing near the doorway. Hands folded in front of him. I wonder had he noticed.

And then I noticed everyone staring at me. I had stopped talking.

I smiled and tried to regain my composure. "Please," I said. "Let's give our authors your full attention."

Something I was going to have to concentrate on doing.

But the audience was back to being a crowd and not wondering what was wrong with me. Reluctance on their faces, I saw most of them comply and put their mobile devices away.

I made the introductions for Nicole. She was my featured author, and I wanted to make sure she got the most time presenting her book.

I wasn't going to slight Deacon Brown. I had read over his book after he dropped them off, and it wasn't bad. I was pleasantly surprised.

But I'd had the event all planned in my head and on paper before Koby brought him aboard. So I led with Nicole.

"I'll read a short excerpt from my book and then I'll take questions," Nicole said after she spoke briefly about her journey to becoming an author. She did such a good job, she had everyone's rapt attention by the time she opened up the book to read.

"The waitress," she started, *"a young hip thing who looked more like an actress than a college student (she was probably both), poured two glasses with water and lemon, then left them to view their menus. The menu was full of items Lisa could barely pronounce, even as a journalism major. The music was soothing and people of all shades were filling the room. She was impressed. If this was the first date, what in the world would he do on the second?"*

Nicole was just hitting her stride when the lights in the room went out. In fact, I turned around and looked. All the lights and the power were out in the store.

Everyone in the room gasped.

And there, to my surprise, were a lot of people in the room. It had filled up. Whatever siren Mother Tyson had sent out to help her nephew for his appearance at the Books & Biscuits author event had worked.

But those gasps swiftly turned to panicked screeches. And then everyone seemed to get up at once. At least that was how it felt because I couldn't really see anything.

People were bumping into one another, turning and bumping into chairs. Some even were knocked over.

"Keaton!" I heard Koby call out my name. Then I heard a crash. It came from the area where I knew he'd set up the food table.

"Oh no!" I screeched. "Koby!"

"I'm over here," he said.

"What happened to the lights?"

"I don't know," he said just as another crash came. "I'm checking on them."

"Get us some light!" someone yelled out.

"What is going on?" I recognized Nicole's voice.

"I'm so sorry, Nicole," I said and tried to make my way over to her.

"Hey, watch it!" I didn't know who said that, but I agreed. I was getting bumped from every side.

Then there was a flash of light from somewhere behind me. I turned toward it and walked only a couple of feet before running into someone else. Having a crowd had been a good thing. Now it made me worried someone was going to get hurt.

"Ouch!" And it looked like that someone was me. "Stop poking me," I said, turning around.

"You think you're so smart." The person spoke in a strained whisper that seemed to be coming from somewhere other than in front of me, so I turned around. It could have been anyone in the room, but it didn't sound like anyone I knew. Then they poked me again. Harder this time. Right in the area of my left kidney.

How could they even see me? I couldn't see a thing.

"Stop snooping around," they said, poking me with each word.

"Ouch!" I screeched again and tried to step away.

"Stay calm." A shout came over the commotion. That voice I knew, and I wished I were closer to him. Daniel Chow. And then there was a stream of light. He'd turned on the flashlight on his cell phone.

And then someone gave me a push. I'm guessing whoever had poked me. The push was hard enough to make me take a tumble over the chairs that were in front of me. I bumbled into a few people before tripping and nearly landing on the floor. I caught myself just before ending up facedown.

Others latched on to the idea of getting some light into the area with the help of cell phones. With it not being pitch black anymore, I turned to see if whoever had poked and pushed me was still around. There were lots of people around. No one looking suspicious as I scanned . . . Oh wait, I'd have to take that back. Katy was standing in a corner staring at me.

Chapter Thirty-Five

WE WEREN'T ABLE to get the lights back on. Koby discovered that someone had messed with the electrical panel outside.

That gave me the shivers.

Fooling around with electrical wiring had been what caused the demise of Austin James.

I had watched them come in. One by one. Katy Erickson. Lacey Bell. Kim James. Ray Patton. Moses Brown. Rocko Jackson. All possible suspects on my list in the murder of Austin James, but I hadn't been able to keep an eye on them as I started the event. I wasn't supposed to have to, according to Koby. No one would try anything in the crowd, and because we were supposed to be the ones scrutinizing folks afterward.

Now it seemed that one of them, at some point, had gone outside and rigged the panel to explode. Or short out. Or whatever they did that made the place go black.

"Why?" I said to Koby. "Why would someone do that to us. To our shop?"

He'd ushered the last of the guests out of our dark bookstore and café and came over to me with his flashlight. Avery Moran had stayed with us. He stood behind me lighting candles.

Even with the little light we had now, it didn't feel like we were going to be able to erase the darkness.

Koby hunched his shoulders. "I don't know," he said. "Because, unless someone stole something out of the store, nothing happened."

"You won't be able to tell if anything is missing until you get the lights back on," Avery said.

I could see Koby's face in the shadows. It didn't look he thought that a possibility.

"What's wrong?"

"Nothing," he said. "I was just thinking there was no need to cast the entire store and all of its occupants into the dark just to shoplift a book or two."

"Nothing other than me being poked and pushed."

"What?" Koby and Avery both said at the same time.

I told them what happened.

"You've got to be kidding me." They said that at the same time, too.

That made me take a pause. "I'm not," I said.

"Why didn't you say something?" Avery asked.

"Say what?" I asked. I did remember reacting to the poke. "I did kind of let out a sort of muffled scream."

"A muffled scream?" Koby held up his hands. "What is that?"

I held up my hands, mirroring his.

Koby said, "You could have said, 'Help. Someone is attacking me.'"

I turned around and looked at Avery. The soft light from the candle flickering in his face. Concern etched in it.

"I don't know," I said, turning back to Koby. I wanted to apologize to Avery. He'd come to help, but wasn't sure what to say. He couldn't have helped me if I had asked.

So, I looked at my brother instead and hunched my shoulders. "No one could see in the dark."

"They certainly saw you," Avery said.

"Yeah. I guess they did."

"I wonder how," Koby said.

"I did see a flash of light behind me before I got poked," I said.

"Seems like they stuck close to you, knowing the lights were going to go out."

"Whoever it was must be pretty good," I said. "Got out without anyone seeing them. Rigging the panel to go off at a certain time."

"Yeah, they were good. That James' crime scene was proof of that."

"You guys were snooping around the crime scene?" Avery asked.

"Only after the police had left," Koby said. "It was pretty elaborate. Coffee. Frayed wires." He shook his head. "And tonight they didn't disappoint."

"Disappoint?" I said, nearly shrieking. Koby reached out and rubbed my arm to calm me.

"I don't think they knew the exact time the panel would blow," Avery said. He'd taken a look at it with Koby when the lights first went black. "But they knew the ballpark and then they just stayed close to you." He looked at me.

"Who was around you?" Koby asked.

"I don't know. I was excited about the event. I had told myself no more snooping until after the event."

"No more?" Koby asked.

"Yeah. I mean I had let myself get distracted with Katy, Lacey and Kim."

"Ah," Avery said. "You think the murderer is a femme fatale?"

"They all were wronged by Austin."

"I thought Koby said you were worried about the deacon—what's his name?"

"Moses Brown," I said. "And I was—am. There just were so many people here tonight that are on my suspect list." I blew out a breath. "I'm surprised I could push them out of my mind at all. Or that I wasn't overcome with anxiety. Murder suspects everywhere I turned."

Avery chuckled.

"You had your Daniel Chow here to protect you," Koby said. "Where is he now?"

"He left," I said. Wasn't that obvious?

"You didn't tell him what happened?"

"We were so busy trying to smooth things over and get people out."

"That you forgot?"

I rubbed my back, then my knee. I'd been poked in one place, and scuffed up in the other when I fell over the chair.

"No. I didn't forget. I just . . ." I flapped my hands. I was upset over more than being poked and prodded. I hated that I'd gotten caught up in the murder business when I should have been minding my own business. I was worried that the fiasco may have hurt business. I knew Nicole and Moses had been upset. And I was worried because now it seemed someone had a warning for me.

"I wonder who did that and why," I said.

"They said it because they don't like you snooping around." Avery pursed his lips. "I agree with them."

"And you didn't recognize the voice?" Koby asked.

"No."

"So," Koby said, and I could see the workings in his sleuthing brain turning, "it must have been someone we haven't talked to."

"And someone I don't want to talk to. Ever." I wanted to move past that conversation. He wanted to talk murder. "What are we doing about the lights?" I asked.

"I got someone coming over."

"Who?" I frowned. "From the power company?" I glanced at the time on my phone. It was awfully late for them to make a service call without any downed wires or anything reported.

"Sort of," he said.

"Koby."

"I had that card, and he was available, you know."

"No. I don't know," I said, something inside telling me I needed to start worrying. "What card?"

"That we got from Lacey."

I raised my eyebrows. "Lacey?" I gulped. "You mean a card as in the business card Power Company Guy gave to Pastor Lee the day of the murder?"

"Exactly."

"You mean the guy we thought may have been involved in the murder?"

He frowned at me. "We haven't thought that in a long time," he said, a lack of understanding obvious in his voice.

"That makes him no less suspect." I raised my arms up and rolled back my neck. "Geesh, his partner in crime was here earlier. Maybe they planned this together."

"Partner?" He nodded once he realized what I meant. "You mean Rocko."

"Yes. I mean Rocko."

"I think we're good," he said.

"Oh. Yep." I nodded my head and then, in one not-so-coordinated movement, started shaking it from side to side. "No! But I *would* be good if my brother would stop inviting possible murderers to our place of business."

WE WERE NOT going to have lights in the store for at least four days. That was Power Company Guy's pronouncement after he took a look at the damage.

Four days of lost business. Maybe more. We couldn't even do a do-over of the author event because Nicole was leaving early Thursday morning.

Whoever had rigged our electrical panel really had done a job on it. The entire thing was going to have to be replaced and then reinspected.

Power Company Guy, whose name was Steve, came soon after everyone left. Flashlight in hand, he was in his own car and took more time talking with Koby, in my opinion, than he did examining the panel. And it wasn't even any talk that I thought was worthwhile. Not about the panel. Not about the murder. Just chitchat. If guys do that. And Avery, my other protector, joined right in, although soon after the verdict, he left. No more protection needed for the night.

Still, even the news about moving forward wasn't good. Nothing he could do that night. Not in the dark, and not without getting parts.

And then, to my surprise, but apparently not Power Guy Steve's, Rocko showed up. Steve acted as if he expected it. And then the three of them started with the chitchat.

I couldn't believe my brother. He was always about talking to people about the murder, and here he was not talking about it with two people we had questions about. Two that we'd considered suspects. And even though two thirds of my protection detail—Avery Moran and Daniel Chow—were MIA, I decided to jump in.

"Rocko," I said. "I thought you didn't know Brother Ron."

All three of them looked at me. Surprised, I guessed, that my statement had come out of nowhere. But it had been in my mind since I saw them walk in together for the author event.

"Brother Ron?" he asked.

"From Grace Spirit Revival," I said.

"Oh," he said, nodding. "The guy that came with the pastor, Kim and me?"

"Yes," I said, as if he didn't know. And I had questions about Kim next, just waiting for him to answer my first round of queries.

"Ronaldo."

I shrugged. "Okay. Ronaldo."

"Why would you think I don't know him?"

That stopped me. What was I supposed to say? That my brother and I had gone snooping around in your booth, found the phone number to the church and then went out and had a conversation about you with Brother Ron?

"I had heard about the church," my brother stepped in. "And had promised I'd stop by there and check it out." He was so good at coming up with a lie . . . uh . . . a cover story. "And we'd got to talking about what happened at Everlasting."

"And how did my name come up?" Rocko asked.

I looked at Koby, telling him to continue. Please.

"He said he hadn't too long ago gotten the call." Koby looked at Rocko, fight in his eyes as if everything he was saying was the truth. "From you about Austin James' death. "

"Oh yeah. Pastor Lee had asked me to call and let them know."

"Why?" I asked. Now that my brother had smoothed things over, and I didn't have to lie about anything, I had more questions.

This time Rocko shrugged. "I don't know. He just told me to tell whoever answered the phone that it was done."

"Done?" I asked. "As in dead?"

Rocko frowned. "Finished. Done like finished."

"What was finished? Or," I said, tilting my head, "*who* was finished?"

"I—I don't know." He turned up his mouth like he was thinking. "I'm sure it wasn't anything sinister like what you're thinking."

"What am I thinking?" I asked.

"That Pastor Lee had something to do with Mr. James' death."

"I didn't say that," I said.

"You were *thinking* it," he said.

He was right about that.

So, I said, "Maybe Pastor Lee and Kim James had something to do with it."

That made him frown.

I wanted to add, *"And you . . ."*

But I was too afraid to do that. Lights being out at our place made the entire corner dark. It was late out, and my and brother and I might be in the company of murderers or accomplices to murder.

I had to shake my head at myself. I didn't know when I'd gotten so gung-ho about taking part in finding the murderer or about speaking up. I was always the reluctant one. Maybe it had stemmed from all the shenanigans that had gone on in my bookshop.

"Those two are the nicest people," Rocko said. Then he squinted his eyes at me. "Wait. Are you the one who has been trying to act like a detective and solve the murder?"

I looked at Koby. I let him know it was his turn to talk again.

"We're just worried about our employee."

"You too?" Rocko said, raising his eyebrow at Koby.

"Pete?" That was Steve. "You talking about Pete?"

How'd Steve know Pete?

I swear. Everyone in this murder knew about each other and already knew each other.

"Yes," Koby said, not picking up on where I'd taken the line of questioning. "We don't want to see him wrongly accused of anything."

"But you can't go around accusing other people of the murder either," Rocko said.

"We haven't accused anyone," I said, getting back into the conversation. "We've just found that Austin James did a lot of wrong to a lot of people."

"Did he?" Rocko asked.

"Yes," I said. "Even to Pete. And that even led Pastor Lee to not want him—meaning Pete," I said to make clear who I was talking about, "back in the church."

"But Pete wasn't ever a member of the church." There went Steve again. Knowing things that he probably shouldn't have known.

"It wasn't Pete that he asked to leave," Koby said, stepping in and correcting my statement. "It was Mama Zola."

"Oh," Steve said. "Your foster mom."

"One of them," Rocko said. "Right?"

Well, aren't they chummy, I thought. Knowing all this stuff about Koby.

Maybe they knew we'd been snooping, too, and one of them was the one who poked me.

"But Pastor Lee made that right," Rocko said. "Your foster mom, Ms. Jackson, can come back to the church now." His brow furrowed, it seemed like he cared. "And Pete, too, even though he wasn't a member."

It wasn't Pastor Lee who'd made it right. At least not of his own volition. It had been Mother Tyson who made it possible for both of them to come back. Although Mama Zola hadn't acted as if she wanted to. Not even wanting to speak to Mother Tyson to say thanks for her help. And Pete, as far as I know, even with the history he had with the people at the church, had only gone there that day to support Mama Zola.

"Austin James was causing a lot of bad vibes all around," Steve the Power Company Guy said.

"But like the pastor said," Rocko said. "Now it's finished."

Chapter Thirty-Six

WE DIDN'T HAVE a business to run for the first Saturday in months. It didn't stop Koby from getting up early, though. And letting himself into my house.

We'd spent Wednesday's daylight hours straightening up around our shop. Things had been left in disarray after ending in darkness the night before. After we'd gotten everything back to normal and locked the place—including our electrical panel—up tight, we headed our separate ways.

Koby left there to go to check on Mama Zola, who hadn't been in the store for a couple of days. I went home and put on my MY WEEKEND IS BOOKED T-shirt and curled up with a copy of something other than my usual mystery book. I didn't even want to read about another whodunit. I had read until nearly eleven thirty, not worrying about getting enough sleep. I had planned on spending my Saturday just as lazily as I'd spent my Friday evening.

Remy was lying in front of the back door when I came

down the steps, following the aroma of fresh coffee. I wasn't a coffee drinker, but the smell of it sure was an eye-opener.

Roo was lying next to Koby's beautiful yellow Lab, just as content as if she had her catnip-filled cat scratcher.

Koby was there to get my fur in a dander and tax my brain.

"I want to talk," he said when he saw me emerge into the kitchen.

Of course, in short order, I found it wasn't Books & Biscuits he wanted to talk about.

It was murder.

I pulled out a kitchen chair and Koby set a large, wide-mouth cup filled with black coffee in front of me.

"No, thank you," I said and let out a yawn. "You know I don't really drink coffee. And plus that looks lukewarm."

"I'm not done yet." He went back over to the counter and picked up a tall oil drizzle bottle.

"What's that?" I asked.

"What do you smell?" he asked as he poured it into the dark brown brew.

I took a whiff. "Mmmm. Caramel."

"Anything else?" He sat the bottle on the table and went to the fridge.

"Vanilla," I said, leaning over it.

"All homemade," he said.

"Sounds divine," I said, ready to take a go at the coffee-based drink. I wrapped my hands around the cup and brought it up to my lips.

"No," he said. He sat a tall glass of ice he'd retrieved from the freezer on the table, took the cup from me and poured it over the cubes.

"Oh my," I said.

"So you drink coffee now?"

"I am certainly going to drink that." The coffee syrup

had made it a creamy, amber-colored drink that looked so inviting. I pulled it close to me and took another whiff.

"Go ahead," he said. "Taste it."

"Oh my," was all I could say after taking a big gulp.

"So we have to determine who killed Austin James."

He would have to ruin the moment for me.

"Can we talk after breakfast?" I looked around the kitchen. A glass bowl of batter sat on the countertop next to a large shopping bag that he'd brought from home. I knew what was in that. An iron. "Waffles?" I grinned. "Are we having Belgian waffles?"

"Yes. And bacon."

"Of course, bacon," I said. Shifting in my seat. Ready to get comfy and eat.

"But we have to talk at the same time."

"Why?" I whined.

"So much has been going on and now they are after our shop."

"And me. They are after me, too, remember," I said, taking another sip of my drink. "Mmmm. I'll probably need more of that." I pointed to my glass.

"No problem," Koby said and pulled his waffle iron out of the plastic shopping bag. "And of course, I wouldn't forget about what happened to you."

"I think we should, in our morning discussion, put a big emphasis on what to do to keep me safe," I said.

"Agreed." Koby started working his waffle-cooking magic, and the sizzle of the griddle made my stomach grumble. "So? Austin James?"

"He was always causing trouble for people," I said. "Seems like to everyone he was around."

"I agree," Koby said. "First, for the people from the trading firm."

"Right."

"Like Pastor Lee," Koby said, "a person we didn't ever really get to talk to."

"I know you wanted to," I said, a hint of sarcasm in my voice. "But his only involvement, I think, was that he was glad to have Austin James out of the way." I nodded. "I think that's what he meant by 'it's done.'"

"What?" Koby asked. "James's reign of terror?"

"Exactly," I said.

"Yeah. I still wish we'd talked to him." Koby gave me a smirk. "And then there was that other guy that was named in the paper."

"Who?" I said. I took a sip of my iced coffee and tried to think. It had been so long since we'd read that newspaper article about them getting fired, then indicted, that not much other than the crime stuck in my mind.

Koby shrugged. "I can't remember his name. But he was probably someone we should have looked into."

"Why?" I said. As if we hadn't looked into enough people. "He, whatever his name is, had no connection to the potluck dinner the church had."

"But he had a history with Austin James."

"Yeah. It was what has gotten Pete named and put at the top of the suspect list. A connection he had with the man more than ten years ago."

"Exactly," Koby said.

"But"—I held up a finger—"Pete also was at the dinner with Mama Zola."

"Okay. Got you," Koby said. "And I guess that's the best way to narrow our search down."

"Sounds good." My stomach grumbled again and Koby laughed.

"You've got a waffle coming now."

"Sorry," I said and rubbed my belly. "All this talking is too much work and is making me hungry." Although if Koby hadn't been at my house cooking, I would have probably skipped breakfast.

He practically rolled his eyes at me. "We've only just started the conversation," he said.

He sat a giant waffle in front of me, grabbed a tub from the refrigerator, dug me out a scoop of whipped butter and plopped it on top. It started to melt right away and so did my salivary glands.

"Where's the syrup?" I looked around. "And I need a fork."

"I got you."

He grabbed silverware out of a drawer, closing it with a bump of his hip. He handed me a knife and fork and slid a bottle of maple syrup across the table.

"So," he said, picking up where he'd left off, "they'd be the only suspects from his time at the trading firm."

"Who?" I asked, my mouth stuffed with waffle. "And where's the bacon?" I hadn't even smelled any cooking.

"Oh yeah," he said. "Bacon." He grabbed a pack out of the shopping bag the waffle iron had been in and got my cast iron skillet from the shelf. "Pete and Pastor Lee."

"Pete and Pastor Lee?"

"Trading firm suspects."

"Right." I nodded. "Except Pastor Lee had already quit Hatton & Lyndale when Austin James started siphoning money."

Koby took his eyes off the bacon and looked at me. "So that only leaves Pete?"

"Mmm-hmm . . ."

"That's not good."

"What about the clients that lost money when he was handling their business?" I said.

"That's our second. First, the people who worked at the trading firm. Second, those that lost money because of him."

"Okay," I said.

"That included some church people, too, didn't it?"

"I think so," I said. The sizzling bacon was making it hard to concentrate.

"They could have easily held a grudge."

"A long grudge, but yes."

"No longer than the people he worked with."

"True," I said. I cut another piece of waffle and dragged it through the gooey syrup.

Koby turned off the stove and put the bacon on a paper towel. I reached out my hands, and he smiled and handed me the plate. "We'll have to figure out who they were," he said, pouring more batter onto the griddle.

I frowned.

"Not every client he had, right?" I worried about my brother when it came to investigating. He liked to be excessive. "Just the ones that were part of his church. Because he had already started the church before he left, right?"

I should have been keeping a notebook. I was not good at keeping up with names and all the things we'd found out. This murder was like a spiderweb, everything, in this case *everyone*, connecting together. Only it didn't make for such a pretty sight.

"Yes, he had," Koby said, pouring more batter onto the hot griddle. "And that was a megachurch."

"Yes. A megachurch. Thousands of people." The syrup was starting to churn in my stomach. I shook my head. "I don't know, Koby," I said. "That is so many people. I don't know how we'd find out which church members were also clients."

"Easy," Koby said. "We'll ask Pete."

I didn't like that answer. We were trying to help exonerate him. It would only seem reasonable that he'd point the finger at someone else.

"And after the job connection, then matching clients with church members, third, we'll just match church members."

"That's a lot of matching." I dropped my fork on my plate and pushed it away.

"And don't forget people like his wife," Koby said. "And all the women he was dating."

"All?" I couldn't remember anyone whose name we knew except Lacey and possibly Katy. Although I got the impression there were many more. "That would leave our list of suspects three miles long."

"What do we have so far?" Koby asked.

"A whole lot of nothing," I said.

"I mean suspects. Motives."

"I think we should go the other way." I took a slice of bacon from the place and took a bite.

"The other way?"

"Yes. You know, work backwards." I stuffed the rest of the slice in my mouth and wiped my hands on a napkin. "Figure out who in the church now was around back then."

"By 'church,' you mean both Everlasting and Grace Spirit Revival?"

"Uh. No," I said. "Why would I mean Grace Spirit Revival?"

"Because they got a phone call saying it was 'done.'"

"Oh yeah. Right." I raised an eyebrow. "Unless the killer, or should I say *killers*, were really the people telling us that story."

"Steve and Rocko," Koby said.

"Yep." I pulled the plate of bacon closer to me and took another piece.

"Steve has a connection to nothing," Koby said. "Not the trading firm. Not the megachurch. Not Everlasting. And he is not a woman."

"Rocko has a connection to Everlasting."

"And he's close to Pastor Lee, it seems," Koby said.

"But that's it."

"So maybe they are not the killers."

I thought about the night of the author event. It seemed like it had been longer than two days ago.

"Well, if you asked me who the killer might be . . . ," I said.

"I am asking," Koby said.

"I would narrow it down to three people."

"Really," Koby said and raised an eyebrow. "Who?"

"Lacey, Kim and Katy."

"You think a woman did this?" Koby said.

"A woman scorned," I said.

Chapter Thirty-Seven

WE HAD GONE through a boatload of suspects. Never getting much further than questioning them. Still I felt like we knew a lot. Enough to piece our mystery together. In my mind, I'd done that already.

"What about the ability to use electricity to kill someone?" Koby asked.

"You think a woman couldn't do that?" I asked, disbelief or concern likely written into my face. Maybe both.

He practically rolled his eyes at me. "You know I didn't mean that. I'm just saying none of them have any electrical background. Like Deacon Moses."

"True, but most people know that water, or in this case coffee, doesn't mix well with electricity."

"True," Koby said.

I blew out a breath, getting ready to say something I wouldn't have thought on Tuesday. "Deacon Brown didn't do it," I said.

"Guessed you'd say that, seeing you think it's a woman."

"You don't think it is?" I asked.

"I'm still piecing everything together," he said. "Tell me, though, why else you ruled him out."

"He was too busy grinning at the author event to have had anything devious on his mind."

"He was pretty happy to be there."

"He was," I said. "Even Mother Tyson commented on it." I sighed. "I think I am going to have to invite him back. Let him have his time at the podium."

"Okay, back to murder," Koby said. Business talk should be number one in his train of thought. It wasn't. At least not today.

"And I know what you're thinking," he said.

"No you don't," I said.

"You're thinking that I'm not thinking about our business. But I am." He held up a hand to stop me from saying anything. "This is hurting our business, so it is important."

He was right.

"So, back to murder," he said again.

"Okay. Where were we?" I looked at my brother and he raised an eyebrow. "Oh. I know. A woman and electricity."

"Right," Koby said.

"I was thinking," I said, "that maybe the killer didn't need to know much about electricity. The thing to know was that he had a pacemaker."

"Because even if the killer didn't get it right, the jolt would be enough to mess with the device."

"Enough to kill him." I nodded my head, harder than intended, but that was exactly what I was thinking. "And with that said"—I blew out a breath—"Kim is probably the one who did it."

"The wife?" Koby said.

"Yes. You can't see that?" I squinted my eyes, now feeling unsure of my conclusion.

"No." He shook his head. "I mean, yes." He nodded. "I can see that."

"Because she was the only one who had a connection to Austin James from the time he worked at Hatton & Lyndale to the time he was trying to make a comeback and hanging out at Everlasting Missionary Church."

Koby thought about that for a moment. "You're right. Why haven't we talked to her?"

"I don't know," I said. "I was thinking I wanted to do just that the night of the author event."

"And you didn't say anything to me about it?"

"We got all turned around," I said.

He glanced at his phone. "It's still early. Maybe we could find her and—"

"We don't even know where she lives," I said. "Where she works, a phone number. Nothing."

"We could find that out," Koby said. "We could Google her. We could ask someone at the church."

"Like who?" I said, just as my phone rang. It startled me. I rarely talked on it, always keeping it charging on the kitchen counter.

"Hello," I said, having to put our conversation on hold.

"Hi," came the voice on the other end. "This is Mother Tyson."

"Hi, Mother Tyson," I said. I could see out the corner of my eye how Koby's face lit up.

"You can ask her," he said and gave my arm a push. His voice lowered. "Ask her about where we can find Kim."

Holding the phone away from my mouth, I told him to shush. "I can't ask her that," I whispered.

"Ask me what?" Mother Tyson said. "Who are you talking to?"

"Hi," Koby said, leaning across the table to get closer to where I held the phone. "This is Koby."

"Hi, Koby," Mother Tyson said. She had warmed to him since that first day we'd met.

"Keaton wanted to talk to Kim and was wondering if you knew how to get in touch with her."

"Kim?" she said.

There was no stopping my brother. I put it on speaker.

"Yes," I said, giving my brother a look that said I'd get him later. "Kim James."

"You want to talk to her about what?"

"About shoes," Koby said. The look on his face showed that he was having a good time.

"What are the two of you up to now?" Mother Tyson said.

"Nothing," Koby said. "At least not me. I'm just trying to help my sister. She's the one always nosing around in other people's business."

I swatted a hand at him.

"Do you know how to get in touch with her?" I asked.

"Oh." She paused for a moment. "I might see her to-day," she said. "That's why I called."

"Oh?" I said.

"I'm having a tea, a small, impromptu get-together this afternoon. I wanted to invite the two of you."

"A tea?" Koby said, turning up his nose.

"Yes. I'd already asked Keaton to help me out with something." She paused. "You remember, Keaton?"

"Yes," I said, then mouthed "Lacey" to my brother.

"I can't come," Koby said, "but Keaton would be happy to stop by."

"Aww," she said. "I'm sorry you can't make it. Are you sure?"

"Yes," Koby said. "I have to meet the electrician at the store to work on getting our electricity back up and running."

"I'm so sorry about that," Mother Tyson said. "I heard it may have been sabotage."

Church gossip. I shook my head. Doesn't take long to get around. I was sure Rocko had told her—and probably a whole host of other people—about it.

"What time?" Mother Tyson continued. "You may still be able to stop by."

Koby's eyes widened. He hadn't thought he'd need to answer to his excuse (read "lie") of why he couldn't attend. I wasn't even sure Steve had gotten all the parts we needed or was going to come to work on a Saturday.

"I just need to be available all day," Koby said.

I jumped in to help my brother out.

"I'll be there," I said. "What time?"

"Around two. Is that good?"

I glanced at the clock.

"That'll be fine," Koby said, speaking for me.

"OMG," I said after I'd hung up. "Why can't you go, too?"

"I am not doing a tea thing. Isn't it for women only?"

"No," I said. "Don't you remember Pastor Lee had it at his house before?"

"Oh. Yeah. I do remember that." He shook his head. "But this one is not at his house. Plus, I don't want to be nice to the people at that church."

"What? Why?"

"They threw Mama Zola out."

"No they didn't." I frowned. "And Mother Tyson, who is giving the tea, got her back in. And Pete."

"Aren't you supposed to be talking to Lacey?" he asked, looking for another excuse not to go.

"Yeah. So?"

"So, then I'd be left alone with all those women while you were off with her. No thank you."

"It might be other guys there."

He gave me a look that said that was doubtful.

"So you're not going?"

"I'll take you. Pick you up. You just stay long enough

to find out about Kim. You'll be around enough people that you'll be safe."

"You worried about my safety?"

"Always."

"And what about Lacey? Don't talk to her?"

"Of course talk to Lacey," he said. "I do feel bad for her. I guess Austin James really did a number on her heart."

"Maybe I could get my mother to talk to her, too."

"There's a good idea," Koby said. "After you get info on Kim."

"You don't expect me to interrogate her all by myself, do you?" There was a frightening idea.

"No. Just get her number. Or where we can find her. We'll talk to her together."

"Oh. Okay."

"And be careful around her," he said. "I do think you're right. We might have been overlooking her all along."

Chapter Thirty-Eight

KOBY PULLED UP in front of the house and put the car in park.

He had waited while I showered and put on something I thought would be appropriate for a tea. I wasn't sure what that was. Or even if I should wear a hat. Or a fascinator. Not that I had one. I opted for a mid-calf-length flowered skirt, flats and a light-knit sweater set, only I left the cardigan off. I figured I might need it down by the water, but for now, the one layer was good.

Surveying myself in the mirror, I looked like I did most any other day.

Oh well.

He and Remy had migrated from the kitchen to the car by the time I was ready. I climbed in, talking fast, still trying to convince him to come with me, even for a little while. But he wouldn't budge. I laid my cardigan in the back next to Remy and pulled down the sun visor to make sure my hair looked alright, and before I knew it, we were there.

Seemed like Koby wanted to hurry and get rid of me.

"There aren't any cars around," Koby said as I opened the door to get out. Remy pulled his head out of the window and stuck it between the seats. I gave it a rub.

"I'm early," I said and looked at the clock on his dashboard. "See?" I pointed to it.

"Still seems like people should already be arriving," he said.

"Well, I can use the time before anyone else gets here to talk to Lacey," I said. "She lives here, remember? Then I'll be free to see what I can get out of Kim."

"Remember, you don't have to try to interrogate her without me. Just find out where we can find her. Stay safe."

"Okay."

He didn't need to tell me that twice.

Lydia Tyson and her granddaughter's house was big and charming. A large porch with white rails, a yellow door with a silver knocker.

I opted for the doorbell.

"Come on in," Mother Tyson said, pulling the door open as wide as the grin on her face.

"Hi," I said. "I see I'm a little early." I looked around, but there wasn't another person in sight.

"They are always late," she said. "I doubt if any of them will be on time for their own funeral."

I laughed.

"So sorry your brother couldn't come," she said. We were standing in the foyer. A room the size of my living room. "I was looking forward to hearing all about what he was up to and whatever it was that went wrong with your electrical panel."

"To be honest, he was worried about being the only guy here."

"Oh." She chuckled and waved a hand. "Men come all the time to my teas. If nothing more than to spend time with the ladies." She smiled at me. "C'mon," she said. "I'll show you the real reason I wanted to have him here."

She led me down the center hallway to the back of the house. Off to the right was a wall of glass doors. Beyond it a big backyard and a pier that led out to beautiful blue waters.

"Oh, nice," I said, my eyes drifting in that direction.

"That's where we'll have the tea," she said. "Out back."

"Oh no," I said, rubbing my arms. "I forgot my sweater in Koby's car."

"Lacey will have something for you," she said. "We'll ask her."

"Where is she?" I asked.

"She had to run to the store for me. I am always forgetting something." She tugged on my arm. "We're going this way."

I followed her into a huge, chef-style kitchen with white cabinets, a farmhouse sink, and beautifully tiled floors.

"This is a really nice kitchen," I said.

"Yes, but a bit too much for me nowadays," she said. "I can't stand and get around like I used to."

"You do pretty well from what I've seen."

She seemed to blush. "Thank you." She clasped her hands together. "So this is what I want to show you."

She had lined up on the counter about six mason jars of a red liquid. They reminded me of what we served our sweet tea in at Biscuits.

"What?" I asked.

"I tried to make your brother's pomegranate lime sweet tea." She looked at me. "From the other night."

"Oh," I said and let out a chuckle of my own. "You got some of it before the lights went out?"

"Yes, I did," she said. "And it was so good, I just had to try it."

"You know," I said, glancing over at the stove, "when you said a tea, I was thinking teacups and hot liquids."

She laughed. "That's so old-fashioned." She went over to a corner and pulled out a large silver tray. "I really wanted your brother to try this to see if I got it right. Do you know his recipe?"

"No. I am not any good in the kitchen."

"Don't put yourself down now, your bookstore is very nice."

"Thank you," I said, beaming.

"Here," she said. "Let's get the glasses on the tray and take it out back. You don't mind helping me get things set up, do you?"

"No," I said. "Of course not. I'll be happy to help."

Mother Tyson started putting the glasses on the tray. "So now tell me what this talking to Kim James is all about. You know I'm not too fond of her."

"I know you're not. And I don't really know her, but I wanted to ask her some questions."

"Questions?" She pointed to the tray. "Can you carry that for me?"

"Sure," I said. I picked up the tray, not as heavy as I thought it would be, although it would've been nice to have a rolling cart like Koby's. I waited for her to lead the way.

"What kind of questions do you have for Kim?" Mother Tyson asked. She walked back through the way we came and opened one of the glass panel doors that led outside.

"You know we—my brother and I—have been trying to help Pete."

The back wasn't as nice as it seemed through the glass. It was unkempt with spots of tall grass and weeds popping up everywhere. I didn't like walking through it.

"Yes, she said, "that's very commendable of you."

"We just don't want to see him wrongly accused of something."

"Again."

"Right." Then my brow furrowed. "You knew about Pete. What happened to him before?"

"Before what?" She pointed to a table set up near the pier. A pier that had boards that didn't seem too secure and some that were even rotted out. "Sit it there," she said.

"You're having the tea back here?" I asked. It wasn't half as nice as the rest of the house.

"Yes. I know. My guy didn't come to take care of the yard this week."

I remembered she said it was impromptu, so the gardener might have not had time to come. But the deck was a hazard. But I took my mind off that and back to her questions.

"You think that Kim may have some information on Pete?" she asked.

"I'm not sure. But my brother and I agree that she might have some information on the murder."

"I was afraid of that." She drew in a breath. I knew she didn't like us lurking around, as she called it. "What kind of information? Like who the murderer is?"

"Or maybe she's the murderer." I knew I shouldn't have said it as soon as it came out of my mouth. Accusing her without any proof. But I'd said it and couldn't take it back now.

"Oh." Mother Tyson seemed to be thinking about that. "What makes you think that?"

"She has known him since he worked at the trading firm," I said, figuring I could spill the beans with her since I'd already told her why I wanted to see Kim. "She knew all the wrong he'd done cheating people. She knew how he'd been having affairs with different women at the church."

"And with some not at the church," Mother Tyson chimed in.

"Right," I said. "And she knew he had a pacemaker."

"Oh. Right."

"And all those things put together make her a prime suspect in my book."

"I see," she said.

"The only problem, so my brother thinks although he didn't say it exactly, was that we don't know if she knows anything about electricity."

"Electricity?"

"She had to know how to rig the coffee machine."

"And the electrical panel at Books & Biscuits."

"Right," I said. "But I don't want to go accusing her of anything. We just thought maybe we could talk to her."

"And ask if she was the killer."

Hearing it said by someone else did make it seem like a ludicrous plan. Of course she wouldn't admit to being one.

"No," I said. "We would just tell Acting Chief Ross what we know."

"I was surprised he wasn't there the other night. Keeping an eye on Peter."

"Pete?" I said. "He wasn't there." But as I thought about it, Ross should have probably been there. "But now that you've said it, it might have been a good idea to have invited him."

"Oh, enough about murder," she said and waved a hand at me. "I want you to taste the tea and let me know what you think." She handed me a glass. "If it isn't up to snuff, I've got a backup one, bottled. No one will be the wiser."

"Sure," I said, taking the glass from her and taking a sip. "Mmm."

"You like it? My nephew really raved about it. That's what made me want to give it a try."

"Yes. I like it. It's a little sweet, though," I said.

"I can put a little more water in the next batch. Maybe this one is too concentrated."

"No. I like it," I said and took a gulp of it. It wasn't as good as my brother's, but not many people were as skilled as he was making things that tasted good.

"Well, drink up," she said. "I want to be telling the truth when I tell everyone how much you enjoyed it."

I took another gulp. "Everyone is really late," I said.

"Yes, they are," she said. "And I just hate that. Going through all the trouble of getting everything ready and no one shows up."

"I'm here."

"Yes, you are," she said and nodded at the glass, telling me to drink more. So I did.

"Do you need me to help you with the food?" I asked. I hadn't seen or smelled any while we were in the kitchen, but she may have had it catered.

"No." Her smile was tight. "I don't need any help. Thank you."

I took another sip and turned to look out toward the lake. I remembered thinking I wished I had my sweater and then wondered where Lacey was. And then the dock seemed to be moving. I held a hand up to my head.

"I'll have to make more tea," I heard Mother Tyson say. "This is too sweet."

I turned to look at her, but I couldn't. I was feeling dizzy. Things were blurry and seemed confused like I couldn't think straight.

"Mother Tyson," I said. "I don't feel good."

"Oh no," she said. I could see the outline of her coming toward me. "Let me give you a hand."

"No!" I swatted at her hand. I didn't know why, but I was feeling agitated. "I can make it." I tried to calm my voice. "I just need to sit down for a minute." I huffed out some air and stilled myself to stop the swaying.

"This way," she said.

"Which way?"

"I have chairs over by the dock. The breeze might help you feel better."

I didn't remember seeing any chairs by the dock, but at that moment I wasn't trusting my mind to do anything correctly.

"Thank you," I said. "And sorry about snapping at you."

"No worries," she said. "I just wish you weren't so nosy. Sticking your nose into things that don't concern you."

"What?" I said. Her voice sounded familiar, but not from how she usually talked.

"You should have minded your own business."

It was the voice from Tuesday night. The voice of the person who poked me.

"Wait," I said. "You know about electricity." That piece of information popped up clearly in my foggy brain.

"I know a little about a lot of things. Electricity. Yes. And things like drowning. I only wished I could have gotten your brother here to try my tea. I had it all planned out."

"Drowning?" I asked. That, too, registered in my brain clear as day.

"Yes. I wish that I'd paid more attention to getting this rickety dock fixed."

"Is it broken?"

"How else did you fall off of it?"

"What?"

And then I knew for sure it was the same person I had encountered the night of the author event, because the push she gave me felt exactly the same.

Chapter Thirty-Nine

I REMEMBER THAT I felt like I was floating. It was quiet. And peaceful wherever I was. And I didn't feel dizzy anymore. I felt calm.

Until I heard barking. I found it to be very annoying and I just wanted it to stop.

"Woof. Woof."

It was making the dizziness come back.

Splash!

And then there was yelling right before I felt the collar of my sweater tighten around my neck. I was being pulled somewhere. The sunlight in my eyes.

And then another *splash!*

"Good boy. Good boy."

It was Koby.

What was he doing? Who was he talking to?

"I got her now," he said. "Go watch that bad lady."

And that was how I almost died. Again.

* · * · *

AND AGAIN I figured out who the murderer was too late.

Mother Lydia Tyson. A woman scorned.

There wasn't any tea. She'd only said that to lure me and my brother over. She'd spiked the tea with insulin (from her own private stash), knowing it would metabolize in our bodies probably before being detected. Her story would have been that we had drowned. One trying to save the other one.

And my Hercule Poirot brother, when he came back to drop off my sweater, had no idea I was in danger. Or that Mother Tyson was anything other than a woman sharing a British tradition with a gaggle of Baptist church folks.

Thank goodness Remy did.

Well, we couldn't ever be sure that he knew about Mother Tyson's role in it all, but he knew something was wrong with me.

According to Koby, while he stood patiently waiting at the front door with sweater in hand, Remy bounded off around the house and would not stop when commanded to.

Thank goodness.

He dove right into the water from that pier and grabbed me by my sweater.

The yelling? My brother screaming at Mother Tyson. You would think he would have yelled later and come and got me first.

Lydia Tyson had a long history with Austin James. She'd lost money from her retirement funds in one of his schemes at Hatton & Lyndale. She'd belonged to his megachurch, where he'd spurned her nephew and dated her granddaughter, whose heart he'd broken. And it seemed she had counseled many women, including Katy Erickson, after he had had his way with them.

And, like I remembered right before my fall, she knew all about electricity.

Per her statement, told loudly as she was led out by Acting Chief Ross, she was tired of James. She'd had enough. And then he was going to try it again at Everlasting.

"I should have killed Calvin Lee, too, for letting him in the door!" Koby told me she'd said. Balling his fist up to imitate her. He said that it took two men to drag her out and get her into a police car.

I believed him. She sure could handle me.

"IT'S GOING TO take about two thousand dollars to get you back up with power," Steve said. We were standing outside Books & Biscuits staring at the electrical panel. Steve had everything he needed to get the job done. He just needed our approval. "And that's with the discount I'm giving you."

Koby gave a low whistle and looked at me. It had been a whole week since the incident and we still didn't have any lights.

I shrugged. "Acting Chief Ross said we might could get victims of crime money," I said. "That might help."

"I don't even know why she did this," Koby said. "What was she trying to accomplish?"

"Looks like Mother Tyson just wanted to give you a warning," Steve said.

"One that you didn't heed." It was Detective Chow. Or should I say Police Chief Chow. He'd been installed as the head law enforcement agent in Timber Lake while I'd lain around for a couple days after almost dying.

And right behind him came Mama Zola and Pete.

"They never listen," Mama Zola said. "And every time something bad happens."

"I'm so sorry that happened to you," Pete said. "I feel like I'm to blame."

"You're not," Koby said, and although he didn't let me answer for myself, those were the words I would have said.

"Not at all," I added.

"Boy, did I pick a church to belong to," Mama Zola said.

"It's not your fault either," Koby said.

"Right," Police Chief Chow said. "The fault lies in these two because they don't listen."

"I try to listen," I said. "But Koby . . ."

"Put the blame on me," he said. "Ha!"

"Yes. On you," I said. "We can't go looking for murderers. It doesn't end well."

"Next time," he started to say.

"Next time?" we all, including Steve, said, practically screeching.

"Yes. Next time. If there is a next time, we'll have to figure out who the murderer is faster before they can get the drop on us."

"You mean *on me*," I said. "Soon I'm going to be so traumatized I'm going to have to schedule time on my mother's couch."

"Or come to church with me and pray a lot," Mama Zola said. "That is, when I find a church to go to, because I'm definitely not going back to that one."

"Amen," Pete said. "Amen."

Epilogue

BOOKS & BISCUITS was finally opening again. Electricity back on and everything secure. No one would be able to tamper with it again. At least not as easily.

Koby came by, with Remy, to pick me up. An hour earlier than he needed to, excitement bubbling in my bell, I was up and ready to go. Both of us were excited about getting back to business.

And it seemed so was Pete. At least that was what I thought when I saw him standing in front of the store when we walked up.

"You're here ea—" I couldn't finish my sentence. Pete grabbed us both and squeezed. "Oh my," I said.

"Thank you. Thank you," he said and buried his head between our shoulders. "I know I wasn't much help and if you hadn't have helped . . ."

"It's okay, man," Koby said. "That's what friends are for."

Pete pulled away from us and looked at Koby then at me. "Are we friends?"

I smiled. "Of course we are," I said. I thought about that. It probably surprised him, since I'd been the one reluctant to hire him. But he'd turned out to be a great employee, even with all of his quirks.

"Thank you," he said and went in for another hug. Koby and I stepped back.

"It's okay, Pete," Koby said, chuckling. "We're going to need our breath to work today and your hugs are squeezing it all out of us."

"Oh. I'm sorry."

"Let's get to work," Koby said, smiling.

And work we did. The day was busy. Lots of people stopping in, it seemed more interested in what happened than in books and food. But Koby knew how to change their direction. The smells coming out of his kitchen were so good, it made the people stop and stay for a while. They bought food, of course, and even some books.

And then right after Pete went out for lunch, Daniel Chow showed up.

Election over, we had all known he was a shoo-in, but what really surprised me was who he came in with. Katy.

"Welcome to Books & Biscuits," I said and put on a smile. I was happy to see Chow. I wasn't sure what Katy was up to, but I wasn't going to say that to her.

"I see that look on your face," she said.

I chuckled. Looked like I wouldn't have to tell her what I was thinking. It was all over my face.

"I came because I wanted to apologize to you."

"To me," I said, looking around. "What for?"

"For the lying and the spying." She tucked her head and picked at her fingernail. "Coming to your house. Following you." I raised my eyebrows. "Yeah. I was just trying to save myself and I thought I could get you to help me."

"Help you do what?"

"Hi." Koby came through the archway just as she was

starting to answer my question. He walked over and shook
Chow's hand and gave Katy a look, I'm sure, that mir-
rored mine.

"I was just apologizing—" Katy was saying when I
interrupted.

"Explaining," I said.

"Yeah." She smiled at me. "Explaining."

Koby just nodded, letting her speak.

"I lied about being a reporter." She drew in a breath.
"Soon to be *ex*–Acting Chief Ross had me on his radar."

"As the murderer?" I didn't want to say, "So did I."

"Yes. He'd seen me on the video. And he found out
how Austin James had manipulated me and how I suffered all that mental anguish at his hand. Perfect reason
to kill him."

My brother and I both nodded, not sure what to say.
Chow had a blank look on his face. I was sure one he
perfected as a police officer and maybe because he knew
the whole story.

"I figured if I worked with the two of you, I would
clear my name." She shook her head. "I had no idea it was
Mother Tyson. She'd been so good to me. Helped me
through everything. But she wasn't for me at all."

"No?" Koby asked.

"No." Katy pursed her lips. "She's the one who sent me
around to that door. The one with the sign on it. She knew
I'd be seen on the video, giving the police me as a suspect
and saving herself."

"Wow," I said.

"Yeah. More mental trauma for me to deal with."

"If you need someone to talk to"—my heart now
warming up to her—"you can talk to my mother."

"Your mother?"

"Yes. She's a psychotherapist."

"Oh. I didn't know you guys' mother worked in mental
health."

"Why would you?" I asked, a little annoyed.

"Well, I did follow her and Mama Zola one day . . ."

I put up my hands. "Tell me no more."

"She isn't my mother," Koby interjected, changing the subject.

"But you two are twins," Katy said, looking confused.

"She's Keaton's adopted mother. We're twins, separated and raised apart," Koby said. "We don't know our biological mother. At least not yet."

"Oh. Sorry," Katy said.

"Don't be sorry," I said. "It's okay."

"Especially since we might have a lead on her," Koby said, it seemed to me rather nonchalantly.

We all turned to look at him. My breath caught in my throat.

"What?" I asked.

"That was why I came over. We have a lead. Someone from her high school left a message in Books & Biscuits' direct messages on Instagram."

"Really?" I said. I had to sit down. "They know where she is?"

He shrugged. "They want us to meet with them."

"Be careful," Katy said. "People can be sneaky."

A hearty laugh came from Chow. The first sound he'd made, while seemingly letting Katy have her say. "You are one to talk," he said. "They needed to be careful of you."

"Yes," I said and smiled at Katy. "But you turned out okay." I looked at my brother. "I hope this does, too."

Acknowledgments

Life has its ups and downs, but God has always seen me through. I thank Him for that. So grateful for the opportunity to write books and to share what I know and do with others. And of course, thanks to my mother, Leslie Vandiver, I miss her every day but constant thoughts of her keep her close.

Saying a big thank you to my Penguin Berkley team, especially my fantastic editor Jessica Wade. So understanding and forgiving when I run into problems. She makes my books better. To George Towne, my book designer, who made it cozy and colorful, thank you. And thank you to my awesome agent, Rachel Brooks, who puts up with me and helps me get the books I want to write out into the world.

Big thanks to Ray Patton who lent his name, fun conversations, and food. Say hi to Alex for me! To talented author Nicole D. Miller, who I met at a pop-up. So nice to find other authors and connect. She graciously gave permission to use her name and book in my story and even gave me her favorite line for *Stories for the (Urban) Soul* to quote. Thank you!

How could I do this without Kathryn Dionne? I couldn't. My writing partner, my friend, my sistah! Thank you for all of your help in my writing journey. And thank you for writing such a wonderful cozy novel, *Murder at the Holiday Bazaar*, that I could put in my book.

And to my writing cohorts, LaBena Fleming, Brandi Larsen, Natassha Ricks, Molly Perry and Cheryl Fields: Thank you, thank you, thank you.

Recipes

Killer (Not Really) Peach Cobbler

INSIDE (FILLING)

- 4 pounds fresh peaches, pitted and sliced
- 2 cups granulated sugar
- ¼ teaspoon salt
- ¼ teaspoon cinnamon
- Dough scrappings (optional)

OUTSIDE (CRUST)

- 1 stick of cold unsalted butter
- 1¼ cups unbleached all-purpose flour
- ⅓ cup sugar
- ¼ teaspoon salt
- 1 teaspoon vanilla extract
- 2 tablespoons very cold water

FILLING: Peel peaches and place in a pot with sugar, salt, and cinnamon to a pot and stir to combine.

Cook on medium heat for five minutes (or less), until the sugar is dissolved. Remove from heat and set aside.

CRUST: Cut butter into ¼-inch cubes and place in food processor with flour, sugar and salt. Pulse to combine. The mixture should resemble coarse cornmeal, and visible butter pieces are the size of small peas when ready.

Place dough mixture in a small bowl and mix with vanilla and cold water, working it with hands.

Transfer the dough to a work surface, pat into a ball and flatten into a disk. Wrap in plastic wrap and refrigerate for at least 30 minutes.

The dough can be cut into strips or used as a whole to top the cobbler. If desired (old-fashioned cobbler), place some of the dough scrappings into the mixture before topping it.

Place in oven at 350°F until crust is golden brown.

Billy Ray's Oxtails

- 5 pounds oxtails
- One white onion
- Lawry's Seasoned Salt (to taste)
- Black pepper (to taste)
- Garlic powder (to taste)
- Onion powder (to taste)
- 2 tablespoons soy sauce
- ½ clove of garlic

Split each oxtail into three pieces and season with seasoning salt and pepper, garlic and onion powders. Place in plastic bag with soy sauce and marinate in fridge overnight.

The next day, place oxtails in pot of water (cover the oxtails) and add garlic clove and more seasoning salt. Boil for about an hour and a half. Then place in a 350°F oven for an hour (to help keep meat on bones).

Mama Zola's Hot Water Cornbread

- 2 cups yellow cornmeal
- ¼ cup granulated sugar
- 1 teaspoon salt (add more to taste, if desired)
- Boiling water
- 2 pats of butter or margarine
- Vegetable oil

Combine cornmeal, sugar and salt in a medium-sized bowl. Add boiling water to the bowl and stir to a thick consistency.

Melt butter and pour into cornbread mixture.

Add oil or butter to skillet and heat over medium-high heat until hot.

Spoon in cornbread mixture to size of small pancake. Flip when bubbles on top start to burst. Each side should be well-browned.

TODAY I WAS going to touch the stars.

Lying on my back, I stared up at my bedroom ceiling. When I'd moved to my own place, the only things I'd taken from my childhood home were the star-shaped glittered cardboard cutouts my grandmother and I had made when I was seven. I hung them as a reminder of what she'd told me—always shoot for the stars.

She'd also told me, on days I had to make ice cream for the store, don't sleep past five a.m.

I sat up in bed and looked over at the red glow of my digital alarm clock.

Four thirty-nine.

Up ahead of time. Already, the day seemed promising.

A smile escaping my lips, I pulled back the covers and stood on the bed. On my toes, I reached up and felt the coarse bumps from the glue on the gold-glittered star that hung the lowest. Closing my eyes, I walked the length of the bed, socked feet sinking into the mattress, and ran my fingertips along the points. Inhaling happily, I jumped off the bed and padded down the hall into the bathroom, humming a tune.

Yes, today was the day that I was going to realize my dream.

As I brushed my teeth, I stared back at my reflection in the mirror and could almost see all the excitement oozing out of me. Running my family's ice cream shop hadn't *always* been my dream, surely not the one I'd left for college and earned a degree in marketing and an MBA for. But when my dad's sister, Aunt Jack, had moved to North Carolina and left our little business without a manager, my grandfather had chosen me, his only granddaughter, to run it. He'd put the key to the shop in a box with a key ring that said "Manager" and a card that said "Carte Blanche" and placed it under the Christmas tree. Tearing into the red-and-gold Ho-Ho-Ho wrapping paper that holiday morning, I'd felt just like a kid—wide smile, nervous giggle and my insides squealing with delight.

That had been nearly a year ago.

I let out a long sigh as I put away my toothbrush and closed the medicine cabinet. I pulled a plastic cap over my short-cropped black hair and stepped into the shower.

Yep, today I was confident about opening the shop, but that confidence had been born out of trouble. After the baton had been passed to me and I came up with the plan to turn our little shop around, I found out the hard way just how quickly plans could go wrong.

I closed my eyes and let the hot water from my brand-new luxury spa showerhead—the only modern amenity in the old Victorian rental—fall down on me.

I had opted to revamp the store, modernizing it with what I deemed strategic, moneymaking renovations. It had a full glass wall at the back of the dining area, a 1950-ish soda shop motif (complete with a black-and-white checkered floor), an open-view kitchen where customers could see their ice cream being made and a menu based on the recipes my grandparents, Aloysius Zephyr Crewse and Kaylene Brewster Crewse, had used when they opened shop in 1965.

I didn't have my grandmother's original recipe box—no one seemed to know what had happened to it. But I did have photocopies of some of the recipe cards she'd used, and, having worked alongside her for my entire childhood, tugging at her apron strings, I was pretty sure, for the recipes I didn't have, I could remember most of the ingredients and churn out her bestsellers, or at least be pretty close.

Known for being the methodical and analytical one, I had carefully mapped out a blueprint to restore the business to what I called its glory days—when all we sold was ice cream—but all my planning and practical graduate coursework had gone straight out of the window by week two. I learned firsthand about real-world time delays.

I'd never worried so much in my life. My plan had been to relaunch the shop at the Chagrin Falls Annual Memorial Day Blossom Festival. But between the wrong glass shipping for my partition wall, a prolonged crop of rainstorms and an overbooked contractor, it would be closer to our little village's October Pumpkin Roll before I could flip the sign on the shop door to OPEN.

I say "closer" because my vision still hadn't been actualized. The plexiglass wall needed to partition off the kitchen still hadn't arrived. And the supplier of our fair-trade cane sugar had gotten into a ten-car pileup—no casualties, but tons of the white grains had been overturned across the highway, making me have to wait to get the first batches started until another truck could be loaded. It turned out to be only a two-day delay. Thank goodness it had arrived in time.

I reached over and flipped the showerhead to pulsating, letting the water beat down and wash away those thoughts of all the hiccups that had tried to give my ice cream dream a meltdown.

I basked in the spray for a few more minutes before I turned off the water, stepped out of the shower and wrapped a towel around me. I slid my hand across the condensation on the mirror and grabbed a bottle of face moisturizer.

Smearing the liquid under my eyes and across my forehead, I couldn't help but grin, thinking about how our little business, with me at the helm, was going to come full circle today. We were back to selling ice cream and *only* ice cream.

I pulled off my shower cap, ran a comb through my hair and felt the first of the butterflies flapping around in my stomach. I whispered a little prayer and headed back to my bedroom to get dressed.

My grandfather had often reminisced about how hard it had been for him and my Grandma Kay to start that little shop. Just relocating to the village of Chagrin Falls, a suburb of Cleveland, from the South, had been an ordeal. My grandma hadn't gotten used to the snow and cold when they took on the business of digging in a frosty freezer every time she served a customer. But then she'd made it her own. Over the years, she came up with flavors that captured everyone's fancy—smooth and lemony luscious ice box pie, sprinkle-splattered cake batter and, my grandfather's favorite, pralines and cream—folds of gooey sweet caramel and salty praline pecans swirled into her homemade vanilla bean ice cream.

But selling ice cream in a place where four seasons sometimes slid into two—either hot or cold—meant our family business had hit more bumps than the almond-filled rocky road ice cream my Grandma Kay used to whip up for her famous cakes. So, to keep up, other family members had stuffed the shop shelves with non–ice cream items in an attempt to keep it viable all year round.

Crewse Creamery had become more of a novelty shop— T-shirts, Chagrin Falls memorabilia, hot dogs, lemonade and candy. "No one wants ice cream in the wintertime, Bronwyn," my aunt Jack had said, calling me by my full name, something no one did, while setting up an Ohio lottery machine she'd purchased. "We have to follow the money. Diversify."

With Aunt Jack's changes, our family business had been teetering on the point of no return, especially after she stopped making ice cream by hand. She ordered mix for soft serve and frozen tubs all the way from Arizona. Homemade ice cream had been what set us apart from all the other ice cream shops. But she said it made no economical sense to continue to make it half the year when she could get a year-long contract to supply ice cream to cover the late spring and summer months. Luckily, she'd found love on the Internet and moved to follow her man to the Tar Heel State before the first shipment arrived.

My radio alarm clock had popped on at five and was issuing a weather alert when I got back to my room. *Cold. Wet. Dreary.*

Pulling back the sheer curtains at the window, I took a peek outside. I couldn't read the still-dark sky, and the dry ground illuminated by the yellow glow of the streetlight didn't give a hint of what the forecaster warned.

I pulled out a sweater as the old radiator clanked and hissed, held it up and thought better of it.

"Cold weather may be blowing in," I said, folding the sweater up, "but churning ice cream and waiting on customers is gonna make me work up a sweat." I smiled. "Yeah, lots of customers. Lots of sweat."

I stuffed the sweater back into the drawer and, opening another one, pulled out one of the shop's custom T-shirts. I layered it with a button-down flannel shirt—always best to be prepared—and snaked my way into a pair of jeans. On my knees, I rustled through the floor of my closet. I pushed work shoes down into my knapsack and dug my UGG boots out of the back.

I was ready to start my day—*the* day—the first day of our family's new and improved ice cream shop.

First stop, though, my parents' house.

I grabbed my puffy coat and a hat from the coat rack, picked up last year's Christmas gift from PopPop and stuffed it in my jeans pocket and plodded across the old wooden floor and down the back stairs that led out from my second-story apartment.

The sky spit down droplets of rain on me as I walked outside. Right now it was hit or miss, but something was brewing, I could tell. The wind let out a low howl, blew the autumn leaves across my path and gave me a shiver up my spine. I pulled the hood up on my coat, shoved my hands into my pockets looking for gloves. Nothing. I balled my fists up and tried to keep my fingertips from freezing. The weather forecast was rarely right, at least for Cleveland and its surrounding areas, and—fingers crossed—I hoped the wintery forecast for the day would be a miss.

Around my hometown, snowfall could come with the daffodils in April and not so much for sleigh rides and decorated trees in December. It wasn't odd anymore for Christmas to arrive with sixty-five-degree weather, which was what I was wishing for today.

Ready to find
your next great read?

Let us help.

Visit prh.com/nextread